Daniel E. Bandmann, Barnard Gisby

An Actor's Tour

Daniel E. Bandmann, Barnard Gisby

An Actor's Tour

ISBN/EAN: 9783337194048

Printed in Europe, USA, Canada, Australia, Japan

Cover: Foto ©Andreas Hilbeck / pixelio.de

More available books at **www.hansebooks.com**

AN ACTOR'S TOUR

OR

Seventy Thousand Miles with Shakespeare

BY

DANIEL E. BANDMANN

EDITED BY

BARNARD GISBY

WITH PORTRAIT AFTER W. M. HUNT

BOSTON
CUPPLES, UPHAM AND COMPANY
The Old Corner Book Store
283 Washington Street
1885

PREFACE.

" What, shall this speech be spoke for our excuse?
Or shall we on without apology? "
— *Romeo and Juliet, Act i, sc. 4.*

A TOUR around the world, not to emphasize travels
of three times that extent, which would have been
sufficient within an easily appreciable number of
decades to have rendered a man an object of unusual
interest to his acquaintances, and a phenomenon in
general society, can nowadays have no such effect; and,
in offering this book to the public, the author does not
delude himself so far as to imagine that on such a score
he is proffering anything of exceptional importance.
To-day every one is a traveler; many have made the
circuit of the world.

Science has wrought marvels as by the hand of
a magician, yet by no wand of enchantment, but by
patient conquest and mastery of the mighty energies
of nature. Steam and electricity, if they have not
diminished, have at least revolutionized, conceptions
and thoughts that have prevailed in relation to the
world, encircling it with a network of appliances that
makes communication and travel between the most
distant places possible, so that with a not very considerable amount of money and a few months of leisure
the most ordinary mortal may become a rival of Captain
Cook. Puck, it would seem, was endowed by the
transcendent genius of the immortal Bard with a

wonderful prescience of the drift of human events, when he said : —

> "I'll put a girdle round about the earth
> In forty minutes."

Those, however, who wish to build a reputation on travel had better attempt something less common in that direction than a trip around, or simply extensive journeyings to and fro over the well-known highroads of, the world, and be quick about it, as the chances of success are each day becoming fewer, the possibilities of originality decreasing; still, however, there remain grounds for hope that adventurous spirits may come here or there on an unexplored spot, if only they have the courage, resolution, patience, and heroism to turn aside from beaten tracks into untrodden solitudes : to follow, in brief, the footsteps of a Livingstone, a Stanley, or a Greely. Modern science, by its discoveries, explorations, inventions, and adaptations of natural forces to the service of man, has produced two opposite impressions on the mind. In the first place, it has made man conscious of the limitations of the world as a whole; proved beyond a doubt, so far as longitude and latitude are concerned, that humanity lives and moves and has its being in a very small place; that the orb which is its home is "cribbed, cabined, and confined"—an atom-world in the immensities of space and the eons of eternity. Schiller, perhaps, was thinking of the growth, development, and progress of the race, no less than of the individual, when he sang of "The Child" : —

> "Happy infant! to thee an infinite space is the cradle.
> When to man's age thou shalt come, narrow thou'lt think the wide
>   world!"

But science has not stopped here. In the second place, it has opened man's eyes to the infinite interests and ineffable wonders there are within the bounds of his habitation; discovered worlds where least he dreamed of them: in the merest atom of dust, in the minutest molecule of matter, every square inch of circumambient atmosphere, each drop of water; in the iris of an eye, a pulse-beat, the faintest note of sound; in the sunbeam, a ray of light, a phosphorescent gleam; in a blade of grass, "a primrose by a river's brim," the "flower in the crannied wall"; in the fungi, the worm, and the ant. In each of these science has revealed a microcosm, and brought man face to face with what cannot be otherwise regarded than as the transcendent marvel of the whole creation — the perpetual miracle of the universe — the presence of law, order, fitness, beauty, or life, in the least as in the greatest things.

The author of this book purposed, however, no such task as the building of a reputation as a traveler. His sympathies and profession have chained him almost exclusively to the civilized world, and seldom allowed of his passing out of well-trodden paths into the byways or the trackless regions of the earth, even to gratify the passion of discovery, to manifest a transient interest in savages or

> "The sweetest innocent(s)
> That e'er did lift up eye,"

suckled at the soft, fruitful breast of nature herself. But, notwithstanding this, it is thought the book may have some amount of interest from the fact that no other professional man has ever undertaken a world-tour like that of which the story is told in these pages, accompanied by a group of a dozen actors and

actresses, performing the loftiest works of Shakespeare,
and other great masters of the drama, before the
various nations of the earth, and with results most
gratifying to all concerned. Not to speak of great
monetary gains, mindful of what Timon of Athens
has said: —

> "Gold? yellow, glittering, precious gold? No, gods,
> I am no idle votarist. Roots, you clear heavens!
> Thus much of this will make black, white; foul, fair;
> Wrong, right; base, noble; old, young; coward, valiant.
> Ha! you gods, why this? What this, you gods? Why this
> Will lug your priests and servants from your sides;
> Pluck stout men's pillows from below their heads.
> This yellow slave
> Will knit and break religions; bless the accurs'd;
> Make the hoar leprosy ador'd; place thieves,
> And give them title, knee, and approbation,
> With senators on the bench: this is it
> That makes the wappen'd widow wed again:
> She, whom the spital-house, and ulcerous sores
> Would cast the gorge at, this embalms and spices
> To the April day again."

There were rewards of quite a different nature that
the actor, true artist as he is, found of highest satisfaction, namely, the proofs he witnessed everywhere of
a deep-rooted sentiment in mankind that responds to
the beautiful; a love of art when represented at its best,
and a passionate admiration for that supreme master of
the drama, to the interpreting of whose plays he has
devoted the best years of his life — Shakespeare.   To
this there were no exceptions worth mentioning.
Wherever he played there was a public, wishful to
appreciate the marvelous creations of dramatic genius.
The Muses of the stage were there: Thalia, with power
to open the sweet fountains of laughter: Melpomene,
the sorrowful wells of tears.   Local and provincial some
plays may be, but the highest conceptions of the drama,

performed with the insight, culture, sympathy, devotion, and enthusiasm of the true artist, are ever a universal language. The story of three and a half busy years of the actor's life is given in this book, which has been written in concession to an outside pressure that a record of a tour more extensive than any other actor has made might be laid before the public, and it is hoped that it may afford pleasant reading to all, and be to thousands of his supporters throughout the world a welcome *souvenir* of the days of hard work, but of rare happiness, which he spent among them. His aim in life has been to give pleasure to others, and, at the same time, to exalt the actor's art and ennoble the theatrical profession, maintaining that scholarship, culture, imagination, sympathy, sensibility, and love of the beautiful, are nowhere more necessary than on the modern stage; in pursuance of this he has assumed many characters, and he now sincerely trusts that those who may at any time have been interested in, or pleased by, him as Narcisse, Hamlet, Othello, Iago, Macbeth, Richard III, Shylock, or some other of his *rôles*, will be glad to recognize an old acquaintance with a new face, even though that new face is his own: and give a hearty welcome to these pages, in which he tells something of his professional experience: that, as an author, he may meet with the same generous sympathy that it has been his privilege to enjoy as an actor.

All that need be said of the editor's part and lot in the matter is that the services here rendered have been given in great admiration for an actor who is, at the same time, an artist; sincere and deep regard for a man who is, at the same time, a gentleman; and in that pardonable pride of numbering among one's best friends a member of the dramatic profession who has both great genius and large generosity. The book is left to public judgment, which will be the true arbiter of its worth and fate, but should it be its destiny, here or there, to fall into the hands of a critic of the type Douglas Jerrold had in view when he said : "Oh, yes, he'll review the book as an east wind reviews an apple-tree," it is hoped that there is something in it that will save it, even though "east wind" criticism may blow upon it, from being carried into that limbo of authors — the world of forgotten literature.

BARNARD GISBY.

BOSTON, November, 1884.

CONTENTS.

CHAPTER I. — AUSTRALIA.

NEW SOUTH WALES. — SYDNEY.

CHAPTER II. — AUSTRALIA.

QUEENSLAND. — BRISBANE.

CHAPTER III. — NEW ZEALAND.

SOUTH ISLAND. — DUNEDIN. — CHRISTCHURCH.

CHAPTER IV. — NEW ZEALAND.

NORTH ISLAND. — WELLINGTON. — NAPIER. — AUCKLAND.

CHAPTER V. — TASMANIA.

HOBART TOWN.

CHAPTER VI. — AUSTRALIA.

VICTORIA. — MELBOURNE.

CHAPTER VII. — AUSTRALIA.

SOUTH AUSTRALIA. — ADELAIDE.

CHAPTER VIII. — INDIA.

CEYLON. — MADRAS.

CHAPTER IX. — India.

CALCUTTA. — I.

CHAPTER X. — India.

CALCUTTA. — II.

CHAPTER XI. — INDIA.

BOMBAY.

CHAPTER XII. — CHINA.

SHANGHAI.

CHAPTER XIII. — CHINA.

HONG-KONG.

CHAPTER XIV. — CHINA.

CANTON.

CHAPTER XV. — Malay Peninsula.

SINGAPORE.

CHAPTER XVI. — India.

CEYLON.

AN ACTOR'S TOUR.

CHAPTER I. — AUSTRALIA.

NEW SOUTH WALES. — SYDNEY.

"Little shall I grace my cause,
In speaking for myself: Yet, by your gracious patience,
I will a round, unvarnish'd tale deliver."
— Othello, Act i, sc. 3.

"All places that the eye of heaven visits,
Are to the wise man ports and happy havens."
— Richard II, Act i, sc. 3.

Early passion for travel — The Baldwin Theatre, San Francisco —
Clara Morris — A new acquaintance, Louise Beaudet — How she
came to play Lady Macbeth — Charlie Ackerman — *Compagnons de
voyage* — The Pacific Mail Steamship Company — Sydney — Commercial and material prosperity — Artistic spirit — "Art needs
repose, not action" — The theatres — The "colonials" — The bishop
of Melbourne's opinion of the "colonial" youth — The "larikins" —
Old friends — A month at the Opera House — A story of two old
tragedians — Judge Wyndier — His delight in Shakespeare — A
judicial experience — Grand situation of the city — Edward Greville
— Port Jackson — A man-of-war — The Public Gardens — Hawkesbury River — The Blue Mountains — Lovet's Leap.

FROM the earliest age, when, indeed, I was quite
a small boy in the dear German Fatherland, I had
a great desire for the adventure of travel, and one
of my chief delights was to wander, in imagination, with travelers over the grand, new lands of
America and Australia, or through the ancient
and enchanting countries of the East. That

juvenile passion was only deepened and strengthened by years, and so it has come to pass that I
have been all my life a traveler; and of men who
have devoted themselves and their talents to the
dramatic profession I have, on several occasions,
made more extensive tours than others.

It was not, however, till May, 1879, that I conceived the idea of a grand theatrical tour around the
world, the story of which I am now about to narrate.
The time at my disposal for anything like literary
pursuits, and the desire to put what I have to say
within a readable compass, no less than the unity
of the narrative, render it imperative that I should
keep exclusively to an account of this tour, except
in those cases in which it seems necessary to refer
to former visits to the same countries, and in
which later and earlier experiences are inseparably
linked together, and more recent impressions
recall those that are more remote. At the time
the idea took possession of me I was playing an
engagement at the Baldwin Theatre, San Francisco,
in which I was supported by one of the best
companies ever gathered together under one
management. It included, amongst others, the
following ladies : Adelina Stanhope, Jeffreys-
Lewis, Lina Cary, Lily Andrews, Clara Jane
Walters, Clara Morris, Louise Beaudet; while
James O'Neil, Bradley, Morrison, and Bishop,
were amongst the gentlemen of the company.

Clara Morris was at the time playing my Ophelia,
out of respect to me because I had encouraged

her in the young days of her career, when, twenty years before, in Cleveland, she played my Queen in Hamlet. Of all the ladies of the company Louise Beaudet was the most talented, the one whose mind grasped most readily and completely the spirit and motive of the character that for the time being she impersonated. It was therefore arranged that she should play throughout the tour the more conspicuous feminine characters of Shakespearean, or other, drama that might engage us.

My relations with Louise Beaudet began in rather a romantic way, and I state the circumstances here because they are necessary to a full understanding of the reasons that led me to give her so prominent a position in my company throughout this tour, which, by the way, has caused some sensation in the dramatic world. Up to the time at which I became acquainted with Louise Beaudet she had only played the *ingénues*, but had just left an opera-bouffe company to join the drama. She came into my room one evening, at the Baldwin Theatre, during the period in which I was performing Narcisse (a play based on the Pompadour episode in French history), to ask me some questions about the representation of the part of Jessica in The Merchant of Venice, and that of Lazarillo in Don Cæsar de Bazan, for which she had been cast, not feeling sure of the ground she had taken. I was at once impressed with the girl's wonderful intelligence and personal attractions. Although *petite*, her figure was graceful, her eye sparkling with fire, and her *tout ensemble* told me at once that there great talent was hidden.

I said: "Why do you not play more serious parts?"

The idea struck her with surprise that I should think such a thing possible.

"Do you indeed think that I could play serious parts?" she exclaimed.

"Of course, I do," said I.

"Well, do you know, I once thought so myself, but people would not believe me because I am so little."

Just then the call-boy entered, saying, "Curtain's up, sir," and I had only time to add: "Call upon me to-morrow afternoon, and I will give you my opinion."

She came next day, and I gave her the part of Lady Macbeth to read. She laughed outright.

"You want me to read that!"

"Certainly, I do."

"But Lady Macbeth is beyond me; as well ask me to stretch forth my hand and touch the stars! It is so difficult!"

"I know all that better than you, gentle maiden," said I; "but that's the very reason I want you to read it. By that, I shall be able to judge what is in you infinitely better than if I had given you an easier piece. Do as I wish you, and allow me to judge. I wish to gauge your talent."

She at once began, and I was not deceived. Here, under the cloak of singular modesty, I discovered very rare ability. After a few lessons, she was able to play Lady Macbeth at the Baldwin Theatre, and all San Francisco came to laugh over "Little Beaudet," and my friends thought I was just going to have a lark with them. But their opinion changed after they had seen her. One of the best critics in California, the veteran dramatic editor of the *Morning Call* and the able critic of the *Evening Bulletin*, together with the editors of the *Chronicle, Atlas, Argonaut,* and others, pronounced a unanimous verdict upon the performance as being a *perfect* picture. Louise Beaudet afterward played Pauline, the manager having refused her the part of Juliet because Adelaide Neilson was to appear in it, and her success as Lady Macbeth had been sufficient to create anxiety lest she, if she got the chance, might by her brilliant acting mar the novelty of Neilson's impersonation of Juliet. But she scored another marked success as Pauline; as she did afterward in all her parts. Then, having made a brief trip through Oregon, where she played Doris Quinault in Narcisse, Ophelia in Hamlet, and Desdemona in Othello: and I, having fulfilled an engagement in German at the California Theatre: we sailed from San Francisco, on August 2, by the steamer Australia, for Sydney.

There were many friends to see me off,

among whom, and perhaps the most prominent, was the genial Charlie Ackerman, who seems destined to make a grand career in the political history of the United States. But he was there to see others off besides myself. Charlie is one of the cleverest and handsomest men in California, and beyond this he is a man of huge generosity of heart. Always ready to do a kind action, and to be of service to his fellow-man, he had interested himself in a family who had come down in the world, through the husband's misfortunes, and who were in very straitened circumstances. In a way that only his generosity knows how, he had got money together to send this family to Sydney, where the husband and father had gone to better his position. " You will take care of them during the trip for my sake, my dear boy," said Charlie, "and see that they arrive safely at Sydney."

Now, Charlie is a man that no one can refuse to oblige. I would do anything in the world for him, and, of course, I promised, not knowing at the time how rash a man may be, even in such slight obligations to a friend. I pictured a lady with a couple of grown-up children to whom one can give occasional courteous attention and assistance ; but conceive my amazement when my dear friend, at the hour of our parting, introduced me to the mother of not less than seven — blessed offspring! the youngest not over twelve months old, and just teething, the oldest about twelve years, inclined to be pretty. To my further amazement

I found that three of them were troubled with
defective speech, and that one had to guess their
wishes and demands, and that the poor woman
had not even a nurse with her. At that I was
greatly pained, and immediately got a good-
hearted Irish woman out of the steerage to
help her.

I did my utmost in a thoroughly conscientious
way, as also did several members of my company,
to alleviate the poor woman's hardships — no easy
task under the circumstances, for, alas! those
seven dear children had whims, fancies, and wants,
that there seemed no possible means of quieting
or satisfying. But at last they were landed safely
in Sydney, and were received by the happy husband, who was overjoyed to póssess once more the
wife of his bosom and handful of chicks; and I,
gentle reader, as you may well imagine, equally
overjoyed in finding myself free of such immense
responsibilities.

Apart from such cares as were imposed on me
by my friend Charlie (heaven forgive him!), the
journey from San Francisco to Sydney was more
like a picnic than anything else, for the Pacific
Mail Steamship Company is one of the most
obliging, courteous, and safest in the world,
and has reduced journeying to the antipodes to
a luxury.

The time of my arrival in Sydney was not
auspicious to my plans, for I no sooner landed than
I heard of the destruction by fire of the Victoria

Theatre, and this necessitated considerable altera-
tion in the programme I had marked out for
myself. In Sydney itself I saw immense change.
I had not been there for upward of ten years, —
a long period in modern history, — yet I was
surprised by what had been effected in it. I
will give my impressions of the entire change the
country has undergone, so far as the manners and
moral life are concerned, later on, but I could not
shut my eyes to one important fact, that Sydney
had improved commercially most marvelously.
There is no need to look further than Chicago,
Denver, or San Francisco, for instances of rapid
progress in business and population: and the same
thing impresses one in Sydney; and, later on, I
found it was the same with Melbourne, Brisbane,
and other cities; they are severally making rapid
strides toward becoming a metropolis worthy of
any country and nation.

But I found that, with this rapid commercial
development, what I may call the art and poetry
of life have not kept pace. A purely material-
istic prosperity has wellnigh destroyed the
artistic spirit. Sydney impressed me as having
retrograded in this respect during the last ten
years, and I fear it is still on the road to greater
decline. Art has suffered immensely in Sydney
from its increased prosperity, and perhaps this
must often be the case, for the spirit of commerce,
steam, and electricity is not a wholesome medium
to advance the Beautiful. They are very useful

and productive to mankind, but Art wants repose,
not action. Together with many other improve-
ments toward the comfort of society, the Sydney
theatres, like all others throughout Australia, have
advanced in matters of exterior beauty and utility;
but they have sadly declined in love for the
legitimate and sublime. A low class of entertainments, especially opera bouffe, sensational
rubbish, and variety-shows, finds greater favor now
than what used to be looked forward to with the
most intense delight and pleasure, a legitimate
play performed by competent actors and actresses.
Australia, in the middle period of this century,
could boast of the best stock-companies in the
world, and every famous actor considered it his
duty to make a tour through this great, rising
country. Thus it had visits from Joe Jefferson,
G. V. Brooke, Charles Kean, Edwin Booth, Ristori,
Anna Bishop, Kate Haynes, Mrs. Scott-Siddons,
Ilma di Murska, Camilla Urso, Wilhelmj, and
many others; but lately it has taken to strange
freaks, and fancies it will treat with perfect indifference men of established European reputa-
tions, and takes a mad delight in charlatanism.
Thus, Mr. Henry Ketten, who was certainly not a
great pianist according to European opinions,
was adored all over Australia and made a fortune,
while Wilhelmj was a decided failure and lost
money.

The cause of this is easily understood when we
compare the Australians of former years with the

Australians of to-day — "colonials," as they like
to call themselves. Formerly, Australian sentiment and public opinion were a mixture of the
best English, German, and American ideas, and
the country was peopled by those who retained
the good, solid tastes of the homes they had left;
by those who really loved the beautiful and sublime in art, and readily supported those capable
of representing these, and that with a generosity
and hospitality that made the artist's life more a
pleasure than a labor; but these men have gradually disappeared from the scene, and their children, the so-called "colonials," have stepped into
their shoes.

As an evidence of the love for the drama in
Australia formerly, I may mention the following,
which occurred during my first visit. Charles
Mathews, the matchless comedian, who was then
in the country, was announced on one occasion to
play in a small town, and, being prevented by
floods from getting there in time, he arrived at
nine o'clock in the evening to find that the
citizens (who had assembled at the theatre at
half-past seven, and waited about the place
for over an hour) had retired in disgust, or
at least great disappointment, to the bosom
of their families, and not a few of them to
their virtuous couches, indifferent alike to the
pleasures and cares of the world. Now, Mathews
was announced to play in another town on
the following day, and had, therefore, either to

skip this town, or to play in spite of Morpheus.
The first he did not wish to do, for he sincerely
respected the people of the place, and was the very
last man in the world to voluntarily disappoint an
audience or to fail in an engagement; while he
was equally wishful not to break the continuity
and order of the remaining arrangements of his
tour by staying in the place more than one night.
He resolved, therefore, to send the bellman round
the town to announce his arrival by loud ringing
of bells and a few oracular words such as a bellman delights to utter; and even got the band to
make the circuit of the streets. Need I say that
by those means he actually got the people out of
their beds and to the theatre, which was crowded
to suffocation before ten o'clock?

Now, all is changed or changing, and I am
sorry to say that I cannot appreciate the
" colonials " of to-day: neither their taste in
art, nor their sentiments in life. I will not ven-
ture a criticism upon the race, but I fear it will
not be a great one, except circumstances should
arise to materially alter their mode of education
and general principles. The bishop of Melbourne,
in one of his lectures before the Young Men's
Christian Association, observed that the character
of the colonial youth is "superficiality of feeling,
crafty cunning, sharpness, and irreverence "; and
I agree with him *in toto.* Of late years a class
of vampires has crept up, which is known in that
country as the "larikans." They are perhaps

better described in this country as the "hudlums," and yet that word is only a weak designation of these low creatures. One can tell a "hudlum" a mile off: his character is stamped Cain-like upon his brow; but it is quite different with a "larikan": he is a man who imitates the gentleman, wears kid gloves, a spotless white cravat, and has a flower of the rarest kind in his buttonhole; and, withal, would think it a great lark to waylay a child or knock down a centenarian. In short, a race has risen that knows nothing of the ideals of its forefathers in Art, character, conduct; which has no true, strong manhood; and hence the decline of the drama in its loftier aspects, the increasing demand for sensational amusements; for, in brief, all performances which please the eye, work upon the senses, but do not move the heart, exalt the character, or inform the mind.

In all this there is a marked contrast in the people of New Zealand and Tasmania, as I shall more fully point out later; the people of these countries are just as opposite in their feelings and tastes to the people of Australia as light to darkness. The reason is this: these are younger countries, and those who are settled in them still have living memories of the lands they have left; and, further, they are principally peopled by Scotchmen, whose love of Shakespeare and the sublimities of the drama is inherent and abiding. Having produced a Burns, they know how to appreciate a Shakespeare. I was fortunate, however, in finding some of the good old colonial race still living, and I was received with great hospitality and cordiality by my old Sydney friends, both on and off the stage. I played one month at the Opera House, running Hamlet a fortnight, and then the rest of my *répertoire*, giving several nights to Othello. In the early days of Sydney theatricals there were two tragedians of whom they tell the following story. One of them had a wife of whom he was jealous, and used to address her at times in a manner the reverse of affectionate. The performance in which they were engaged was Othello, and before the third act began the wife of the actor had caused once more his displeasure, and there was a quarrel; so the other actor, who played Iago, interfered, and told Othello that he should speak more respectfully to his wife.

"What's that your business?"

"I choose to make it so!"

"You do, do you? Look here " —

"Your cue, gentlemen!" cried the call-boy.

The two actors rushed on the stage, and after the exit of Desdemona, which part was impersonated on the occasion by the object of their dispute, the following scene took place: —

OTHELLO. — "Excellent wretch (*aside, to Iago,* curse you)! Perdition catch my soul, but I do (*aside,* hate you!) love thee! and when I love thee not (*aside,* d—n you!), Chaos is come again."

IAGO (who overheard all). — " My noble lord (*aside, to him* — beast !) " —

OTHELLO. — " What dost thou say, Iago (*aside, to him* — blackguard) ? "

IAGO. — (*Aside,* "If you call me blackguard again, I 'll hit you.") (*Aloud*), " Did Michael Cassio, when you woo'd my lady " —

(OTHELLO muttered, during Iago's speech, " How dare you interfere in my family affairs, you scoundrel ? ")

IAGO. — (*Aside, to him,* " Another word and I 'll smack your face.") (*Aloud*), " Know of your love ? "

OTHELLO. — " He did, from first to last : Why dost thou ask ? "

IAGO. — " But for a satisfaction of my thought ; no further " —

But, alas ! before Iago could finish the sentence with " harm," Othello had again ejaculated some disrespectful words, and Iago's hand without further hesitation came in contact with Othello's face, and Othello's dignity being offended he returned the blow. This peculiar behavior on the part of the two actors of course aroused the audience to take part in the dispute, and " Go it, Othello ! " came from a dozen voices, while " Cheer up, Iago ! " was shouted by a dozen others ; and this encouragement, which never fails to influence men whose " angry passions rise," seemed to have acted on the combatants like oil on coals of fire, for soon they rolled down the stage into the orchestra, smashing by their fall the big drum and causing considerable consternation amongst the musicians and their instruments; till at last they were parted by the superior strength of the conductor, assisted by several others, and the shouts and laughter of the audience made an end of the play. This was, perhaps, the first and only occasion, in the history of the drama, on which Iago protected the wife of Othello instead of calumniating her; and, as a reading of the play, it cannot be considered an improvement, even though our sympathies may wholly be with Desdemona.

In society I met my friend Justice Wyndier, who was but a struggling barrister when I was in Sydney in 1870, but who now is considered the strongest and most eminent judge in Australia. The juries love him: the criminals fear and hate him: no bad test of a judge's capacity. It is an actual fact that in circuits where Judge Wyndier presides he generally frees the country for years to come from vice and crime.

Legal engagements do not exclusively occupy his attention; he is one of the best Shakespearean scholars in Australia, and, as might be supposed, I had additional pleasure in meeting him from this fact. He never misses a good performance, and has the highest intellectual pleasure in observing a new reading of a great dramatic conception or the effort on an actor's part to reach a lofty ideal. He has often told me that he has learned a great deal from fiction, and by a constant study gained from it considerable advantage and much assistance in his profession, for it has immensely increased his knowledge of mankind.

I recall one circumstance that he related to me bearing on this point, and showing how in real life it is, as we so often find it related in fiction, that many considerable, and even momentous, issues turn on some small thing, the thing that common minds do not observe, but which never escapes the all-searching vision of the true student, poet, or philosopher, of humanity.

On one occasion, when on one of his circuits, he saw a prisoner leaving the dock who had been indicted by the grand jury, and was to be tried the following session. The man's face made a strange impression on him: it seemed an embodiment of all brutal passions. However, business was pressing, and, without asking or knowing what the man had been committed for, he turned to it and thought no more of him. The next session his brother judge changed circuits with him, and it was the session following when he again presided, and this very criminal was brought before him. The jury, at the first trial before his brother judge, could not agree, and so a new trial had now to take place. In this trial Judge Wyndier brought out the guilt of the man (who had killed his benefactor in the bush for a few miserable pounds) so clearly and convincingly that the jury found him guilty without leaving the box, and he confessed his crime in toto before execution. One important point Judge Wyndier observed was that the murderer did not ask a certain witness, whose evidence was most important, any questions. So at last he insisted that he should speak to him, and ask him why he did not recognize him at the former trial. The prisoner did so, and the witness said: " Because you declined to ask me any questions, and I now recognize you fully by your voice." The judge had had this impression all along, and the witness, without knowing it, hit upon the judge's device.

Another prominent citizen of Sydney, whose name will be handed down to posterity in the history of the development of the Australian colonies during this century, is my friend, Edward Greville, who has honorably served his country as a member of the New South Wales parliament for over fifteen years. He was the first to introduce telegraphy into the country, and his energy and enterprise were unresting till every nook and corner of the Australasias was brought, by this means, within the circle of the civilized world; and traveling through the country has led me to entertain the opinion that in not a few cases — so perfect are the telegraphic arrangements, and so moderate the rates — the news of many European and American affairs is fully known throughout the length and breadth of these colonies before the merest tidings have reached certain rural districts of England, Scotland, or

Germany. Messages can be sent to any place within the bounds of Victoria, New South Wales, Queensland, or New Zealand, for twenty-five, from one colony to another for fifty, and a cablegram to Tasmania for seventy-five, cents.

Sydney, as a city, deserves much praise; it has, more than any other city in the Australian colonies, an old-world look, which at once opens the heart of the traveler to it; and though, from what I have said, it will be seen that it is not an El Dorado for actors, it is impossible to overlook, or not to be moved by, its many natural beauties and the grandeur of its situation. The harbor of the city has, and deservedly, a world-wide reputation: it is a question if there is more than one other equal to it. But even if the rest of the world were not aware of the fact, the Sidonians take good care that everybody who visits their shores shall be awakened to a consciousness of its superb beauty; consequently the questions first put to you when you speak to any one are : " Have you seen our harbor? and what do you think of it?" The crew of a man-of-war that lately anchored in its beautiful waters, having heard of the inquisitiveness of the people, and being anxious to please them all, hit upon the following plan. They attached a board to each side of the warrior-vessel, upon which they inscribed the following: " We have seen your harbor, and we think it sublime." The view as one steams into Port Jackson can never be forgotten by the traveler; the distance from

the entrance to the city is over twelve miles, and
the spectacle is beautiful from whatever point one
views it. It is remarkable in this, that all along
are little bays that retreat from the main body of
the water, which add in a marvelous way to the
charms of the general impression, and offer immense facilities for growing traffic. The largest
ship can moor alongside the docks of Sydney; and
it is no exaggeration to say that the entire fleets
of the civilized world could lie within the waters
of this splendid harbor. The city is spread out
over low hills at the upper end, and presents a
striking contrast to what have been well described
" the prosaic and painfully systematic cities of new
countries." Its irregularity reminds one of Boston,
and many of the more ancient towns of England
and the continent. In the city itself there is
nothing of great interest except the Public Gardens.
Sydney, like most of the Australian cities, has
most lovely gardens, laid out with scrupulous
taste and wisely kept. In the suburbs, too,
there are beautiful drives, and splendid private
residences scattered all along the banks of the
harbor; the wealthy Sidonians spend their days
in truly idyllic scenes, and nowhere are there more
stately homes than are to be found on the slopes
of the glorious harbor. The chief places of
interest in the neighborhood that invite a visit
from the traveler are Hawkesbury River and
the Blue Mountains: though, as a German,
I may perhaps be forgiven for expressing

a more moderate opinion of the former than
Anthony Trollope, who said it is superior to
the Rhine, and has in the way of natural beauties
"nothing equal to it, nothing second to it." I
admit it is a scene of great beauty. Lovet's Leap,
in the Blue Mountains, is one of the most entirely
desolate and awful pieces of scenery in the world.
It is said to have no true story about it, though its
appearance is such as to suggest a dozen tragedies
to one's thoughts and imagination, and it is hard
to convince one's mind that they may not have
happened, for it seems so pre-eminently a place
that may have witnessed deeds of darkness;
however, it is said simply to owe this designation to a surveyor of the name who inscribed it
so on his map of the district.

CHAPTER II. — AUSTRALIA.

QUEENSLAND. — BRISBANE.

"Thus far into the bowels of the land
Have we march'd on without impediment."
— *Richard III, Act. v, sc. 2.*

Privileges of the theatrical profession — A story of the colonial bishops — The city — The Bank Buildings — The Brisbane River — A magnificent engagement — The climate — The houses — Storms — Moreton Bay — Stranded — Sand-sailing — Sharks — A boy's heroism — Goulburn — Cherries ripe! — Wagga Wagga — Albury.

EARLY in November I left Sydney for Brisbane, for an engagement in the School of Art, the theatre there, also, having been burnt down.

Brisbane is the capital of Queensland, and two lines of steamers run from Sydney — the Australian Steamship Navigation Company and Messrs. Smith, Howard and Company. The journey takes from thirty-six to forty-eight hours, and the fare is a few pounds, while those connected with the theatrical profession, I may as well say here once for all, have the privilege in Australia, as in most other countries, of traveling at reduced rates. There is a good story told in Australia *à propos* of this. It seems that some time ago the bishops and archdeacons from all parts of Australia had to attend synod at Sydney, and one of the former, having an eye to economy (and perhaps the income of his bishopric was not more than that

of a good, fat English rectory), asked the Australian Steamship Navigation Company this simple
question: "Will you make a reduction in our
tickets?" To this the reply came by telegraph:
"You may be carried same as theatricals." So
these bishops and archdeacons, no doubt dressing
with greater care and putting on a little additional
solemnity, — for these colonial divines are by no
means given to solemn grimness on ordinary occasions, — availed themselves of the privilege of the
theatrical profession and journeyed to and from
synod at reduced rates. I have heard that it is
said amongst the people now, when they are from
home, that "they are on a theatrical tour," but I
don't know how true that is; a sly hit at ritualism
may perhaps be intended.

Brisbane, as a town, contains nothing of interest.
The Bank Buildings are the finest in the place,
and the river is a rather pretty sight as it winds at
the foot of the low hill on which the town rises.
My visit, however, was satisfactory in every way.
I played a magnificent engagement, and Louise
Beaudet, who had become a great favorite in
Sydney, and whose reputation had preceded her,
enhanced her position considerably here. November in Brisbane is pretty hot, but what struck me
especially was the early rising of the sun. One
hardly can get away from that fiery, powerful
ruler of the day during November, December, and
January, in Queensland; it burns and shrivels one
up. In India the houses are built in such a

manner that as soon as one gets inside the fiercest
rays of the sun are powerless to reach or harm,
but in Queensland the same careful precautions
are not taken. Queensland enjoys, during eight
months of the year, the loveliest climate imaginable ; the other four months the people suffer
much — I must do them justice, their suffering
is great. The reason is, their houses are built
for these eight delightful months, and for the
rest they do the best they can. I have, in all
my travels, never known what lightning and
thunder were till J visited Brisbane. It is
nothing rare to see a cabman fall from his seat
struck by lightning, and the horse, with cab and
occupant, going on a spree all by itself, till some
courageous passer-by stops it. Horses don't like
lightning and thunder, but in Brisbane they seem
prepared for all sorts of eventualities. The rain
falls in marvelous torrents, and the atmosphere
after one of these storms is extremely refreshing.

During my stay in Brisbane a very touching
incident happened worth recording. The city
lies near the river forty miles from Moreton Bay,
which has two outlets, ten miles distant from each
other, one on each side : there are high and low
tides, and ships of a certain tonnage must catch
the high tide, or they strand. Stranding is not
dangerous, but rather unpleasant. Our captain,
anxious to get his vessel into the river in time,
forced his speed in hope to catch the tide, but
unfortunately he was too late, and we stuck in the

sand of the bay and had to wait for the next tide.
This was my first experience of sand-sailing and I
don't want another. The river is about a quarter
of a mile wide, and is infested with sharks, and
some say crocodiles, which have been seen to swim
across the river and disappear. Yet, in spite of
the interdict of the government, persons, especially boys, will bathe in its dangerous waters. On
one occasion a party of boys bathed along the
bank at the foot of a hill on the top of which the
house of a Mr. Drury, a prominent citizen, is
located. Suddenly the boys on the shore heard
their friend, young Drury, a lad of about twelve
years of age shriek, " A shark ! " Rushing to the
river's edge they saw to their amazement two
sharks after young Drury, who was fighting them
as he swam toward the shore. Quick as thought
one of the boys, about ten years of age, sprang
into the water to his friend's assistance, and
succeeded after much effort in getting him near
to the land, but they had not quite reached it
when he saw one of the monsters turn fiercely
toward his friend. He struck out with all his force
and gave the monster a powerful blow — then in
another instant both the boys were on shore. But
when on shore the boys saw to their horror that
the entire right side of young Drury had been
literally stripped. The father was sent for, and on
his arrival the boy said: " Oh, papa, dear, don't
scold me, I could n't help it. It was not my fault.
Don't tell mother." The doctor was sent for, who

consulted with some of his *confrères*. Amputation was inevitable, and need I say that the sweet boy did not survive it? The boy who showed such marvelous courage as to jump into the water to rescue his friend was interviewed by a reporter, and when he had finished, the brave boy said: "I say, Mr. ——, you're not a newspaper chap, I hope, who will put that stuff in the daily. Now, don't do that: I don't want anything of the sort: the one thing I wanted was to save poor Drury; but, alas! he's dead and if my dad hears about it, he'll give me a thundering whipping." Surely this is the stuff heroes are made of.

From Brisbane I returned to Sydney; thence overland to Melbourne. One night I gave dramatic readings in a little town called Goulburn, which is surrounded by beautiful gardens and farms. The hall was packed and the audience greatly delighted with the performance. During the day we went to an orchard in the neighborhood, where we feasted ourselves on the most delicious European cherries of all dimensions, flavors, and colors, gathered fresh by our own hands from the trees. We tried to pay liberally for our pleasure, but I am sure we never could pay sufficiently for the quantity of delicious fruit we consumed that day; for once we felt we had feasted with the gods.

From Goulburn we went to Wagga Wagga, made famous by the Claimant, a thriving little town, where they now have a beautiful theatre.

Then on to Albury, where we saw the vineyards, and which is the line of demarcation between New South Wales and Victoria. On my arrival at Melbourne I at once considerably supplemented my company to travel through New Zealand, a country which I had not seen and was anxious to visit.

CHAPTER III. — NEW ZEALAND.

SOUTH ISLAND. — DUNEDIN. — CHRISTCHURCH.

"Good things should be praised."
— *Two Gentlemen of Verona, Act. iii, sc. 1.*

"Pleasure and action make the hours seem short."
— *Othello, Act ii, sc. 3.*

The Bluff — New Zealand ports — Invercargill — Dunedin, the queen of New Zealand cities — The Scotch — Port Chalmers — Two systems of railroad — The city buildings — The situation — Farming in Otago — Frozen meat — Mountain scenery — The roads — Convict-laborers — A convict-artist — The waterworks — Drinking-fountains — The suburbs — Heresy and orthodoxy — A grim bishop — Dr. Byng and the liberal clergy — The High School — Children at the theatre — Dramatic readings in the Temperance Hall — Shakespeare in English, German, and French — Speeches — "Blue-fire" — "The ghost began to cough!" — The hotels — Means of transit — Horse-breeding — Daily papers — Professor Alexander Wilson — A great success — Farewell to Dunedin — Timaru — Christchurch — Public buildings — The spirit of the place — Orthodox religiosity and Art — The Honorable Mr. Romilly — The climate — The only natural attraction — The Public Gardens — The Museum — The moa — Lyttelton — The Canterbury plains.

I LEFT Melbourne in December by the Union Line in the steamship Rotomahana, a vessel which can run sixteen knots an hour, and which makes the distance between Melbourne and the Bluff, the first point in New Zealand, in less than three days. Vessels run twice a week, and the Union Line has a powerful fleet of between twenty and thirty vessels. They make what is called the "round trip," leaving Melbourne direct for the Bluff, which is a small port at the extreme south of New Zealand, where they remain all day in the

harbor and start at night for the next port. The
ports they touch are as follows: Port Chalmers,
for Dunedin; Port Lyttelton, for Christchurch;
Wellington, Napier, Gisbourn, Auckland, then to
Sydney, which takes three days and a half. The
return journey is made along the entire line of
New Zealand ports to Melbourne. On the west
side of North Island commencing with Wellington there is a smoother sea, and a steady communication with Picton, Nelson, New Plymouth,
and the Bay of Auckland; there is also communication to the western parts of South Island,
including Greymouth. From Sydney there are
direct steamers running to Wellington, and to
the ports on the west coast of South Island.
The round trip from Melbourne to Auckland
costs fourteen pounds; to Sydney, twenty pounds;
to intermediate places, according to distance.

I arrived on Sunday afternoon, December 17,
at the Bluff, and left with my company completely
organized for this special trip through New Zealand early the next day. The point we made for
first was Invercargill, a small town, populated
principally by Scotchmen. The principal occupation of the people is farming; they live and often
grow rich by the produce of the land. The
town has no great attractions: indeed, the only
marked feature it seems to have is that it always
rains there, or, if by any chance it stops, it blows
terribly. The town has two theatres, but the
people are exceptionally slow and sluggish for

Scotchmen. I played five nights so as to rehearse some of my pieces, and then took my company to the queen of New Zealand cities — Dunedin. I can hardly speak too well of this beautiful, generous, and hospitable town. Commercially it is the most important city of New Zealand, and has a population of nearly fifty thousand, chiefly Scotchmen. No city in the world reflects more credit on the enterprise, capacity, and perseverance of the Scotch race. Its harbor, Port Chalmers, is very fine: indeed, no fact impresses the traveler in New Zealand more than the number of good harbors it possesses. From Dunedin there are two complete systems of railroad: one extending south to the Bluff; the other to the capital of South Island — Christchurch. The buildings of this city are the finest in the colony. The city stands on the top of a hill, and is surrounded for many miles by the most fertile tableland in the world.

The farmers of Otago are the richest in the colony, and in recent years many new industries have sprung up, and now other produce finds its way into the world's markets besides wheat, hides, wool, and canned beef, namely, frozen meat, which, in refrigerators, is sent out to England by sailing-vessels and steamers. The profit arising from this new trade is enormous and is doing much to revive Otago from the commercial depression of the last few years. There are districts of country near Dunedin equal in beauty to the most beautiful mountain-land in Bavaria, Scotland, or Switzer-

land, especially the fourteen miles' drive over the
" Blue Skin " road, named after a famous Maori
chief, or because the tips of the mountains are
generally blue. The roads all over New Zealand
are in perfect order, and can only be compared
with the celebrated shell-road of Mobile.

The reason of this is, New Zealand utilizes
its criminals for making roads, wharfs, and for
building public institutions. These unfortunate
men are to be seen in all directions where public
works are progressing, and it is wonderful to see
their perfect state of health and vigor. The
motley dress is the only indication of their state ;
the same may be said of criminals in Tasmania
and in the Hawaiian Islands, for these are following the example of New Zealand in compelling
those whose crimes have rendered them outcasts
of society to work for the public benefit.

As I looked on these men at their work they
reminded me very much of the convicts of the
state-prison of Kingston, in Canada, where I was
greatly struck with the humanity of their treatment. What different treatment this ! and how
much more likely to result in what should be the
real end of all punishment, namely, the reformation of the criminal, from that I witnessed on a
visit to a Melbourne prison, where I saw hundreds
of poor wretches sitting in rows in a large open
space securely walled in, and protected by armed
wardens, before immense piles of stones, breaking
them into pieces in solitude ; the terrible silence

only broken by the sound of a hundred hammers or by the meal-bell. I spoke to one of these unfortunate fellows in Melbourne, who was permitted to come out of the ranks to see a gentleman whom I accompanied on my visit to the prison. He was a Mr. ——, who had been a cashier in one of the Melbourne banks, and a great swell in the society of the place. He had embezzled many thousands of pounds, but returned most of the money as a *repentant*, by reason of which he got only seven years. When we saw him, he was breaking stones like the rest, and I could not help feeling pity for him. I asked him: "How do you like it?" He simply said: "I have to do it, whether I like it or not." Still, I could not keep back the thought that the method of punishment that consigns a man of this stamp to stone-breaking, ignoring altogether his aptitudes and talents for higher labor, which utilized might be much more profitable to society, is itself a criminal act on the part of the legislature of the country, and needs reformation no less than those for whose punishment it is designed. The sheriff told me that this man was an excellent worker, and that he was always ahead of the others in getting through his allotted task.

In the same prison the governor showed me some of the most exquisite pen-and-ink sketches that I have ever seen, done by a German who had been committed for forgery. These were chiefly copies of celebrated pictures, both landscape and portraiture. The governor and his family, feeling pity for a man so highly gifted and brought so low by his folly and crime, and respect for his remarkable talents, tried in every way to reclaim him and to plant in his heart true moral principles. He was treated with special care, and taken into the governor's own service in the capacity of clerk. He soon got his punishment reduced, and rejoiced over his success. "Now you have a new chance, my friend," said the governor, "and may the protection of God be over you, and may I never see you again except as a friendly visitor. Here is an extra five pounds for you. Take care not to enter bad company; keep away from vice. Good-by." Like timely advice gave the governor's worthy wife, as she, too, said "Good-by"; while even the governor's children, who had come to find marvelous pleasure in the man's "ink-paintings," as they called them, raised their young voices high, crying, "Good-by, good-by!" as the grateful artist passed away through the prison gates. Would he be strong? would he stand that fearful trial a man has to stand who once more faces the world from a term of prison-life? For a month all went well; but then he was back at the prison again, not as a friendly visitor, but sentenced to a heavier punishment and for a longer period than before, and for a like offence. The governor feared he would have to look upon him as a perpetual lodger.

"What fools these mortals be!"

The waterworks at Dunedin are so arranged as, perhaps, to be the most lovely and refreshing in the world. They are a marvel of taste, and imply the highest sense of the beautiful, allied with perfect design, in a matter of great use and importance to a populous city. Here is a long, winding road, by the side of which a rivulet of clear water runs, either gently sloping bank being ornamented with ferns, for which New Zealand is celebrated — ferns of all dimensions, from a few inches to twelve, and in some instances fifteen, feet in height. The road rises to an elevation of about five hundred feet, and all the way along the rivulet makes a quiet, sweet music as it glides down over the stones, till, when you reach the top of the hill, there are two large basins, in circumference about a mile, around which there are lovely walks, most comfortable seats placed every hundred yards, and drinking-fountains for refreshment. I have been in many watering-places in Europe, and have seen most towns that lay themselves out to catch the summer pleasure-seekers, but nowhere else have I been so impressed by the perfect fitness, harmony, and beauty of the arrangements, both for the healthful and for the health-seeking invalid. I think it is Ruskin who has said that a people's reverence is never more seen than in the care and respect they pay to Nature's fountains — the sweet, pure springs she opens for man's need, joy, and refreshment among the hills of every land. New Zealand, in this

respect, deserves the highest praise of all countries
I have visited, for, go where you will throughout
its cities and towns, you find this care taken to
save from pollution, and to give a fitting and
beautiful home and appointed place to, that pure
stream that brings gladness and refreshment, but
no pain and misery, to man. The care shown in
this respect gives one, on entering any New Zealand city, the impression of a perfect hospitality,
the like of which I have never felt anywhere else.
The people seem to have grasped the great truth
of charity which the world's great Master and
Teacher has enshrined forever under the image
of "a cup of cold water."

The New Zealanders are, perhaps, the heaviest-
taxed people in the world, but also among the
most generous and hospitable.

There is another beautiful outskirt to this
lovely town, stretching to the sea about a mile and
a half from the city, where, especially on a Sunday
or on a public holiday, thousands of people go
seeking health and pleasure on its smooth, sandy
shore. It is in fact a lesser Brighton, Margate, or
Yarmouth, and reminds one much of these as one
sees so many hundreds of happy children building
sand-castles along its beach or deliciously paddling
in the merry waves.

As extremes generally meet, so Dunedin is the
centre of free-religious thought and of episcopal
orthodoxy in the Australasias. The head and
front of the former is represented in a Mr. Stout,

who is considered one of the ablest lawyers in the country, and who, with others earnest in modern religious liberalism, gives, every Sunday evening, lectures to crowded audiences in the Lyceum, and encourages the people in their love of intellectual and religious freedom, science, art, and the drama; while the latter is represented by the lean and hungry bishop of the Episcopal Church, struck with miscalled holy horror at the bare thought of amusement and the stage.

But there are many happy exceptions to this type of divine amongst the clergy of the city: one especially, the Reverend Dr. Byng. This distinguished clergyman encourages the people to uphold everything in the way of beauty, art, and the drama, of a legitimate character. He treated me with great kindness during my stay, coming to most of my performances; and on several occasions I had the pleasure of dining with him. He is the minister of the most influential church in the city, and in the strongest way urged his people to give us an earnest support. Wellnigh the whole clergy of the Episcopal Church did the same, notwithstanding the grim bishop at their head, and it was no uncommon sight to see a dozen clergymen at a time occupying stalls. On one occasion, when I gave a reading, in grateful acknowledgment of the great public support I had received, at the High School, before five hundred scholars and masters, the platform was crowded with ministers of every denomination, and the chair was occupied by the Reverend Dr. Steward, one of the leading divines of the Presbyterian Church.

On another occasion I allowed all the children who could show a certificate of good behavior a free-pass into the theatre if they were accompanied by their parents, and the success was so great that I had to repeat the experiment. It was done from my sympathy with the children in their studies, for I have an infinite pleasure in the joy, wellbeing, and progress of the little ones who fill our homes with such sweet laughter and teach us the unselfishness of love; and also as a compliment to their parents. It must not be supposed, however, that the New Zealander is mean and cares much for a free-pass for his child: none are more generous than he. But I never witnessed more real enthusiasm than in these sweet, happy children, during the evenings in which they crowded the theatre. The play was Hamlet, which took immensely in Dunedin.

On the afternoon of January 18, I also gave a series of dramatic readings in the Temperance Hall for the benefit of the teachers and pupils of the public schools. Mr. Robin, chairman of the Dunedin school committee; Dr. MacDonald, rector of the High School; the Reverend Dr. Byng, and other distinguished men, were on the platform; while in the body of the hall there were several members of the synod, and the Reverend Fathers Walsh and Nieuport. The readings included Hood's Dream of Eugene Aram, Marc Antony's

oration from Julius Cæsar, Shylock's speech from
The Merchant of Venice ; respecting the last, I
may say, that, out of consideration for the scho-
lastic character of my audience, and hoping to
encourage the young people in their study of the
modern languages, and also to show something of
the cosmopolitan quality of Shakespeare's genius,
and that his thoughts and ideas retain their music
and beauty in every tongue, I recited it not only in
English, but in German and French.   I concluded
with the trial scene from the same play.   There
was great enthusiasm, and the reception I met
with was gratifying in every way.   At the conclusion, Dr. MacDonald, rector of the High
School, rose and said : —

"I move a vote of sincere thanks to Mr.
Bandmann for the reading which he has given
this afternoon.   I am certain that I can assure
him in your name that it is with exquisite
intellectual pleasure we have heard some of
the noblest passages from the literature of our
own country powerfully interpreted to us by a
master of the dramatic art — one who is eminent
in action, gesture, and utterance.   There is another
way in which we can return him our thanks.   In
our schoolwork, reading intelligibly possesses an
educational value of a high order ; but it is also
true that, in the multiplicity of competing subjects in our schools, this important art of reading
does not receive that amount of cultivation which
it evidently deserves.   We shall take care to

return our thanks to him by further attention on the part of those who have distinguished themselves by devotion to the cultivation of this subject. I ask this meeting to thank Mr. Bandmann for his graceful courtesy in coming forward this afternoon to give us these beautiful readings."

To this neat little speech I made the following reply : —

"*Mr. Chairman, Ladies and Gentlemen,* — You have taken me by great surprise, for I am not a speaker, and was not prepared to hear so many kind utterances on my behalf. Had it been otherwise I perhaps should have done — what we actors have to do — namely, studied my part; but I hope you will take the few words which I have to say for what they are really worth. I can assure you that they come from my heart. I thank you sincerely for the many kind things you have said of me. As to my coming before you to give a reading, I can assure you that it gives me great pleasure to find that it has given you pleasure. If my humble efforts will lead to greater attention in the utterance of speech, I shall be very proud of it. I am glad to hear the rector recognize that elocution is defective, not only in your town, but all over the world. I do not know why that should be the case. It seems as if language were written and read, but not spoken. One of our principal professors said as much, years ago. He said: 'Speak as you

write, but do not write as you speak.' There
is a great deal of meaning in that. It is as a great
author once told me was the case with the English
language: 'You spell it donkey, and pronounce
it ass.' The English language is very arbitrary;
we all know that. The German language is not
so, but a regular one, yet with my countrymen
every few miles you find a different patois. The
most educated people speak bad grammar, while
they write the language perfectly. So it is not
only in your country that sufficient stress is not
laid upon the art of elocution. It is different
with Frenchmen, for they care much more for
refinement and finish of speech. No one in France
is considered an educated man unless he speaks
accurately. That is not so in other countries.
I have heard educated people speak the most
dreadful dialect, and yet they would write most
elegantly. I can assure you that elocution is a
great art, and is not one easy to learn. It is a
child which requires to be fostered and nursed,
and if attention is not given to it in the days
of childhood, and to what is said from morning
till evening, a habit of indifference is acquired,
and when we are older it takes many years of
hard work to do what might have been accomplished in a few years in early life. I have
given this afternoon's reading with the greatest
pleasure, and I feel great satisfaction at seeing
so many children around me. If they have
enjoyed themselves I am thoroughly rewarded."

Both of the foregoing are taken from the Dunedin *Morning Herald* of January 19, 1881, as I have no other record of them, though a much fuller report of Dr. MacDonald's speech was given in some of the papers.

I stayed over two months in Dunedin, and played my own and Louise Beaudet's entire répertoire. I had to repeat Hamlet fourteen times, it was in such favor with the Dunedin public. One evening the property-man, whose duty it was to get a proper blue-light for the appearance of the ghost, being unable to procure the lime-light, made up the deficiency with blue-fire; but the druggist, who had told him that it would neither produce smell nor smoke, had very much deceived him, for, of all the foul, offensive, mephitic stenches that might accompany a ghost from the unseen world, that was surely the worst. As Falstaff says, "there was the rankest compound of villainous smell that ever offended nostril." That night, I think, the audience must have imagined that a whole world of lost spirits was playing a prank with them. But, oh, misery! it did not end there, for, strange to say, the ghost began to cough! then Hamlet, then every one at the back of the stage, then the entire audience in front of the stage, and when finally the curtain dropped, there was the most perfect oratorio of coughing ever heard inside a theatre, accompanied by such a rushing to the windows and doors and general stampede as wellnigh threatened to ruin the entire play. But I was not altogether without presence of mind. I immediately sent for my agent, who was trying to pacify the crowded house, and bade him buy twenty pounds of bronchial troches, and to send four girls with trays of these through the entire house, with my compliments. The audience laughed and accepted the remedy good-naturedly, and although an occasional cough was heard here and there from an oversensitive throat, the performance was finished, as usual, amid universal approbation.

Dunedin has two theatres, each able to accommodate about fifteen hundred people. It has, also, a magnificent public hall capable of seating three thousand. The hotels are conducted on the most approved principles, and some of them are very handsome buildings. The town has all the modern appliances of transit, such as horse and steam street-cars; and it is even ahead of New York in one respect, for it has already adopted the cable system of the San Francisco street-belt-cars, by which means one can travel with safety up almost perpendicular hills. There is also a fine service of hansom-cabs, with splendid horses, which would be an ornament to the metropolis of any country. Indeed, horse-raising is one of the proudest occupations of New Zealanders; they supply the entire Australasias with most noble breeds, especially of draught-horses.

Three good daily papers are published in the city: the *Otago Times*, the *Morning Herald*, and the *Evening Telegraph*.

The High School is an admirable institution, and will bear comparison with the best colleges of older countries. Dr. MacDonald, the rector, and Professor Alexander Wilson are both Edinburgh graduates, and thorough Shakespearean scholars. The latter possesses very remarkable critical faculty, and the use to which he puts it, in endeavoring to raise the public taste, is worthy of the highest praise. He thus renders many kindly services to actors of real merit who visit the city, while I enjoyed the privilege of meeting him socially.

But the best of friends must part, and the hour came when I had to say farewell to the noble, generous, and hospitable people of Dunedin, and to quit their fair, beautiful city. My visit was a great success, for the two months of my stay brought me a clear profit of upward of fifteen hundred pounds (seventy-five hundred dollars), and, beyond this, there was the happiness of being taken to a people's heart, welcomed to their best society, and made glad in their joy, which constitutes the true riches of life, — of an actor's life no less than of others, — and will ever remain among my most precious memories.

I brought my engagement to a close on the evening of February 26, and during an interval in the performance I did my best, in a little speech before the curtain, to acknowledge the favors I had received. I know that I failed, — we actors seldom succeed in speeches, — but, inadequate as it is to express the sentiments I then felt and still cherish for the noble Dunedin people, I will include it here, because everything I tried to say then I would like to repeat now ; but I fear my art has not improved in such matters. I copy it from a report of my last performance at the Queen's Theatre, which appeared in the *Otago Times* of February 27 : —

"*Ladies and Gentlemen,* — There is an old proverb, ' When the heart is full the tongue runs free,' but I do not think that that proverb is applicable to me in this present instance, for I assure you were I to say everything that my heart feels, it would take a much longer time than you or I have to spare this evening, for my heart is full of thanks and gratitude for the kind manner in which you have treated me. Believe me, what I say is sincere. There is no blarney about it. In fact, I should not like to be near that blarney-stone at present. I speak sincerely. My thanks —my grateful thanks — are due to you for the excellent manner in which you have treated me from the moment I put my foot on the stage in Dunedin. I have traveled all over the world and have been in many towns in Germany, England, America, and Australia, but I cannot mention a single town where I have been received with sincerer feeling, with more enthusiastic kindness, than in Dunedin. With a few exceptions my houses have been good ; and the honor you have bestowed on me great ; and the warmth and enthusiasm displayed by you thorough and full-souled. Now, have I not every reason to be grateful? Not only on the stage, but also off the stage, I have been very happy. You know very well (this is no flattery) that your town is one of the most beautiful in the world. In fact, I prophesy that the time is not far distant when this will be the resort of tourists from Australia and Europe, who will travel to see the grandeur of the place. I have traveled in Italy, Switzerland, and other countries, but I have seen nowhere grandeur so beautiful as I have seen around your enlightened, hearty, and progressive town. I go out of this town well pleased. Why should I not be well pleased? I go away with honor and money, and I have every reason to be satisfied.

"I thank the press. I think the press has treated us with universal kindness. Gentlemen of education, scholarly, Shakespearean men, have come forward on this occasion to write, not only criticisms, but essays. I am proud they have done so. I have also to thank the company. They have worked very hard. When you come to consider that we have played twenty different pieces, I think you must believe that they have toiled very hard to make this season a success. Every one — there is not a single member of the company who has not willingly and gladly put his shoulder to the wheel, to earn the patronage and applause of the Dunedin public. And now, ladies and gentlemen, it is hard to say farewell; but when I come back (for I shall decidedly come back) I hope you will then have retained the same kindly feeling you have shown me on this occasion."

My company and I left fair, beautiful, and charming Dunedin on the next day for Timaru. Timaru is a small, thriving town of about fifteen thousand inhabitants, located on the sea-coast in Canterbury, South Island. It is easily reached from Dunedin, as the railroad from the Bluff to Christchurch passes through Timaru. I gave a series of dramatic readings in the public schoolroom, at which Mr. R. B. Walcot, the chairman of the school committee, presided; and we played four nights to crowded houses, at double prices, amid the most intense enthusiasm, and then passed on to Christchurch, also in Canterbury, where we opened the first week in March.

Christchurch is situated on an open plain. The public buildings and residences are principally of wood. It is a cathedral city, and in appearance and public spirit, or rather its want of it, the very antithesis of Dunedin : there, everything is undulated, picturesque and progressive; here, everything is even, methodical, and more or less conservative. The people live in an atmosphere of dull, very stupid, bent-down piety, similar to that which characterizes the communities of the old cathedral towns of England, and there is a stiffness and rigidness about the place that reminds one especially of Lincoln, Worcester, and Gloucester;

together with an absolute lack of spontaneous
enthusiasm and lively intelligence, which is at
once noticed by any one who visits those cities.
I don't know whether the same fact has impressed
other travelers, but I think it must be felt by all
observing minds, that in cathedral cities coarseness
and vulgarity are more prominent than in others;
and that variety and negro shows, and exhibitions
of monstrosities, are more popular, and find most
favor, where orthodox religiosity is the most
fervent.

To a very considerable degree · this is true of
Christchurch; the inhabitants are formal and
cold; they lack the fervor of the Londoner,
the intelligence of the Scotchman. Yet the
people seem anxious to appreciate a good performance, and during my visit far exceeded my expectations in the support they gave me; but, the truth
is, they usually live under such ice-cold formalism
and rigorous social conditions, that their minds
have sunk into a habitual and settled dulness,
that, do their utmost, they can't rouse themselves
completely out of it without the aid of violent
sensationalism; and though I believe they sincerely aimed to do so, on the occasion of my
visit, they did not succeed in reaching the standard of the Dunedin public in sentiment and taste;
with whom Art is a supreme interest of life; the
legitimate drama an institution of daily edifica-
tion and delight; and the practice of hospitality
a habit that confers an unspeakable happiness

on others and gives a marvelous grace and beauty to those who cultivate it.

But it happened that, in spite of the usual dead-level of the place, I did an excellent business for one month, and left, after paying all expenses, with a considerably clear profit. Socially, too, I had a very good time in Christchurch, for I was fortunate in meeting there an old friend, the Honorable Mr. Romilly (whose brother, Samuel Henry Romilly, married my friend, Lady Arabella Southesk), son of Lady Elizabeth Eliot, daughter of the Earl of Minto, and of Lieutenant-Colonel Frederick Romilly, who had come from Wellington on government business.

The climate of Christchurch is everything that could be wished — beautiful, mild, constant. During the winter months New Zealand has heavy snowstorms and considerable frost, but Christchurch is generally free, even in the depth of the winter season, from severe weather, though it comes in for its full share of rain.

There is one natural feature even in Christchurch that does much to relieve the otherwise monotonous physiognomy of the city. It is as though Nature, knowing how dull and helpless the people are in themselves, had in sheer pity bestowed upon them one charm complete and beautiful, as her gifts so often are : for, running through the centre of the city, is a small, winding stream, clear and lovely, the home of innumerable trout and salmon ; the banks of which are surpass-

ingly charming, being lined with willows rivaling
those that render so delightful the meadows at
the back of the colleges at Cambridge, and the
sight of which recalls many an English landscape.
The Public Gardens are large and prettily laid
out; while the Museum contains the finest collection of Dinornis skeletons — a class of large and
terrible extinct birds — of any museum throughout the world. The most famous is the moa, so
called by the Maoris, an enormous, wingless bird,
long extinct, but celebrated in the hunting-songs
of that strange people ; the finest specimen is over
twelve feet high, and its legbones exceed in size
those of the African elephant.

Lyttelton, the port of Christchurch, is a magnificent harbor, built at the cost of two hundred
thousand pounds, and is connected with the city
by a tunnel that passes through a small mountain-
range. Lyttelton itself is a most beautiful place,
but entirely monopolized for purposes of traffic
and shipment.   Christchurch is almost exclusively
dependent on the agriculture of the outlying
districts of the Canterbury plains, and since for
the last few years this has not been very prosperous, the city has suffered severe commercial
depression.

CHAPTER IV. — New Zealand.

North Island. — Wellington. — Napier. — Auckland.

"Therein I spake of most disastrous chances,
Of moving accidents, by flood and field;
Of hairbreadth 'scapes i' th' imminent deadly breach;
. . . .
And of the cannibals that each other eat."

— Othello, Act i, sc. 3.

The seat of the government — The public buildings — The climate — The Museum — The theatre — The governor, Sir Arthur Gordon — Lady Gordon — A "Judas" — Wanganui — Napier — The situation — The Scotch element — Judge Kenny — Auckland — Changes in ten years — The Duke of Edinburgh — Story of an English officer and a Maori girl — Civilization and the Maoris — A noble warrior-race — Hongi Ika, the great chief — His memorable last words — The War of 1845 — Heke — His address to his people — Maori superstition — Divination — The *tohungas* — The *mataika* — Heke's fort at Mawhe — Te Atua Wera — His exhortation — "The European God" — A runaway slave — Kawiti — Te Kahakaha — Heke's heroism and grandeur of character — A painful problem — England and her colonies — The Earl of Pembroke — Too little consistency in government — The Maoris and religion — The Old Testament preferred to the New — The massacre of Poverty Bay — The Hau Haus — Te Kooti — Ropata — Class distinctions — Cannibalism — Immortality — Marriage — Tattooing — The way a chief shows favor — Names — Tobacco — The *mere ponamu* — Love of warfare — Story of a Maori law - student — The King Country — Half - caste — The Thames gold-fields — Lake Taupo — Rotomahana Springs — Mountains — The Ruahine range — The Manawatu — New Plymouth — Coaching across country — Taranaki Province — An amusing incident — A Maori salutation.

FROM Christchurch I took my company to Wellington, situated at the southwest point of North Island, which for years suffered so much from the effects of the Maori War. The journey by sea takes about twelve hours. Wellington Harbor is the finest, with the exception of

Auckland, in New Zealand, and the city stretches over its shores with a background of fine hills. The houses are all built of wood, perhaps as a slight precaution in the eventuality of earthquake, to which awful occurrence experience has shown the locality is liable. A severe one occurred some years ago, in which several lives were lost, and enormous damage done to property. The seat of the New Zealand government was formerly Auckland, but on account of its more central position it was removed to Wellington, to the great disgust of the Aucklanders. The Government House, a very simple structure, and the public buildings are of wood, and somewhat primitive in character. The climate, on account of the peculiar position of Wellington, lying as it does unsheltered on an ankle between the two islands, and exposed to storms and foul weather on all sides, is the worst in the country. It rains eight months out of the twelve, and, when it does n't rain, there are often fearful gales. They say a Wellington man can be recognized in any part of the world — he always puts his hand to his hat when he turns the corner of a street.

The Museum contains a very large collection of Maori curiosities, including a meeting-house erected by the Maoris in one of their villages, from which it was removed and re-erected here. It shows a wonderful proficiency in design, carving, and art-workmanship.

The theatre is a plain building and will accommodate fifteen hundred people, and, like most of the theatres of the country, has only stalls, dress circle, and pit. My engagement was only of nine nights' duration, under the special patronage of the governor of New Zealand, Sir Arthur Gordon, who, with Lady Gordon, came nearly every night to the theatre, and from whom I received the following letter, in which he signified his preference for certain plays: —

> "GOVERNMENT HOUSE, NEW ZEALAND,
> "19th April, 1881.
>
> "*Dear Sir*, — In reply to your letter of the 14th inst., I am directed to inform you that his excellency will have much pleasure in being present at some of your representations in Wellington.
>
> "The plays which, in accordance with your invitation, his excellency would name, are: Much Ado About Nothing, The Merchant of Venice, and As You Like It.
>
> "His excellency would suggest Tuesday, the 26th, for the first of these plays, unless a night later in the week would be more convenient for its representation. The Merchant of Venice and As You Like It his excellency would prefer to see either at the end of next week, or the beginning of the following week, by which time Lady Gordon will have arrived in Wellington.
>
> "These suggestions are, of course, intended to depend upon your convenience.
>
> "I am, dear sir, yours faithfully,
> "F. P. MURRAY, *Private Secretary.*"

At Wellington I found an old member of my company, who had played the traitor to me, left behind by his bogus manager who had induced him to leave my service, in very reduced circumstances. He asked me to reinstate him in my company. "How can you, sir, expect such a thing? you know you have been a 'Judas' to me!" I exclaimed. "Well, then," he replied, "be like 'J. C.,' forgiving, and take me back." I did as he wished.

From Wellington we ran up to a place called Wanganui, located at the foot of several hills on the west of North Island. There is a railroad to it now, but formerly you had to go by coach, or in wretched little tugboats by sea. By road, for sixty miles of the route, partly along the sea-coast, it is most lovely scenery; but after the coach leaves Foxton there are twenty-four miles of desert country, the most terrible imaginable; these passed, however, and there open before you plains of the most fertile pasture-lands. The people in Wanganui are the worst in the country; the church and drink are their only means of passing their leisure, and they alternate between these; if anything, the latter is in most favor with them. But, fortunately for the colony, most of them are going mad — out of every hundred madmen in Taranaki state-asylums seventy-five are from Wanganui.

The manager of the theatre showed me the stage and auditorium, and I found it a very neat and compact little building in these respects.

"But where are the dressing-rooms?" I asked.

"The dressing-rooms? Oh! yes, there is a room here," said he, "which is generally used for that purpose."

"A room," I said; "I require four — one for my own use, one for Miss Beaudet, one for the other ladies, and one for the gentlemen."

The man looked thunderstruck.

"The people who come here generally manage that for themselves," said he.

"But I don't; and except you can offer me four respectable rooms, I decline to act."

The four rooms were run up, and the manager, no doubt, thought me a — bear!

On leaving Wanganui, we went to Napier in Hawke Bay Province — an eight hours' run. It is a charming spot, surrounded on three sides by sea, and has most beautiful hills; still it is not very healthy, on account of morasses in the neighborhood. The people are enterprising, intelligent, and hospitable. The Scotch element predominates, and wherever that excellent element is prominent in the colonies, thoroughness and worthiness in dramatic art are sure to find support.

At Napier I met Judge Kenny and his wife — very delightful persons. Judge Kenny is a descendant of an old English warrior-family, and Mrs. Kenny is a relative of Charles Kean. My reception in the little town was most enthusiastic and remunerative.

We next made for Auckland, which takes exactly twenty-four hours to reach from Napier. I had been in Auckland some ten years before, but there had been so many changes, and the town exhibited such an altered appearance, that I hardly recognized it. My previous visit was at the invitation of the Duke of Edinburgh, who, as captain of the Galatea, was cruising in the Australian waters, and whose friendship I enjoyed. The duke was, at the time, and I believe still is, fond of playing the violin. He asked me to be present at one of the rehearsals of the Auckland Choral Society, in which he was playing. The music was not first-class, but I remember that, during the rehearsal, I saw two ladies of remarkable beauty; they were neither European, nor did they appear half-caste, and I could not make out to what people they belonged. They had the appearance of being, in every respect, perfect ladies, with large, ravishing, lustrous eyes and slight olive complexion.

After the rehearsal was over, the duke said: " Well, Bandmann, I suppose you thought the music poor, but did you observe those two ladies? "

I answered: " Who could help doing so? they are so wonderfully beautiful."

"Indeed they are," said he, "but thereby hangs a tale."

" Then, pray, let me hear it," said I, "for I have puzzled my brains to place them amongst the nationalities of the world, and have given up the effort in utter failure."

"I am not surprised at that," continued the duke, "for I never met any one unacquainted with the secret to reach the right conclusion. Well, you shall hear all I know of their history. These handsome girls are the daughters of an officer in the English army, who was sent many years ago to New Zealand on government business. He met a Maori girl and lived with her; she bore him these two daughters, and, for the sake of legitimating the children, he married the mother. The children received a European education, and graced their father's house with their beauty and intelligence; but one day, after twenty years of matrimonial bliss, the mother suddenly disappeared, having, in a paroxysm of religious fanaticism, followed an old Maori chief into the woods, taking with her only a blanket to cover her loins. From that day no more was heard of the old woman, but the girls are well married and live happily with their husbands."

Of all cities in New Zealand, Auckland (formerly called Waitamata) suffered most from the Maori War, and that proud warrior-race, which was subdued, has not been crushed: though every year its numbers are lessening from contact with an alien civilization. It is computed that at one time there were no less than four hundred thousand Maoris in New Zealand; half a century ago they had dwindled greatly, and now there are known to

be less than a tenth of that number. Could the
story of this race be fully written, it would probably be one of the most marvelous romances of
history. They have been called "the noblest of
savages," and in many ways certainly are the most
notable of barbarous races. They are pre-eminent
in warfare; skilled in military strategy; zealous
upholders of their own creeds of honor; incomparable for bravery, possessed of many remarkable
qualities in social life, great vigor of mind,
extraordinary oratorical powers, and patriotism
absolutely fearless of death.

A tradition is current among them that, long
ago, when Hongi Ika, the great warrior-chief of
the Maoris, saw that death was inevitable from a
wound he had received in battle at Mangamuka,
he gathered his relations and people about him at
Mawhe and addressed them thus: "Children and
friends, pay attention to my last words. After I
am gone, be kind to the missionaries, be kind to
the other Europeans, welcome them to the shore,
trade with them, protect them, and live with them
as one people; but if ever there should land on
this shore a people who wear red garments, who
do not work, who neither buy nor sell, and who
always have arms in their hands, then be aware
that these are a people called soldiers, a dangerous
people whose occupation is war. When you see
them, make war against them. Then, O my
children, be brave! then, O friends, be strong!
Be brave, that you may not be enslaved, and

that your country may not become the possession of strangers."

The Maori chief Heke, in the War of 1845, fought in the spirit of these words, spoken by his relative, Hongi Ika. When the hearts of the other chiefs failed them, and their courage forsook them, at the sight of the numbers and warlike appearance of the English army, Heke is said to have called the people together for a "great talkee," and when the tribes drew back, to have uttered these remarkable words: "I will fight these soldiers. I will cut down the flagstaff. I will fulfill the last words of Hongi Ika. Be not afraid of these — 'all men are *men*' — [a Maori proverb]. The soldiers are not gods; lead will kill them; and if we are beaten at last we shall be beaten by a brave and noble people and need not be ashamed." Still the chiefs hesitated to join Heke, in fear of the strength of the foe, saying, "We will wait till a battle has been fought, and if he is successful then we will join him."

Heke, therefore, started on the expedition with his people and those of his elder relative, Kawiti. They made for Kororareka to fight the English soldiers, and to cut down the flagstaff which, after the Treaty of Waitangi, the governor of New Zealand caused to be erected at Maiki. The Maoris, notwithstanding their general intelligence, are fearfully superstitious, and this flagstaff had become an object of the greatest abhorrence to them;

a hundred superstitions had grown about it, and it was a symbol of every conceivable oppression and injustice. They imagined it kept traders from their harbors, that it was a sign that their island had been taken by the English, and that their nobility and independence were no more. One thing they were certain about, namely, that they got less tobacco and fewer blankets than formerly, and their hearts became sad, and, at last, they attributed all their ill-fortune to the flagstaff, and they resolved that they would by a practical experiment decide the point; so Heke went and cut it down. It was a daring act, but it was rewarded; for soon after the flagstaff was cut down the customs-duties were repealed, and tobacco and other articles became cheaper. What better confirmation could the Maoris have had of their impression of the evil potency of the hated thing? The flagstaff down, fortune seemed to smile on them, and they concluded there must have been a mysterious connection between the flagstaff and their ill-luck; yes, its existence had been the source of all their evils. Would it be erected again? Well, if it were, they knew what course to take. Soon after the flagstaff was re-erected, and again cut down at great risk. But it was erected a third time more securely, and this time, O hateful sight! the military were stationed around it. The courage of Heke, however, was equal to the occasion; he resolved that he would down with it, though the act might cost his life, and so started on the expedition. On the night before the battle he and his followers are said to have had recourse to divination, by using miniature darts made of rushes or reeds, which the Maoris strongly believe in, though it would seem that the *tohungas* (priests) can make the sign favorable or otherwise.

The dart for Heke was fortunate, but the darts for the foe and the flagstaff not so, and there was great joy in the Maori camp. Afterward Kawiti, being himself a tohunga, threw a *rakau* (dart) for his own sake, then one for the foe; either was straight and fair, but either turned the wrong way up, which is the sign of death. Then Kawiti said: " It is good. Here have I two darts ominous of success and bravery and death — our enemy will prove very strong and brave, they will suffer much from us and so will we from them. I am not displeased, for this is war and not play."

Throughout the night Heke and Kawiti, good generals as they were, spoke with great eloquence to their men, to give them resolution and courage. One thing seems to have surprised them greatly throughout the war, that the soldiers in the enemy's camp paid no attention to omens, and did a thousand things tremendously "unlucky."

The man first killed in a battle is called the *mataika*, and the one who succeeds in doing the deed is ever afterward held in great distinction, and the young Maoris will risk everything to obtain the honor. Some of them seem to possess a charmed life, having been known in eleven different affrays to have won the distinction of killing the matáika. Indeed, the aptitude for this sort of business seems to increase with each success.

While the battle of Kororareka was going on under Kawiti's leadership, Heke took the fortress of the *pakehas* (the English), and cut the hated flagstaff down for the third time. There were losses on both sides, and at last the Maoris set fire to the town of Kororareka, which had been evacuated by the pakehas, and this was the first exciting incident that occurred.

Heke soon afterward built a fort at Mawhe, being resolved to fight the pakeha soldiers on the spot where the memorable last words of Hongi Ika had been addressed to the assembled Maoris. At the completion of the fort, the spirit of Ngakahi (a familiar spirit the Maoris believe in) entered into Te Atua Wera, the greatest priest among them, and spoke to Heke and his followers by his lips: "Be brave and strong and patient. Fear not the soldiers, they will not be able to take this fort; neither be you afraid of all those different kinds of big guns you have heard so much talk of. I will turn aside the shot, and they shall do you no harm; but this *pa* (fort) and its defenders must be made *tapu* (sacred). You must particularly observe all the sacred rites and customs of your ancestors; if you neglect this in the smallest particular, evil will

befall you, and I also shall desert you. You
who pray to the God of the missionaries continue
to do so, and in your praying see you make no
mistakes. Fight and pray. Touch not the spoils
of the slain; abstain from human flesh, lest the
European God should be angry, and be careful not
to offend the Maori gods. It is good to have
more than one God to trust to. This war-party
must be strictly sacred. Be brave, be strong, be
patient."

During the siege of the fort, a slave frightened by the English guns ran away, but met
in doing so Kawiti and his people, who were
on their way to relieve Heke. He shouted: "Oh,
the soldiers have a frightful gun! it comes roaring
and flaming!" At which Kawiti stopped him with
these words: "I know all about all sorts of guns:
all guns will kill, and all guns will also miss; this
is the *ahua* (nature) of guns; but, if you say one
word more, I will split your head open with my
tomahawk." Then the slave, fearing Kawiti's
tomahawk more even than the "roaring and
flaming gun" of the foe, ran back to the fort
with the news of Kawiti's approach.

To be taken a prisoner in war is considered
a great disgrace by the Maoris, and in all cases
where it is possible they will even enter the
enemy's country to fire volleys on the spot on
which any *toa* (chief or hero) of importance has
fallen. This is called *paura mamae* (powder of
pain and grief).

Everything goes to show that Heke was brave in the highest degree, and there are incidents recorded in the progress of the war that show him to have risen to the height of a sublime heroism. The news reached him that Te Kahakaha had fallen in the fight, and we are told that he was so affected by this that he threw his arms and garments (no doubt these last were not of a very elaborate description, for he does not appear at any time to have been " clothed in purple and fine linen," and, I imagine, never spent much time about his toilet) aside, and rushed naked along the line of the foe to the place where the old man had fallen, and the words exchanged between them are most touching: " Father, are you slain ? " asked Heke. Te Kahakaha answered: "Son, I am slain; but in whose battle shall I die if not in yours ? It is good that I should die thus."

Then Heke hastened to Te Atua Wera, and besought him to assist in removing the old chief to a place of safety. Te Atua Wera refused, because Heke had transgressed some sacred rule or other. " But is not this battle ? " roared out Heke, and here he seems to have reached, when we consider the rude conditions of the man, a height of grandeur and sublimity seldom equaled. " What care I for either men or spirits? I fear not. Let the fellow in heaven look to it. Have I not prayed to him for years? It is for him to look to me this day. I will carry off the old man alone."

We all know the result of the Maori War, but it is surely well to perpetuate by every means possible the memory of the nobility and heroism of a race fast becoming extinct; while, perhaps, one of the most painful problems history suggests is whether by a different treatment they might not have risen to be a more numerous and greater people than they have at any time been.

A great wrong has been done somewhere, and the questions arise: " How was it done? and by whom?" I am not able to answer these, and perhaps they can never be fully answered; but history shows that, in not a few cases, England has not been sufficiently wise and politic in the management of her colonies. " In the good old times," says the Earl of Pembroke, "of conquest and colonization (I like to be particular about my dates and places), the civilized nations of the day followed a simple policy in regard to the savage races with whom they came in contact, which may be roughly described as going their own way, and punishing the natives if they did n't conform to it, without troubling themselves much about what the aforesaid natives thought or felt on the subject. If they understood the meaning of it, so much the better for them; if they did not, it could not be helped. Holding themselves to be morally and intellectually far superior to the savages, they maintained that it was the savages' business to understand and conform to their notions, and not their business to regard the savages. As for giving savages the rights of civilized men, it was seldom thought of; savages were to be treated as such." All this, the earl tells us, is changed, and that, all through the checkered course of England's Maori policy, there has been an earnest desire to treat the native as a man and a brother, and to give him the status of a civilized man wherever it was possible to do so; but the result has been far from satisfactory, and perhaps the old method would, after all, have been best. There may be some truth in the earl's opinion, for it would seem that there has been too little consistency in government, and that sometimes the Maoris have been flattered and caressed, and at other times received the most contrary treatment, until, shrewd as they are, they scarcely know what to expect, and are often in doubt as to whether a little affray amongst themselves, or uprising against the pakehas, in which a few lives are lost and the war-spirit of the race shows itself in wild fury, altogether bereft of its old heroism and glory, will result in additional facilities being afforded them to obtain tobacco, whiskey, and blankets, or in a severe castigation by the ranga-tira pakehas (the rich, foreign gentlemen). It is certainly a misfortune for a savage, or at best a half-civilized, people to be in doubt on such a point. The policy of the government should be one sufficiently clear and decided for them to understand and respect its authority, and, at the same time, enlightened, just, and considerate.

So far, however, as can be seen, the Maoris have only suffered from intercourse with Europeans, and are fast dying out — drink, tobacco, and clothing are more destructive to them than the powder and shot of the pakehas. They are, in a word, dying from contact with civilization. The "sugar and flour" policy is doing its work; being given necessaries, they are killing themselves with luxuries.

The Maoris have, perhaps, the least religious faculty of all races. The idea of a Supreme Being does not seem to have occurred to them: at least there is no word in their language representing it. The missionaries have adopted *Atua*, for the purposes of teaching, which has several meanings, such as : a dead body, a ghost, a malevolent spirit, but not a Supreme Being. *Maui, the Atua,* who is said to have fished up the island, is conceived to have died long ago. With them religion is war; and, while they have a most limited nomenclature of religion, they have a very rich vocabulary relating to war. Their adoption of Christianity, if indeed they can be said to have adopted it at all, was prompted by no higher motive than a desire to have "two gods on their side"; and their conception of deity never rises higher than that of a dynamical force. One who lived long years amongst them has said : " I was there at the time when both Protestant and Roman Catholic missionaries were first beginning to make their way in the country ; and the Maoris of my tribe used to come to me and ask me which had the greatest *mana* (fortune, prestige, power, strength), the Protestant God or the Romanist one. I was always a good Churchman and used to tell them that the Protestant God could lick the other into fits. There was an old Irish sailor about five miles from me who used to back up the Roman Catholic God; but I had a long start of him, and, moreover, *was the best fighting-man* of the two, which went a long way. In a short time I had about two hundred of the most muscular, blood-thirsty, hard-fighting Protestants you could wish to see."

He further tells how, on another occasion, a great warrior-chief, the commander of the *Taua* (war-party or expedition), saluted him thus: "Look here, young fellow! I've done the incantations and made it all square with my god; but you say that you've got a God stronger than mine, and a lot of our young fellows go with you; there's nothing like having two gods on our side, so you fellows do the proper business with him and then we'll fight." Religion, with them, is a means to an end, and that is the best the principles of which incite to the killing of the greatest possible number of foes. For this reason many of the Maoris have a decided preference for the Old Testament over the New; they are fascinated by the war-element in its narratives, and prefer the bloodthirstiness of the conception of God in the earlier pages of the Scriptures to the conception of the divine love in the later.

The massacre of Poverty Bay was the act of some three hundred *rangatiras* (native gentlemen) of this type. They are said to have known their Old Testaments well, and to have turned their New to yet greater use — they made cartridges of them! These gentlemen have formed themselves into a sect called the Hau Haus, in which the worst features of Judaism are mixed up with the vilest native superstitions, and the outcome is a religion of plunder and blood. A ruffian, by name Te Kooti, was the founder of it, and the leader of the Hau Hau expedition; and the foremost chief to oppose them was a Maori of the better type, Ropata. An Englishman asked Ropata, one day : —

"What do you think would be done with Te Kooti if he were taken?"

"Oh! you'll make him a judge," he replied.

"What do you mean?" was further asked.

"Well, the last two rebels you caught you made native assessors, and Te Kooti's a much greater man than either of them, so I don't see how you can do less than make him a judge; but you won't if I catch him."

In these words Ropata made a strong point against the government. The Hau Haus believe the Old Testament refers to the Maoris; they are the chosen people, the Messiah will come of them, and the English are the Philistines. Will Mr. Matthew Arnold agree with this? Te Kooti was finally captured, and not elevated to "the

bench," but condemned to the cell; which did
something to break his spell over his followers.
The Hau Haus, however, are still active.

Class distinctions are very marked amongst the
Maoris; the *tutuas* are the low, worthless, and
poor — the nobodies of society; the rangatiras are
chiefs, warriors, gentlemen — the somebodies of
the world; so the rangatira pakehas (rich, foreign
gentlemen) are highly thought of, while the
pakeha tutuas (the mean, poor foreigners) are
despised. In old times if, by any chance, a Maori
chief gave one of this latter class a good supper,
he was sure to make his breakfast off him the
next morning, for, he would coolly ask, "What
else can I do with such stuff? It's only good
for eating." The pakeha tutua was favored somewhat if the chief killed him first, as sometimes,
by way of a special luxury, he would set his teeth
in his living, quivering flesh, and enjoy his breakfast all the more for the visible agony he saw this
gentle treatment inflicted, never pausing till the
life was out of him, save to exclaim: "How sweet
is man's flesh!" This sort of cannibalism is
at an end, and now the rangatira pakehas are
eating up the native tutuas in quite another
way. The old, barbarous custom, too, of cutting
themselves severely on the face, arms, and breast,
when singing the *tangi* (the song of lamentation for
the dead), with flints or shells, in token of sorrow,
is almost obsolete. In the last moments the
dying person is exhorted to cling to life, in words

which are supposed to have a mystic meaning. Has the idea of immortality, in some dim and vague way, dawned on the mind of the Maoris?

Love-making and marriage as practised by the Maoris are peculiar. The wooing lover, instead of kissing the object of his devotion, after the European fashion, rubs his nose gently over that of the Maori maiden's, and she, if his addresses are welcome, responds in the same way. There is no marriage ceremony, and the question of divorce does not seem to trouble them. A chief's giving a woman to a man constitutes marriage. Both the man and the woman are tattooed on the face, especially on the lips, as soon as they are married, and some very handsome faces are thus completely spoiled.

The highest token of the favor of a chief is for him to take your hand in his and lick it, a ceremony which, though it may be very pleasant to him, is likely to stir unpleasant thoughts in one's mind, for one cannot forget just then the old Maori passion for human flesh, and the question is sure to suggest itself: "What if he passes on from licking to eating, and should gobble one up before one knows where one is?" Some names amongst the Maoris are very suggestive, such, for instance, as those which translated mean, "The eater of his own relations," or "The eater of foreigners," or "The devourer of children"; the last has a strange savor of Dean

Swift's ironical prescription for dealing with Irish overpopulation and poverty, and hints that an idea that was thrown out in the great Dean's loyal espousal of the wrongs of that unhappy country has at some time been a dreadful fact elsewhere.

Tobacco is in great favor with them; even infants sometimes, it is said, refuse the mother's breast and cry for the pipe; and a dying Maori often asks for a pipe and dies smoking.

The love of warfare is so great in them that they have been known, on learning that the enemy was without arms, to divide their own into halves and to send one half to the enemy with an invitation to fight. On one occasion a Maori chief was asked: " Why did you not attack the ammunition and provision wagons of the enemy ? " He replied: "Why, you fool! if we had stolen their powder and food, how could they have fought ?" When a Maori kills a man of note in battle he usually commemorates the deed by adopting his name. The *mere ponamu*, a weapon made of rare green stone, is valued above all else, and a Maori will give all his other possessions to secure one. Nothing, no method of education and training, seems able to destroy the war-element in the Maori character. A friend of mine, a solicitor in Napier, took a liking for a Maori boy of twelve years, and sent him to a good school; he turned out a fine scholar, for he was more capable of learning than many of the European boys; later he took him into his office, where he made great progress in his law studies. All went on charmingly, and he thought himself a victor in this instance, and that he would be able to produce a Maori as faithful and grateful as a European, till one day the youth, in his twenty-first year, suddenly disappeared. The tribe to which he belonged had a little feud with a neighboring one, and the young Maori, pupil of the law though he was, and very near to qualifying himself for its practice, was completely overmastered by hereditary war-passion, and left forever his Justinian and Blackstone for the more primitive, but perhaps, under certain circumstances, not less successful instruments of persuasion, his mere ponamu and tomahawk.

The Maori hates agricultural work. One may travel for great distances through the King Country, a large tract of land between Auckland and New Plymouth, in the very heart of North Island, which is still in the absolute possession of the Maoris, and find not an acre of it cultivated.

The streets of Auckland are full of these people, and some of the most extraordinary, motley-dressed figures are constantly seen there. A numerous half-caste is springing up, which is often, in physical appearance, finer than either the European or the Maori. Auckland is now a town of over sixty thousand inhabitants, and enjoys wonderful commercial prosperity. Six hours' run from there are the Thames gold-fields, which are still in progressive yielding, and about a day's journey takes one to Lake Taupo, which

is twenty-five miles in length and twenty in
breadth; near to which are the hot springs of
Rotomahana, famous for their medicinal qualities;
while south of these are two mountains — the
Tongariro, a volcano, and the Ruapehu, in height
ninety-one hundred and ninety-five feet, and
snow-capped.

In Auckland I met, at the house of my friend
Dr. Scharland, — a gentleman eminent in the
medical profession and for his scientific attain-
ments, — the American consul, Mr. Griffin, uncle
to Mary Anderson, and spent many happy evenings with him.

From Auckland we returned to Napier, and
then journeyed across country into the province
of Taranaki. The scenery through which we
passed was magnificent, which compensated somewhat for the fatigue of the journey arising from
its having to be made by coach and the roads
in some places being rough. The route lies over
the Ruahine range, in which we passed through
several gorges, one over four miles long. The
Manawatu River is one of the grandest sights that
eye ever rested on, and the mind is roused to
a pitch of intense excitement as the coach
descends an incline hundreds of feet deep, — the
roaring water below, the wildest scenery around,
the dark skies above, — in fearful zigzag fashion;
the driver sure of his art driving at such a furious
rate that one imagines every minute one will be
dashed against the rocks, or hurled down the

gorge with coach, horses, driver, and all. One's
hair literally stands on end till one finds one's self
safely at the bottom, facing the river, which in
its awful gloom looks like Acheron with its
hovering shades. A boat took the coach and
horses across, and after a journey of twelve hours
from Napier we arrived at a point where we took
the railroad to Wanganui; from there we went
by coach to Patea; then to Howera, — both
sweetly beautiful country towns. In the latter
there was a shock of earthquake twenty seconds
in duration at five o'clock in the morning on
the preceding twenty-sixth of June. Here I took
a coach and drove over the worst bit of
road in the world, the horses at times actually
disappearing and only showing their ears above
the fearful gullies and holes, and the coach
shaking and tumbling in a manner to which a
small craft on the Atlantic in foul weather is
a cradle. By two days' patient endurance of this
we reached New Plymouth, having crossed by
land the entire North Island, and passed through
scenery with which there is none even in
Scotland or Germany to compare for grandeur
and sublimity.

In New Plymouth, on the first night of Hamlet, a
funny incident occurred. The house was crowded,
and the stage was very small. After Laertes was
killed, and Hamlet had done away with the King,
Hamlet found to his amazement that there was
no room left for him to lie down and die respecta-

bly, so there was nothing to be done save whisper to the King: "Hang it man, move up and let me die!" The King, obedient to the manager's voice that he detected beneath Hamlet's whisper, crawled slowly into the first wing.

It was while walking down from my hotel one day, in the same town, that I suddenly found myself embraced by a pair of brawny arms, and saluted in the following fashion: "O Romeo! wat's de matter wit dee dat you are Romeo?" I looked up and saw a Maori woman with a big bouquet. "O, plees, gif dis to Miss Juliet for der hacting so bufully dast nit." I promised to do so, and thanked the kindly soul, who had seen Romeo and Juliet the night before and wellnigh lost her balance.

From New Plymouth we returned to Wellington, and then passed over to Nelson at the north of South Island. Both New Plymouth and Nelson are most beautiful towns, and their climate, especially that of Nelson, which has earned the name of Sleepy Hollow, is incomparable. Italy is the only country that can come up to it, but Italy itself has not the even temperature of Nelson. From there we made a tour back to Christchurch, Lyttelton, Timaru, Oamaru, and Dunedin; which city honored me with a farewell banquet on the night preceding my departure for Tasmania.

CHAPTER V. — TASMANIA.

HOBART TOWN.

"If you look in the maps of the world, I warrant you will find, in the comparisons between Macedon and Monmouth, that the situations, look you, is both alike. There is a river in Macedon, and there is also moreover a river at Monmouth: . . . and there is salmons in both."
— *King Henry V, Act iv, sc. 7.*

The old convict establishments — A story of the past — Port Arthur — The Derwent River — Mount Wellington — English traits of the people and country — No disagreeable insects — No wild animals, except the black opossum — Produce — Orchards — Whale - fisheries — The seat of the government — Climate — Drives — Fern-trees — Forests — The roads — Salmon - trout — Mineral wealth — The habits of the people — Love of Art — The Government House grounds — The Botanical Gardens — The railroad — Launceston.

IT takes between three and four days from the Bluff, the last station of the South Island of New Zealand, to reach Hobart Town, the capital of Tasmania, an island that lies off Victoria, being separated by the Bass Strait from the main Australian continent. The island formerly bore the name of Van Dieman's Land, which has been changed, by an act of parliament, on account of its unpleasant associations with the place as a convict settlement.

In Tasmania, as in New South Wales, the forefathers of the country were convicts; but they have left little or no trace behind them, for, in all the world, there is not a better class of people to be found than the Tasmanians. It is said that the convicts had a very good time of it in former years, for the goaler used to let them out in the morning, and allow them to come back at a stated hour in the evening. On one occasion a convict was later than the permitted time, and the enraged goaler told him that, if this occurred again, he would be locked out; but tradition says it never happened again, for the lodgings at the goal were so comfortable at night, and the liberty enjoyed for excursions about the island was so complete by day, that the arrangement was in every way delightful. But the story may, perhaps, point in two directions: while it records a fact true to the experience of some few favored convicts, it is more likely intended as a bitter irony on the general system of their treatment. At least, the history of the convict settlements on the island had a darker side, than which perhaps there would be nothing more painful, if the story could be fully written, for philanthropists and political economists of to-day to ponder; and especially would this be so in the case of Port Arthur.

The entrance to the town is very romantic; the Derwent River for miles, and which in some places is nearly two miles wide, is full of picturesque scenes, while it is deep enough to allow, at all times, the largest vessels to enter. A navy might safely ride in the waters of Hobart Harbor; and the town on its edge, with Mount Wellington, four thousand feet high, for a background, is a very fine sight.

The Hobartians are pre-eminently English, and it is not difficult to find amongst them instances of those older types of English character which are even growing scarce in the Midlands of Old England. The streets, the houses, the parks, and everything in the town, have an English appearance; the doctor calls upon his patients in the old-fashioned English gig, and the wealthier farmers drive to market in the same, and this vehicle, which has been spoken of as "that famous test of respectability," is a symbol of the entire conditions of the place; and to a great extent the very climate is English, only it is clearer and more beautiful. Hobart Town, indeed the whole of Tasmania, is like New Zealand in having no disagreeable bugs, mosquitoes, snakes, or wild animals of any kind, except the black opossum, which abounds in considerable numbers. The principal produce of the country is timber and fruit. There are orchards in the neighborhood of Hobart Town that contain over six thousand trees. All European fruit grows in Tasmania, and it may be said to be the fruit-grower and jam-maker for the rest of the Australasias. Apples, which are very scarce in New Zealand and New South Wales, and which do not grow at all in Queensland, attain to an exquisite size and flavor in Tasmania, and the same may be said of its peaches, cherries, and pears. Beyond these, corn and hops are grown for exportation, and there are whale-fisheries. Nearly as large as Ireland, the total population of

the island does not reach one fourth of its number.
Hobart Town, being the capital and the seat of the
government, is the busiest place on the island, and
it is very pleasant to visit because everything is so
neat, clean, and good.   It is a great pleasure and
health resort for the Victorians and people from
all parts of the Australasias, during the summer
and autumn, that is, from December to the end of
April; and the Hobartians hope it may erelong,
on account of the great beauty of the country
and the salubriousness of the climate, become a
health-station for India.   During the season the
town is full, and one can hardly get a room for
love or money.   The Museum, the Library, and
the Town Hall, are built of a fine, white
stone, and are large and imposing structures for
the size of the town, the settled population
being only twenty-six thousand.   The residence
of the governor is one of the handsomest govern-
mental buildings in the colonies and commands
a fine view of the bay.   The drives from the town
are lovely, especially those along the harbor and
the Derwent, up the Huon Road, or to Fern-
tree Gully, which, in picturesqueness, variety of
scenery, and wealth of natural beauty, are equal
to any I have seen in my many travels.   On the
way to the Gully thousands of fern-trees line the
road on either side, rising to from twelve to fifteen
feet, and their wide-spreading foliage overhead
forms one of those beautiful aisles in the vast
temple of nature, the sight of which makes us feel

that man's noblest efforts in architecture are poor
in comparison with those of the divine. There
are wonderful forests spread over the hillsides and
on the mountains of the island, many of the trees
rising to a greater height than the famous Welling-
tonia of California, and growing, not in little
detached groups, but thousands in company, and
forming a forest scenery unique and grand. Some
of the trees are over twelve feet in diameter, and
one tree has been discovered which has reached
the enormous height of four hundred and seventy-
one feet, while the highest tree of California is
only about three hundred and twenty-five feet.

The roads, which were made by convicts, are
of the finest kind and kept in perfect order, yet
to "do" the island requires many departures
from them, and entails great walking, as in all
mountainous countries.

It is to the Tasmanians, and thanks to them,
that Australia owes the introduction of the salmon-
trout. The raising of this valuable fish takes
place about twenty miles from Hobart Town, close
to the Derwent River, and acres and acres of land
are used for this purpose. The different sheds
are most scientifically managed; the spawn was
formerly introduced from the old country, but
now they have experimented with artificial eggs
with successful results. In a few years the large
rivers of Tasmania will be rich in salmon-trout,
and another great branch of commerce will open
to that peaceful and beautiful country. There

are gold, silver, and lead mines waiting to be
worked. The latter discovery raised quite a *furore*
and great rush amongst the mining community a
few years ago. It takes a good deal to excite the
Tasmanians. They are very slow and methodical.
They shut their warehouses and offices from twelve
to one every day, as regularly as they are in bed
by nine o'clock in the evening. But they are an
art-loving people, and the legitimate drama goes
well with them. They treated us with generous
support, filling the pretty little theatre every night
for one entire month. I made many friends there.
Their love of the Beautiful shows itself nowhere
more than in the Government House grounds and
Botanical Gardens, which leave nothing to be
desired; and both are freely open to the public.
In the latter every imaginable flower is represented
and the beds are laid out in exquisite taste, fully
rivaling, if not surpassing, the gardens of Kew,
Versailles, or Vienna.

> "Here could I breath my soul into the air,
> As mild and gentle as the cradle-babe."

Tasmania has its railroad, like all the other
rising Australian colonies, which extends from
Hobart Town to Launceston. The latter is a dull
and uninteresting town, cold and unintelligent.
It had its chance lately on account of the "lead
rush," which brought considerable capital from
Melbourne into the country, but soon relapsed
into its former sleepy state; from which there

seems no chance of its ever again awaking.
From Launceston to Melbourne takes about
twenty-two hours by the Tasmania Steamship
Company; thirteen by sea, crossing the bar, the
rest by river — flat, stale, and unprofitable.

CHAPTER VI.— AUSTRALIA.

VICTORIA. — MELBOURNE.

" Keep a gamester from the dice, and a good student from his book,
and it is wonderful."
— *Merry Wives of Windsor, Act iii, sc. 1.*

The Opera House—"Dead or Alive "—A successful engagement—
Australian passion for gambling—Horse-racing—The "Derby"—
Sir Wilfrid Lawson and Mr. Parnell—The Melbourne Cup—The
ladies are inveterate gamblers — The grand stand — How the
ladies dress—Two hundred thousand people assemble on the course
—The "Cup" and the "Totalisator"—Burke Street—Supporters
of the turf—The squatters—A good squatting - station — The
squatter's enemies — Melbourne pre-eminently modern—Indifference
to the higher aims of Art—Theatrical managers—Public institutions
—The suburbs—Mr. Mowbray, mayor of Melbourne—The Duke
of Edinburgh—Charles Mathews—Sunday in Australia—The art
of cooking — The need of good hotels — Rover and Jessie are
taken on board the Galatea—The German Turn Verein.

ON October 1, 1881, I opened at the Opera
House, Melbourne, a theatre capable of holding
twenty-five hundred people, and as beautiful a
structure as one can wish to see. The house was
crowded in every part, the receipts on that single
occasion being over two hundred pounds (one
thousand dollars), and the reception given to me
and Louise Beaudet was the most cordial. I had
not reappeared in Melbourne for over ten years,
and all my old friends and acquaintances reassembled to give me a hearty welcome. I played
in the first place Narcisse, which had a run of
nearly a fortnight. I then played Tom Taylor's
Dead or Alive, a drama written expressly for

me by the author, and played by me in London
with considerable success. The last week was
devoted to Shakespeare, in which Louise Beaudet
was especially introduced, and won golden
opinions, both as Ophelia and Juliet. The entire
engagement, considering that it occurred in the
worst month in the year, at least for the
drama (namely, the month of October, which
precedes the annual "Cup" week), was a great
success. The reader may ask why that month
should be considered the worst in the year, and
his surprise at the assertion is reasonable, but
those who have been in Australia, and have been
present on the occasion of a "Melbourne Cup"
meeting, will readily understand. No description
can be conveyed by words of the mad passion or
the rage all over Australia for gambling —
especially horse-backing. Racing is, with all
Englishmen, an exciting passion, and all over
England this sport has been kept up to the enjoyment of the people. The "Derby" is a national
festival which England will never give up; the
one occasion of the year on which even the Lords
and Commons, in Parliament assembled, forget
the wrongs of Ireland, the Permissive Bill, and
the irksome task of the "rectification of foreign
frontiers," and commingle with the multitudes at
Epsom, in gayest spirit and the most festive robes.
It is even whispered that Sir Wilfrid Lawson has
been seen arm in arm with Mr. Parnell on the
course, with the gayest ribbons in their hats, and

that they both, at such a time, have little felici-
tous dealings with the book-makers, in which
each tries to forget his political monomania. I
cannot vouch for its truth, but report has it that
once upon a time Mr. Parnell was overheard
thus: —

" Come, Sir Wilfrid, the Permissive Bill be
d—d. The race has begun. Let's away to the
grand stand."

" Nay, nay, Parnell, not quite in such a hurry,
for I was, you know, about to say, Home Rule
be d—dynamited! but come, let's turn in here
(a booth where liquors are sold) and take 'a wee
drap of ould Irish,' and then to the race."

Be this as it may, what would a Cockney do
without his annual Derby? or a Liverpool man
without the Chester Cup? But these English
sports come but once a year, and when they are
over no one thinks of them, except the gamblers,
till a week or so before they come round again.
But it is not so with Melbourne, aye, I may
almost say, entire Australia.

The Melbourne Cup is an event which is talked
about, and looked forward to, from the day after
it has been run to the day in the following year
on which it will be run again. The ladies are
inveterate gamblers, believing with Shakespeare
that "the gentler gamester is the soonest winner."
Thousands assemble hours before the first race
begins, on the enormously large grand stand,
capable of seating upward of fifty thousand

people, so that they may have good places, and do not leave them even during luncheon for fear that they may lose their seats. They are armed with pencils and cards, and note the runs and their bets down in a business-like and methodical manner that convincingly proves that they are old stagers.

They win or lose in their sweepstakes without showing the slightest feeling of pleasure or grief, and they settle their accounts with great spirit. Their excitement and shouts and enthusiasm over the individual races are charming to see and hear, and their dresses and toilets are a spectacle worth chronicling. From Cup day to Cup day these fair, gentle women break their tender heads about what new and elaborate costume, never before seen, they are to wear at the next great meet; and as each is anxious to outshine the other, the motley crowd of diversified costumes is indescribable.

Imagine, gentle reader, the most heavenly day that nature can bless mortals with, neither too hot nor too cold, with a pure, bracing, rapturous atmosphere which makes the young heart beat with joyful gratitude, and the old heart forget that it is burdened with age and trouble; the lawn smiling with the brightest of all green grasses, and the sun warming your inmost soul with pleasure and delight; round you a swarm of human heads, nearly two hundred thousand persons, and everything gayety and happiness.

Among this crowd of holiday-seekers you behold
swarms of women who have been devising every
possible means to dress in all the colors of the
rainbow, and to cover themselves up with heavy
silks, damasks, laces, gold and silver braidings,
feathers, flowers, red and yellow boots, diamonds
by the bushel, and all conceivable designs of
jewelry and ornaments. I saw a woman dressed
as follows: a crimson, heavy, damask silk robe,
wrought with large patterns; a train of almost six
yards dimension; a crimson hat with a crimson
feather; crimson gloves and crimson shoes; a tremendously heavy, gold chain and huge gold watch,
which she took out every few seconds either to
show (as an Irishman would say) that she had it
in her pocket, or that it was of heavy, solid gold.
In this costume she strutted up and down the large
lawn, proud as a peacock showing her feathers; and
while the sun in sarcasm exposed her ugly colors
in its own beauteous, bright rays, this woman, no
doubt, considered herself a queenly person.

Another lady had a similar costume in bright
green, not the sage-green of modern æstheticism,
than which there is nothing more beautiful (unless
you have too much of it), and such an enormous
train that the passers-by had to jump over it.
This, with the exception of a few sensible ladies
who choose comfortable, always-charming muslin,
is the average fashion of the Melbourne ladies
on the Cup day. There is much room in this
paradise of Australian fair women for the genius,
enterprise, and costuming dreams of a Worth.

But the evil the annual Cup produces does not end here: the above is but folly and we can afford to smile over it. The moral damage it does is immense, especially upon the mind of the young, who begin with the age of ten, or even earlier, not only to save, but to steal and rob, that they may be able to bet and to gain a "sweepstake," which, by the way, by no means always follows from said betting; or a "Totalisator" — a sort of bogus lottery institution which gives every one, apparently, a chance, but in which the person who runs it mostly wins, formed all over the Austra- lasias for the purpose of fraud, and which carries on its business in so brazen a manner that the various governments had to step in and check its operations after it had done incalculable mis- chief and poisoned the minds and ruined the pockets of thousands and tens of thousands of weak-headed fools. It is an experience never to be forgotten to see Burke Street the night before the Cup. There is usually over one hundred thousand people on that street, crowded within a space of a few hundred yards, anxious to get a "tip," or to hear some news about the latest chances of the favorite. And as the winner of the Australian Derby — a race run a few days before the Cup — generally also wins this, the excitement that follows that race is immense.

The Cup is the great power of the Australian's universe, and what used to be a picnic and a delightful season of pleasure has become the

tyrant and haunter of the minds of the men,
women, youths, and even children, of that country — everybody and everything are rushed along
in the whirlpool of vulgar madness; entire cities
become depopulated of their inhabitants during
that week, and steamship and railroad companies
exert themselves to the uttermost to meet the
extra demands; and it is no exaggeration to say
that a week before the Cup day as many as two
hundred thousand people flock into the city of
Melbourne, which has, during that period, a
population of over a third of a million.

> "Foolery does walk about the orb like the sun;
> It shines everywhere."

The squatters are the kings of the Australian
colonies, and many of them are great supporters
of the turf. The Cup of last year (1883) was
won by a Mr. White, a sheep squatter, who made
not less then two hundred thousand pounds
(a million dollars) by that little transaction.
Squatters have made enormous fortunes in their
peculiar industry, but sheep and cattle raising
has been brought now to such a fine point
that only rich men can hope to succeed.
Years ago it was no uncommon occurrence for
young men to invest in sheep stations with as
little as one thousand pounds, and after a few
years' successful management, in which they were
favored by rain and the high price of wool in
the market, to sell out at a clear profit of forty

thousand, or even in some cases sixty thousand, pounds.

Now, things are all changed in this respect. Rapid fortunes from the squatter's occupation are still possible to men of small capital in North Australia, but in the South the lines are drawn so close that money stands, at times, as low as four per cent.

A squatting-station of two or three thousand acres of good land cannot be bought under fifty or sixty thousand pounds, and there are stations that are worth double or treble as much.

The squatters' greatest enemies are drought, kangaroos, and especially rabbits. Not many years ago, the Australians complained of not having any rabbits in their country. A few dozen pairs were imported, and now they have become so plentiful and are such a terrible devastation that the farmers and squatters groan under them and are devising all possible means and plans for their destruction. Shot and powder are impotent against this nuisance; even poison has been tried with no very satisfactory result, and a fortune can be made by any one who can devise a sure means of freeing Australia from the tyranny of the rabbit. Some of the squatters have as much as forty thousand acres of splendid land, and make two or three thousand pounds a week by selling fat cattle. It is said that one squatter has spent sixteen thousand pounds in the effort to extirpate the rabbit from his estate; in one year as much as three thousand pounds, but in vain.

New Zealand suffers no less from this pest, and I need not say that the Australian rues the hour in which he introduced this harmless, inoffensive little animal.

With the kangaroo it is quite a different thing; he is only to be found in pairs and herds, and is gradually being driven further North. Besides, though he eats nearly as much as a sheep, he tickles the passion common to all Australians for sport; they get great pleasure out of him, and his hide is useful, and his tail most appetizing. 'T is a wonderful tail he has, containing, it is said, forty yards of sinews. Even his meat is not to be despised. On one of my overland journeys from Melbourne to Adelaide I had some kangaroo-steak, which was quite as tender as that of an ox. My host, a shepherd, who, by the way, had two of the most magnificent kangaroo-hounds I had ever seen, explained that the meat only needed to be kept in water for twenty-four hours, and it became quite tender and delicious. I never made a better dinner than that day, after a sixty miles' ride, off a large kangaroo-steak, a pot of tea, and lots of damper. In some parts of Australia the favorite method with the squatters of hunting the kangaroo is to chase them, not on horseback, but in a buggy, four-in-hand.

Melbourne is certainly a very beautiful city, pre-eminently modern in type. The streets are wide, the houses elegant, the theatres spacious, and the public buildings handsome enough to grace a metropolis.

But the public of Melbourne is no longer what it used to be. In former years the people might very deservedly be denoted among the most intelligent, generous, and appreciative of civilized communities, but now all is unlike the days of yore. The city has become stupid, licentious, ungenerous, and for the most part indifferent to the higher aims and ideals of Art. In public taste and sentiment it has been systematically demoralized by managers, who, in their desire to please and attract, have made their entertainments too cheap and offered too much quantity — quality has ceased to be the rule with them — for too little money, or, as it is the case during the principal part of the year, for next to and sometimes even for nothing. The better section of the public has in consequence become apathetic toward the theatre, and the very name of it creates *ennui*, or evokes bitter contempt. The colonial generation of to-day prefers, at any time, a pipe, a mug of colonial ale, a dice-box, or a billiard-cue, to the best drama in existence. I have seen performances in Melbourne, at the Bijou Theatre, and also at the Royal, before deserted houses, in which the management must have lost heavily night after night. Let no one of my own profession visit Australia with his mind set chiefly upon Melbourne, or even Sydney, for assuredly any one who does so will be rudely shocked out of all dreams and dreadfully shaken in expectations. Australia means a large continent, but the two largest cities are dead to dramatic art and finer æsthetic sentiment.

Melbourne, however, has some fine public
institutions. The Library, the Town Hall, the
Post-office, the House of Parliament, and the
Exhibition Buildings, are all worthy of a great,
rising, commercial city, and in the general plan
and width of the streets it is altogether the finest
city in the South. The Botanical Gardens cannot
be praised too highly; they are the largest in
Australia, and well cared for, affording a delightful retreat from the glare and tumult of the
streets; they are perhaps not so beautiful as
those at Sydney, and are said to be less of
interest scientifically than those at Adelaide,
but they are well adapted to afford rest and
pleasure to the heart and eye of a weary public. Melbourne proper has a population of
about seventy thousand, while in the suburbs
there are over one hundred and fifty thousand;
St. Kilda, Brighton, Kew, Yarra-yarra, and other
places in the neighborhood, being filled with
beautiful houses and fine gardens and lawns.

During my stay in Melbourne I had the pleasure
—and it was to me a very great one—of meeting
many of my old friends again, and amongst them
Mr. Mowbary, one of the largest drapers in Australia, who, on the occasion of my former visit,
was mayor of Melbourne, and with a courtesy
and generosity that showed his true public spirit
and appreciation of the benefits of Art to a community, and that he could find time, notwithstanding the immense claims of business and public

affairs upon him, to think on other things, less tangible but not less important to the wellbeing of a people, gave me a public banquet, at which he said: "I consider it a part of my duty as chief magistrate of the town to entertain distinguished artists." Indeed, all my old connections were revived from the time — ten years ago — of my intimacy with the Duke of Edinburgh, who every evening came into my dressing-room, to which he had a key of his own and could come and go as he liked, and where he could be absolutely at ease and get relief from the strained etiquette of Melbourne society and the detestable follies of that lionizing of royalty to which he was everywhere else subjected.

I remember how, one evening — and I fear it was a Sunday — the duke dined with me and afterward had a game of *écarté*, but finding that rather slow I proposed loo, at that time the favorite game with the Australians, — "Nap" has now taken precedence, — and that I should invite Charles Mathews and his wife, who at that time were playing an engagement in Melbourne. The duke was delighted, and I was about to write a note of invitation, when he wrote the following, which I copied: —

"MELBOURNE, November 6, 1870.

"*Dear Mathews*, — H. R. H. is spending the afternoon with us. Sunday in this place is uncommonly dull and we are thinking of playing a little game of écarté, but should it be convenient to Mrs. Mathews and yourself to join us during the afternoon it would give H. R. H. and us great pleasure, and we might even initiate H. R. H. into the glorious mysteries of loo, to which at present he is a stranger. If you can manage, come to high tea."

Soon after we received the following characteristic reply from Charlie : —

"MENZES HOTEL, Sunday.

"*Dear Bandmann,* — Both myself and Mrs. Mathews feel highly flattered over your kind invitation to meet H. R. H. to help to initiate him into the 'glorious mysteries of loo.' I shall endeavor my best to make him a victim, but as I have invited a friend to a low dinner, I cannot accept your invitation to high tea. You must therefore make our excuses to H. R. H., but we shall be on the spot immediately after our low dinner.   Your

"CHARLES MATHEWS."

We kept up our little game of loo till the next morning, and when we rose neither of us had lost or won much, but we had a pleasant night of it, and H. R. H. liked the game immensely.

Sunday in Australia is, of all days, the most tedious. One is obliged to dine at one, or latest, at two o'clock, for the sake of the servants, and as you generally rise on that day an hour or two later

than usual, you either have to give up your breakfast, or take breakfast and dinner together, or one
immediately after the other. And as the Australians eat meat, and that plentifully, at every meal,
the amount of beef, mutton, and pork, consumed
in one day, and on Sunday, the briefest of days,
unless you sit up all night as H. R. H. and our
friends did at loo, — but perhaps the Australians do
not carry their vices to that extent, — is indescribable. Meat is so abundant and so cheap that the
poorest in the land can afford to have it at every
meal. But the art of cooking in Australia needs
more attention than it receives. In no country
does the Anglo-Saxon mind show its utter helpless-
ness in affairs of the palate and good cooking more
than there, where foreigners are so scarce. The
monotonous sameness of the *cuisine* all over the
Australasias is deplorable — chops, steaks, and
joints, joints, steaks, and chops, three times a day
in seven days of the week, and thirty-one days of
the month, and from the beginning to the end of
the year, is dreadfully monotonous in the end, or
rather because the end is never reached. Poultry
is also plentiful, but it is tasteless — similar to the
American turkey, and the Australian fish is very
poor, except in New Zealand and Tasmania, where
the rivers produce a better quality. What Melbourne and Sydney sadly lack are first-class
hotels, combined with superior restaurants. In
this direction there are positive fortunes to be
made in the future.

À propos of my former visit to Melbourne is
the following: The Duke of Edinburgh was very
fond of two of my dogs (I had six) which accompanied us on our frequent rides together. I
finally promised to give him these: they were
brother and sister, named Rover and Jessie: and
one day took them on board the Galatea just
before she was leaving the city. I gave particular
instruction to one of the marines to tie them up
well. Then, after shaking hands with the duke
and watching the vessel out of sight, amidst the
cheers of thousands of spectators who had
assembled to shout their "God speed you!" to
the sailor-prince, I rode home and took my dinner.
Two hours after I went to the stable to look after
the rest of my family, two horses and four dogs,
when, to my amazement, Rover, dreadfully wet
and dirty, jumped up into my face kissing and
barking, almost mad with joy. I could not
understand how the dog could have come back
to Melbourne, for I had seen it tied up, and the
Galatea out of sight. Two days later, however,
Captain Standish, superintendent of the police
in Victoria, received the following telegram from
the duke, then at Sydney: "A brown retriever
dog, given to me by Bandmann, jumped overboard several miles after leaving Sandrige Pier,
named Rover. Please make inquiries." I at
once telegraphed the news of the dog's return to
the duke, and received the following telegram in
reply: —

"I shall be in Auckland by eighth December. Bring Rover if you get there; if not, send him there by Californian Mail. ALFRED."

The next day I received this letter: —

"UNION CLUB, SYDNEY, 19th November, 1870.

"*My dear Bandmann,* — I telegraphed to Standish to send the dog down by the mail leaving here on the 30th, to Auckland, but if you are to be there in December you had better bring him yourself. He jumped overboard a few miles after we had started, but they did not tell me till half an hour afterward.

"Jessie is a mamma of seven, and two will be left with Mrs. Henfrie, of Alfred House, for you, who has offered to look after them, and you can give her your directions.

"I leave for New Caledonia to-morrow and will be at Auckland not later than the 8th December. Try to be there. With kind regards to Mrs. Bandmann, I remain, yours truly,

"ALFRED."

I did as the duke wished and took Rover with me to Auckland in December, where he was again united to Jessie, and remained quite happy in the keeping of his royal master. But I have never been quite able to understand the remarkable part performed by Rover on this occasion, for he swam for miles in Hobson Bay, which was fearfully turbulent at the time and teems with sharks. ·

Rover, however, had wonderful sagacity, and, I am sure, when he returned, wet and dirty, he meant, so far as he was able by barks and kisses, to tell me all about it. On one of the days subsequently, in which I saw Rover together with Jessie in the duke's company at Auckland, I seemed to see in the dog's eyes a look of deepened intelligence and half-regretful love, as though in such mute language he did his best to say : —

"You know, my dear old master, I was always very happy with you, and I did n't want another master at all, not even though a royal duke. I did my best to show you this by risking my life a thousand times for your sake in Hobson Bay, but you brought me back to the duke and now I mean to stay, for a dog ought to respect a duke, and he's very kind, you know; and then besides, after a doggish fashion, I love Jessie dearly. Although at first I didn't like at all the way in which she seemed to completely forget you and caress her new master, Prince Alfred, still, you know (and here Rover gave a most knowing wink), she's only done just what one might expect a dog with a feminine soul to do. 'T was natural for her to love one who is a duke and a prince best, but 't was different with me; however, she's my sister and it's for me to hide her faults. I've forgiven her and we are very happy together now, for the duke's a right good master."

And Rover, as though it were by volition and actual determination on his part, never afterward took any more notice of me than of a stranger, and was, the last time I heard of him, still with Jessie in the duke's household, and a great favorite with the other dogs and much admired by men.

But to speak once more of my second visit, any account of which would be incomplete were I not to refer to the hearty welcome and generous hospitality that were shown to me by the members of the German Turn Verein, from whom I received the following: —

"MELBOURNE GERMAN TURN VEREIN,
"71 Latrobe Street, East, October 5, 1881.

"*Dear Sir*, — Ours is the largest society, and the only German one, in Melbourne. We possess our own hall; and the committee have charged me with the pleasant duty to give you a hearty welcome. We are proud to have a countryman amongst us whose artistic reputation is world-wide, and who is an honor to our country and to our art.

"The Turn Verein Association, which celebrates every Sunday after good old German fashion, devoting the evening to good music and good singing, and so entertaining its members in the best manner, would consider it an honor if you would accept their invitation to be among them next Sunday, or the following, to enjoy an evening in their society.

"In the name of the committee,

"W. WIESBADEN, *Secretary*."

I accepted this invitation, and shall never forget
the delightful season I passed with the glorious
fraternity of the Turn Verein. It afforded a most
remarkable exception to the monotony of Melbourne Sundays, for on the occasion of my second
visit there was no gallant royal duke to drop in
for dinner and loo, and, alas! dear Charles Mathews
was no more. The souls of the members of the
association were brimful of goodwill toward me,
and the music and singing were fine in the
extreme. But their reception of me as a prince
among them, at their clubhouse, did not fully
satisfy their great desire to do me honor, for after
I had returned to the Oriental, where I had taken
up my quarters, the singing section of the Turn
Verein came along and serenaded me. I invited
them inside the hotel and acknowledged the honor;
but by that time, to my yet greater surprise, the
band had arrived outside, and were, by the most
pleasing melodies, repeating the compliment, and
it was wellnigh midnight before the goodwill of
the members of the Turn Verein had expressed
itself to their full satisfaction; and they left me
to retire to rest amid sweet, dying melodies, and
with a soul deeply and gratefully impressed by the
many proofs they had given of their admiration,
respect, and good-wishes.

CHAPTER VII.— Australia.

SOUTH AUSTRALIA. — ADELAIDE.

"For I am nothing, if not critical."
— *Othello, Act ii, sc. 1.*

"Thou canst not see one wrinkle in my brow;
Mine eyes are gray and bright and quick in turning;
My beauty as the spring doth yearly grow;
My flesh is soft and plump, my marrow burning;
My smooth, moist hand, were it with thy hand felt,
Would in thy palm dissolve, or seem to melt."
— *Venus and Adonis.*

Old friends— Von Treue — Sir James and Lady Edith Fergusson — Dramatic critics — John Oxenford, Tom Taylor, and Mr. Mowbry Morris — Adelaide, a provincial town — More liquor is drunk than water — The resources and possibilities of the country — The Soliloquy and Ophelia scenes from Hamlet in German — The Botanical Gardens — Some of the company afraid of the climate of India, and refuse to go — A young lady who thought she resembled the Venus of Milo or the Venus de' Medici — New members of the company — Captain Sharland sings "The Vagabond."

On November 2, 1881, I followed my company, which had gone on a few days before to Adelaide, South Australia. I sailed on the Orient steamer Chimbaroza, a large, fine vessel, but, as I thought, poorly provisioned, the principal food being frozen meat. This seemed to me folly where there is such a quantity of good fresh meat to be had. The journey only takes forty-eight hours by a large vessel and fifty-six by a smaller one.

I arrived at Adelaide on Friday and opened on Saturday evening in Narcisse. My répertoire throughout all this tour was, in fact: Narcisse, Othello, Hamlet, The Merchant of Venice, Romeo

and Juliet, Macbeth, Richard III, Much Ado About
Nothing, As You Like It, Richelieu, The Lady of
Lyons, The Corsican Brothers; and the following
pieces in which Miss Beaudet greatly excelled,
raising each performance to a very high standard
of dramatic art: East Lynne, A Woman of the
People, Leah, the Forsaken, Camille, and The
Hunchback.

I was welcomed back by a full house, and met
my old friend Von Treue, the German consul, and
a right good fellow. On my former visit to
Adelaide I had the pleasure of meeting frequently
Sir James Fergusson, the former governor, who, with
the late Lady Edith Fergusson, made our stay very
pleasant. It was on that occasion that I also met
Mr. Mowbry Morris, then acting as a third-rate
equery to his excellency, and eating very humble
pie indeed. A few years later he came to London,
and as he was the son of his father, the proprietors
of the *Times* were anxious to do something for
their late trusty servant's son. They made him, well,
— or shall I say gave him the name? — a dramatic
critic! I could not help smiling when I met
Mowbry after this nomination — how he spread
his plumes! He was the most humble, modest,
genial fellow before, but now there was no talking
to him. Poor fellow! he had to show in some
way, and this was the only way open to him, the
dignity of his office. When one remembers such
giants of intellect as my late friends, John Oxenford and Tom Taylor, who used to write dramatic

criticisms for that leviathan of the English press, the *London Times*, and then thinks of the pigmies who at the present day attempt the same task, a feeling of the sad falling-off in power is inevitable, and we cannot but regret that the public, whose taste is formed to no small extent by what they read in their favorite daily, should be left to the tender mercies of such as these; but in the end, and the end won't be long in coming with these in office, the public will, no doubt, from sheer weariness of their weak twaddle, take to criticism on their own account, which will be an immense benefit alike to the theatrical profession and to themselves.

Adelaide is, of all Australian towns at present, the most provincial. It has in recent years grown considerably and has now about sixty thousand inhabitants, but it is slow, dull, and without attractions.   There is more liquor drunk in it than water, and the brain is hampered in its healthful activity, and the heart has lost all its finer sentiments and has sunk into a besotted-ness very unlovely to witness.   Six months in the year Adelaide is unbearable on account of its dreadful dry heat, three months it rains, and the rest are the only endurable portion of the year. South Australia, nevertheless, has inducements for the ambitious; the colony is immensely rich, and only in its infancy.   Give it time, and we shall be surprised by the full development of its resources; enormous quantities of gold and silver lie buried beneath its soil. Up till now, only wheat, iron, copper, and coal, have been cultivated; but the time will come when South Australia will produce every agricultural and commercial commodity in request throughout the civilized world. It will be one of the foremost manufacturing countries, and, together with Queensland, will spread its industry and commerce to Java, Malacca, Siam, India, and the entire Eastern world, as it already has pushed forward to Port Darwin, and soon will reach Cape Ontario.

There are a good many Germans in Adelaide, and on my former visit they gave me a public banquet, and honored me with an address, the chair, on the occasion, being occupied by Consul Von Treue.

"A kinder gentleman treads not the earth."

Anxious to show them that I had not forgotten old favors, and that, so far as I was able, I desired to reciprocate their kindness, I played, at my benefit, the Soliloquy and Ophelia scenes from Hamlet in German, for which Miss Beaudet studied the part most carefully, and, having been coached by me in the language, she played it in a masterly manner. So pure was her elocution that the Germans did n't know that she was an alien.

In Adelaide, as indeed we have found to be the case in all Australian cities, a great point of attraction is the Botanical Gardens. Those here, in size, and the quality of their plants and flowers, would certainly justify any city's pride. They lack the picturesque beauty of those at Sydney because it is rare that a harbor like that which is Sydney's glory is to be found, and the gardens lie close to the harbor, and gain much from that position; but everything that money and skill can do has been done for those in Adelaide. Many rare plants and flowers are found, and the large zoölogical section gives to them quite an extra grace.

It was still early in the month of November that I found myself fairly ready to start with my company for India, when, to my surprise and disgust, four of my people — the first old man, the heavy leading man, the old woman, and the second juvenile — declined to go because they were afraid of the climate. It was rather late in the day to raise such objection, and I nearly found myself in a dilemma; but a man who has his wits about him, and possesses a little insight into human nature, is never left in the lurch. After reason and persuasion were useless with them, I inserted an advertisement in the Adelaide daily papers for ladies and gentlemen willing to be taught the dramatic art and to accompany me to India. I had as many as forty applicants. So I advanced those who had played second parts to the higher vacant positions in the company, and picked four new persons out of the applicants to fill their places.

One of the two ladies I selected was a very handsome girl, and seemed to possess talent. She belonged to a very respectable family, and her parents said they were quite willing that she should go. But the mother never seemed to be at her ease about it, and when the girl left the pier to go on board the Indus, the steamer of the Peninsula and Oriental Line by which we sailed for Ceylon, the poor old woman swooned away. I could not quite understand this peculiar maternal behavior; it seemed to me so contradictory from time to time, and more especially as I had used no particular persuasion, but rather consented to make a trial of the young lady's powers than anything else; for the truth is, though I thought she had a certain amount of ability, many of the young ladies whose services I had to decline when I gave the appointment to her seemed to possess an equal amount, or more; and those who did not impress me at all, nevertheless told me that they would make admirable Lady Macbeths, Juliets, Ophelias, Women of the People, — and had I not a right to take them at their word? In short, one young lady even went so far as to ask: —

"Am I not like the Venus of Milo, or, as some of my friends think, like the Venus de' Medici? At least, am I not gifted with a perfect form, a figure of most symmetrical proportions, admirably carved features, significant expression, and have I not good elocutionary powers? Mr.

Bandmann, please, don't go by what I say; judge
for yourself; only I think one who, like myself,
resembles the Venus of any great master must be
able to do, you know, a simple Lady Macbeth,
Juliet, Ophelia, or Woman of the People. Try
me, and I 'll soon show you where that Louise
Beaudet will be."

Now, of this young lady's "elocutionary
powers" I had n't the slightest doubt after all
this; but do my utmost I could n't see any striking resemblance to the one famous Venus or to
the other, nor even to Venus in any way as she
shapes herself to my thought and imagination.
But, putting all this down to my own mental
obtuseness and perversity of vision, I very
modestly said : —

"But, young lady, supposing all that you say
of yourself is true, don't you think that, after all,
your place is in the studio, and not on the stage?
I think your forte is to be an artist's model."

The look of the young lady I shall never
forget, nor the subsequent deliverance of her
"elocutionary powers."

"You think so, Mr. Bandmann, do you? Well,
I think differently. A Venus worth a pin is
not to be seen simply by one man, though
he should be a great artist, and by the rest of
the world in stone or canvas copies, but by
humanity; and to be gazed at and wondered at, by
all, is my forte. 'T is nonsense to tell me that I am
best fitted for the studio and the contemplation of

one man. I am touched with an enthusiasm for larger things than that, and so I intend to adopt the stage whether or not you think me fit for it. My chance will come, and the eyes of all will be enamored with that form that nature has blessed me with."

What could I say to all this? It would have been in vain to have told this young lady that not a woman living but thinks at some time or other that she's a perfect type of beauty, and that no woman exists that does not imagine herself, somewhere between eighteen and forty, and even later in life, a Venus of some sort or other, only some of them have the good sense to say nothing about it; and as I did n't wish unnecessarily to pain such a bright, clever, ambitious girl, I simply added, with no wish at all to wound her feelings, but to teach a lesson of modesty: —

"Let us grant that you do resemble the Venus of Milo, or the Venus de' Medici, or any other Venus that you prefer, but even then I would remind you in all seriousness that, since their part is a passive part, yours may be so likewise; that the most perfect form, and even great beauty, is no sure test of qualification for the actress's work, or guaranty of success in high dramatic art. That depends on quite other qualities. A Lady Macbeth, an Ophelia, a Juliet, is not made by these, but by the quality of her inner life and soul, and her power to grasp and to live in, for the time being, the personality of another. You understand me, I hope?"

"I do, and I wish you a good-morning, sir!" said the youthful Venus, as she bounced out of the room.

Need I say that all through this interview I saw how impossible it would be to make anything of this clever but conceited girl?

She was beautiful in shape and form, indeed, but possessed of no more soul than a marble statue, and might with truth have said with Audrey in As You Like It: "I do not know what poetical is. Is it honest in deed and word? Is it a true thing?" Her tongue was her only power, and that she could n't rightly use. She offered a great contrast in every way to the modesty and hesitancy of Louise Beaudet, whom she thought she could eclipse, and who has, with few of this girl's external attractions, effected so much. This girl confirmed me in the conviction that power and merit in women are measured by modesty no less than in men: —

> "In the modesty of fearful duty
> I read as much, as from the rattling tongue
> Of saucy and audacious eloquence."

I have since heard that the girl succeeded in getting on the stage, but was a miserable failure, and that the only notoriety she has ever attained is by a very "passive" method indeed, namely, by photography, that she has become the model of a certain, not painter, or sculptor, but — photographer, who finds her a useful addition in the composition of groups, and for photographs of unknown women represented in every conceivable costume: at times with very little, and sometimes with none — "figuring in the nude as an illustration of the beauty of health," as Alice Comyns Carr speaks of Emma Lyon, the famous Lady Hamilton, as once doing. So far has the poor girl's resemblance to the Venus of Milo or the Venus de' Medici served her.

But there were girls, amongst the twenty or so who offered their services to me, of a far different type to this young lady, and certainly with quite as much talent as the one I selected. But to return to her. We had been out at sea a few days, when the mysterious transitions in her mother's emotions were seen in a new light. The young lady fell ill, and the doctor informed me that one of her lungs was absolutely gone and that the other was already seriously affected, and that she was in consumption. I cross-questioned the poor young lady to ascertain to what extent this had been known to her parents and herself before starting, and on my pressing her very hard I found out the whole truth. She had been ill for three years: her parents knew that she could not live and sent her away to die somewhere else, to save the funeral expenses, and the general inconvenience of such an event to the family; hence her mother's remorse at parting from her. The case of this poor girl was the most cruel instance of parental cold-bloodedness and shameful heartlessness that

I have ever known. I was kind to her, and so were all the rest of the company, and I promised to keep her till I should hear from her parents. On arrival in Calcutta I wrote to the father, who was a well-to-do blacksmith, but received no reply. Further trouble was needless, for soon after the poor girl died, and we laid her dust to rest in that foreign land of burning suns to which the cruelty of her parents had banished her.

Two of the other three new members of my company turned out fairly well, especially the woman to whom I taught the parts of the Queen in Hamlet and of Pompadour in Narcisse. She created quite an impression. My company was, in all, twelve strong, and after a most pleasant voyage of fifteen days' duration, we arrived at Point de Galle, Ceylon.

Captain Sharland, in command of the Indus, is a most agreeable man, a very good fellow, indeed, but awfully fond of singing " The Vagabond," resting always on the last high note, a song which is easily possible to have too much of. However, every man has his weakness; Captain Sharland's is " The Vagabond," selected, perhaps, because of his wandering life on the great waters. Save for this he is one of the most excellent fellows I ever met.

CHAPTER VIII. — India.

CEYLON. — MADRAS.

"Corruptiou wins not more than honesty."
— *Henry VIII, Act iii, sc. 2.*

"Honor aud policy, like unsever'd friends,
I' the war do grow together."
— *Coriolanus, Act iii, sc. 2.*

"If I lose mine honor,
I lose myself."
— *Antony and Cleopatra, Act iii, sc. 4.*

"For honor travels in a strait so narrow
Where one but goes abreast."
— *Troilus and Cressida, Act iii, sc. 3.*

Point de Galle — The character and the dress of the natives — The Cinnamon Gardens — Cocoanut-farms — The New Year festival — Native jewelers — A terrific sea — Madras, a beautiful town — First experience of a *pankhâ* — Newspapers — The clubhouse — Government House — A great banquet — A variety-show — One who wears a "Victoria Cross."

WE did not stay long at Point de Galle, as we were lucky enough to get there a day or two before the Pekin sailed for Madras, *en route* for Calcutta, and we determined to proceed in that steamer. As a rule, the Australian steamers for Calcutta have to lay over in Galle ten days, but on this occasion the Indus was before her time in arriving, and the Pekin behind her time in starting, and this twofold want of punctuality considerably furthered the speedy accomplishment of our journey.

We, however, made good use of our time to see what we could of the neighborhood of Galle, and of the island and people of Ceylon. But our experiences were not very happy. Passing along the street, our eyes were attracted by the handsome appearance of some, as we supposed, silver-mounted, ebony canes. We purchased several, paying rather a high price for our staffs, but, alas! we discovered afterward they were ordinary wood only, blackened over.

The manner of dressing customary with the men, and which makes them so closely resemble women in appearance, struck us as something very odd. They wear their hair, usually of the blackest hue, very long, and adorned with large tortoise-shell combs, and many of them have very beautiful faces.

We drove up to the Cinnamon Gardens, which are very charming, stopping on the way at a cocoanut-farm, where we were invited to join in the sports, it being the natives' New Year festival. We did so, and greatly enjoyed ourselves. They brought us cocoanuts fresh cut from the trees, from which we drank the delicious milk. On our way back the driver stopped at a prominent citizen's house, and asked him to give us some cinnamon-oil.

During another excursion Miss Beaudet was induced to buy some sapphires. Three large ones were shown to her, for which the jeweler asked the sum of seventy-five pounds, declaring that they were worth a hundred and fifty pounds, and said he was willing, in proof

of the truth of his statement, to give a receipt for
that amount. Fortunately, however, for Miss
Beaudet, she had left all her money with the
purser on board. So the diamond merchant and
dealer in precious stones, as he called himself,
was asked to come on board for payment. This
he consented to do, and soon after our return
he put in his appearance. But the purser (what
wise and canny persons these pursers on board
ship are!) asked, before he would part with so
much money: —

"What is it for?" He knew that Miss Beaudet
was a stranger to Ceylon, and that the natives are
great thieves.

"For brilliant sapphires, wonderfully beautiful
stones," answered the man.

"I doubt not," said the purser; "but come, my
good man, I know a sapphire when I see it. Let
me look at them."

Without the slightest hesitation, for the man
had grown old in swindling and knew that that
would instantly condemn him, he produced the
jewels.

"Now, purser," said Miss Beaudet, "tell us
your opinion of these jewels. Have I a bargain?"

The purser had no sooner taken them in his
hand and glanced at them than he broke into
a loud laugh that rang through the great saloon
in which we were sitting.

"It's lucky," said he, "that I refused to
give you any money when you went on shore,

Miss Beaudet, for if you had transacted much business with the natives on the principle on which you have entered on this, you would have been bankrupt, maybe, before you left Ceylon. This man — thief rather, I ought to say — has endeavored to swindle you out of at least sixty-five pounds for these jewels; at the utmost, they are not worth more than ten pounds in Ceylon. Leave this fellow to me."

We did so, and the purser got Miss Beaudet out of the scrape wonderfully well. He took the pseudo-jeweler aside and gave him, as he said afterward, " a bit of his mind," and the result was that she got the sapphires for ten pounds; and the man was glad, after he saw the turn events had taken by the purser's interference on her behalf, to end the transaction in this way.

The streets of Galle were literally pestered with dirty children. The natives crowded around us with their various wares. They even surrounded our ship in small boats, and everywhere we went we were met with the cry: " Sab, want some change? Change I you five pounds?" But we didn't want any change; our money, thank heaven! was still safely in our cautious purser's keeping, and we wish it could always have remained there. Experience makes us wondrous wise.

The carriages of the town are very pretty, drawn by Burmese ponies, and can be hired most reasonably; a drive all round the town costs only eight *annas* (twenty-five cents).

But the time came for the Pekin to sail, and I had too little time during this visit to see the glories of Ceylon, the paradise of Hindu mythology: though of those "natural beauties," the inhabitants, I had seen quite enough.

It is a two-and-a-half days' voyage to Madras, where I also made a brief stay. It was early morning when I arrived there, a terrific sea was on, and it seemed impossible to land. The breakwater had been completely washed away by a cyclone a few weeks before, and in the harbor it was almost as tempestuous as in the open sea. At last, however, we anchored, and in time, by means of wretched little Madras boats, and after risking our lives, to our thinking, a dozen times, we got near the shore. But even then we could not land without the assistance of the coolies, who carried the gentlemen on their backs and the ladies in chairs to the land. Whether by pure accident, or purposely as a practical joke, or by the sheer overwhelming character of his burden, I can't say, but a coolie gave a very stout gentleman, who had journeyed with us from Ceylon (who ever journeyed anywhere without a very stout gentleman? and who is there that does not remember that some evil always befell him in particular, as though fate, knowing his proverbial good-nature, took a delight in teasing him?), a thorough ducking, and when at last he got to land he came on his hands and knees, looking, in his drenched, tight-fitting mackintosh, for all the world more like a gigantic seal emerging from the sea than a human being.

"This fellow, methinks, hath no drowning-mark upon him :
His complexion is perfect gallows."

To see the town of Madras necessitates a drive of six miles, and it was so tremendously hot beneath the burning sun that before we got there we half envied the "stout gentleman" his sea-bath. On reaching the town I made at once for the Mount Royal Hotel, where I put up for a couple of days. Madras is a beautiful town, with most lovely trees, and the drives are exquisite, especially the beach drive.

Here I had my first experience of sleeping under a *pankhâ*. The bed was hard, with no pillow, and but one sheet for covering, and the night was cool, yet allowing for all that, I found that sleeping under a pankhâ pulled by coolies is a very pleasant arrangement, and often in India a very necessary protection from the mosquitoes that swarm by thousands. The food served to us was wretched, except the *khûrdi* (curry). The papers of Madras, however, are excellent, especially the *Times* and the *Mail*, as though the journalists, knowing how poor the diet is for the body, somehow hoped to make up for the deficiency by "a feast of reason and a flow of soul." The clubhouse is a fine building.

I went one evening to the Government House expecting to hear a concert, announced

to be given by Mr. Simmonson and his daughters, who had journeyed with us from Adelaide. The concert, however, did not come off,
as a big dinner was previously arranged to be
given to two hundred prominent gentlemen of
Madras and the neighborhood. After the dinner
was over, instead of the usual "speechifying,"
which is too often a dull performance, in which
everybody trying to say smart things ends in saying the most trite and stupid things imaginable,
except, perhaps, in Ireland, where I am told by
a friend that "after-dinner speeches are even
better than the rarest old Jamieson" (though
I imagine that "the rarest old Jamieson" is in
reality the superlative to which the "better after-
dinner speeches" is the comparative), we were
entertained by the most wonderful conjuring-
geniuses I ever met. It was quite marvelous
to see how docile and companionable snakes
become, even the famous *cobra de capello* (what
a wonderful head it has!), beneath a magic spell.

The next day we joined the Pekin for Calcutta.
On board I met dear old Hartigan, who is now
custodian of the high court of Calcutta, one of
the brave, old soldiers who fought in the Indian
Mutiny. Never shall I forget the veteran
warrior's look as he told me (O how his eye
flashed, as if lit up again beneath the fire of
battle! and as if he felt now, as ever, "England
expects every man to do his duty!" and which,
though simple, has been his lifelong creed, and

gloriously exemplified by him) that on one occasion he was attacked by six natives, and had to fight them all, naked, single-handed, with a sabre wrested from one of them. The six fell before his prowess, and for this he received the "Victoria Cross," which the old man wears proudly enough; but it is the pride in which there is the sweet, bashful modesty and delicious simple-heartedness of the little child that feels somehow, though it scarcely knows how, or cares to ask why, when anything exceptional has come to be its own more than another's, that it is a lovely, priceless thing it has got, and is glad on account of it, but without any vanity or boastfulness whatsoever. I have seldom met so great a man so modest as old Hartigan; but I have observed it is somehow, and in some degree always, the way with men who, like him, have stood face to face with the king of terrors, — Death, — and who, for duty's sake, hold not their lives dear unto themselves, but would, if need be, unhesitatingly sacrifice it for their country's good and glory. Hartigan is a true, modern Achilles.

> "By how much unexpected, by so much
> We must awake endeavor for defence;
> For courage mounteth with occasion."

> "I dare do all that may become a man;
> Who dares do more is none."

From Madras to Calcutta is a voyage of two and a half days.

CHAPTER IX. — India.

CALCUTTA. — I.

"And, in the spiced Indian air."
— *Midsummer Night's Dream, Act ii, sc. 2.*
"The setting sun, and music at the close,
As the last taste of sweets, is sweetest last."
— *Richard II, Act ii, sc. 1.*

The Ganges — The city a wonderland of Oriental magnificence — The houses — The *metas* — The drive along the Maidan — All nationalities represented — The Eden Garden — Sir Ashley Eden — Hindu servants — The theatres — The Corinthian — Christmas eve in Calcutta — The Great Eastern Hotel — Their excellencies, the Marquis and Marchioness of Ripon — Lord Lytton — Lord William Beresford and his brother Charlie — A little dinner-party at which the Duke of Edinburgh provided the music — The Calcutta season — Rajahs and maharajahs — The enormous wealth of the Maharajah of Darbungha — His residence, manners, and character — The Cooch Behar — The Woodlands — The love of Shakespeare amongst the Hindus — The works of the Bard prized next to the Zendavesta, the Vedas, the Koran, or the Bible — The Hindus learn English from Shakespeare — The nature of the Hindus — The Brahmo Somaj — Babu Keshub Chunder Sen — Tribute to his character, spirit, and work.

A PECULIAR impression came over me on Sunday, December 18, as we steamed up the holy river Ganges, the stream so dearly loved by every true Hindu, and about which the fervent imagination of his race has woven a thousand beautiful myths, and its no less fervent piety has regarded, for over forty long centuries, as one of the chief objects of rapturous devotion. We reached Calcutta about three o'clock in the afternoon; it was tolerably hot, but not so hot as I expected, by any means, for we could walk the streets most comfortably, even in the sun.

The first impression of Calcutta is most dazzling. The city is a perfect wonderland of Oriental magnificence and grandeur. There are rows on rows of houses heavily built, of a rough, stony, massive appearance, without windows or doors to be seen, and entirely surrounded by elaborate balconies which lead into the interiors, and every house completely walled in, with one or two grand portals through which you gain an entrance. Sometimes two or three houses are enclosed within the same walls. A real Indian house is of four or five stories, and has a certain stately massiveness of appearance — but no windows, to prevent the glaring sun from penetrating into the rooms, necessary light being conveyed from the balcony.

I was much impressed by the appearance of the water-carriers, or *metas*, as they are called, who are perfectly naked, as all coolies are, with the exception of a band around their loins, and who were most energetically engaged in their particular work. These metas carry in large leathern bags, each of which holds about three or four buckets of water, the water-supply to every house in the city, and also water the streets, which keeps them cool and pleasant. At five o'clock, both morning and evening, these fellows sprinkle the drives of Calcutta all along the Maidan up to the Zoo and back again to the Eden Garden. Thousands of coolies are employed in this work, and it is wonderful with what alacrity and quick-

ness it is done. The water is conveyed along the
entire roads by means of narrow canals, so that
they have it ready to hand, and the refreshing
odor this spreads out is most exquisite. Nowhere
else in the world is there an equal sight to be
enjoyed in the afternoon as the drive along the
Maidan. The road stretches from six to eight
miles; on one side a row of palaces, on the other
the Maidan Park, from which the drive takes its
name. Carriages crowd upon carriages, the luxury
and beauty of many of them greatly surpassing
the most fashionable turnouts in the Champs
Elysées in Paris, Unter den Linden in Berlin,
the Prater in Vienna, Rotten Row in London, or
Central Park in New York. Here one meets with
vehicles of every conceivable shape, size, height,
and beauty of design, decorated with an infinite
variety of arms and pedigrees, drawn by handsome
"fiery-footed" Arabian steeds, and attended by a
host of coachmen, grooms, and lackeys of every
nationality, complexion, and livery. A most marvelous panorama passes before you: crowds of carriages on your left, and multitudes of mounted
horsemen and horsewomen on your right. Down-
ward along the Maidan it is the custom to
drive fast; upward slow. Here in these hundreds,
nay thousands, of vehicles of every description,
one sees prince and merchant, maharajah and
babu, Jew and Christian, Moslem and Hindu,
Chinese and Japanese, Parsees and Siamese, all
mixed together in a motley, gorgeous magnificence

of color, costume, and luxury. In the distance
strains of the most melodious music invite you,
and as you draw near it, you halt close to the
Eden Garden (named after Sir Ashley Eden, the
late lieutenant-governor of Bengal), and you alight
to have a stroll in these beautiful tropical grounds,
a wonderland of flora and perfumes, illuminated
by electric lights, and where a fine band of music
plays every evening from eight to twelve pieces,
to the immense enjoyment of the assembled
crowds.   The concert begins punctually at six
o'clock and lasts exactly one hour.   As you look
around and see these long lines of carriages, four,
sometimes even six, abreast, in the midst of which
you detect that of the viceroy, preceded by out-
riders and accompanied by a numerous escort
of splendid Sepoys and a swarm of servants,
who are busy, as their horses' tails, in the endeavor to keep off the myriads of teasing
insects from the fiery Arabian steeds: and then
at the crowds who, by this time, have assembled
in the Eden Garden: you find yourself in a most
bewildering labyrinth of nationalities, and, do
your utmost, it is impossible to get out of it
by a complete discovery of the national genus
to which each belongs, or by an accurate classifi-
cation of the manifold types that confront you.
You will detect the European, the Eurasian, the
Hindu, the Arab, the Singalese, the Burmese, the
Siamese, the Malay, the Albanian, the Circassian,
the Parsee, the Turk, the Chinese, the Japanese.

the Zulu, the Ethiopian; but still, types will remain to tax your thought and to surprise your ethnology.

Seated, or walking up and down the promenades of the Eden Garden for exercise, with their children dressed according to their particular national costumes, and playing their national games, some with and some without their *ayah*, while the sweet melodies of the band flood the cool, perfumed evening air, and plants and flowers of every kind and hue blossom around, you behold representatives of every people of the world rejoicing in a common happiness, and producing an impression upon the senses at once so dazzling and fairy-like that it is wellnigh impossible to believe it a reality, or to convince yourself that you are not, all the while, wandering in some delicious dreamland, or, in an imaginative way, simply moving among scenes of the Arabian Nights. Certainly, never before (nor since) did I behold such glories amid the gathering shadows of departing day, and I remember with what fresh beauty and vividness the scene between Lorenzo and Jessica, in The Merchant of Venice, rose before my mind, and I found myself uttering almost aloud the words of both: —

" LORENZO.   In such a night as this,
When the sweet wind did gently kiss the trees,
And they did make no noise; in such a night,
Troilus, methinks, mounted the Trojan walls,
And sigh'd his soul toward the Grecian tents,
Where Cressid lay that night.

" JESSICA.   In such a night,
Did Thisbe fearfully o'ertrip the dew;
And saw the lion's shadow ere himself,
And ran dismay'd away.

" LOR.   In such a night,
Stood Dido with a willow in her hand,
Upon the wild sea-banks, and wav'd her love
To come again to Carthage.

" JES.   In such a night,
Medea gather'd the enchanted herbs
That did renew old Æson.

" LOR.   In such a night,
Did Jessica steal from the wealthy Jew:
And with an unthrift love did run from Venice,
As far as Belmont.

" JES.   And in such a night,
Did young Lorenzo swear he lov'd her well;
Stealing her soul with many vows of faith,
And ne'er a true one.

" LOR.   And in such a night,
Did pretty Jessica, like a little shrew,
Slander her love, and he forgave it her."

.   .   .   .

' How sweet the moonlight sleeps upon this bank!
Here we will sit, and let the sounds of music
Creep in our ears; soft stillness, and the night,
Become the touches of sweet harmony."

At seven o'clock you drive home, and take
the bath which awaits you. Your evening-dress
will be laid out, even to the studs in your
shirt: for, if you are in moderate circumstances
you will have six; if rich, about twenty-four; if
a rajah, or in society and wealth of a rajah's

status, you will have about a hundred, servants.
Even the poor white man cannot get on beneath
the burning suns of India without at least a
couple of them. Servants are inevitable, and
several, often many, a necessity ; for one will not
do another's work. Your *boy* will not clean your
boots or carry your dirty water, and your *size* will
not open or shut your carriage-door. Consequently you must have a groom, a size, a meta,
a cook, a *kidmeghar* (steward), and a boy, if you
wish to get on passably well. Each understands
the duties of the other, and each knows his station and most persistently keeps it. The boy is
the head-servant and orders all the others to their
duties, or perhaps I ought to write duty, for each
limits his toil to the minimum, and, since he
cannot do less unless he does nothing at all, he
does some one thing. The boys, as a rule, are
Moslems, and so are the sizes, the cooks, and the
grooms. The metas, who discharge the lowest
and meanest duties, are Pariahs. Dinner is
prepared at eight o'clock, and at nine the
theatres open.

The theatres are lofty buildings with only one
gallery, and have a dress circle, stalls, and generally a considerable number of private boxes.
The stalls and dress circle are four or five rupees
(two dollars or two dollars and a half), and the
private boxes are from twenty to forty rupees
(from ten to twenty dollars). I have received as
much as one hundred and fifty rupees (seventy-

five dollars) for one private box, and frequently
seventy-five rupees (thirty-seven dollars and a
half).

The first few days in Calcutta were spent in
preparation for opening at the Corinthian Theatre,
the largest and grandest in the city. The place
was crowded, even more than usual, for thousands
of visitors had swarmed in for the Christmas
festivities. I had little leisure, but I found time,
in the intervals of coaching the new members
of my company and necessary rehearsals, to join
to some extent in the many festive gatherings of
the season. I was present at the Great Eastern
Hotel during a grand illumination on Christmas
eve, which Sir Ashley Eden honored by his
presence. I was introduced to him. The scene
was most imposing, and there was immense cheer-
ing by the natives as Sir Ashley Eden and his
suite and the numerous guests passed into the
banqueting-hall. The appearance of the Hindu
waiters was very charming as, dressed in pure
white muslin with crimson turbans on their heads
and a band of the same color round their loins,
they ranged themselves on either side of the way
along which the procession of the lieutenant-
governor and the guests passed, all of them
crying, "Salam! salam!"

The Great Eastern Hotel is the largest institution of its kind in India. It combines with the
hotel proper an establishment where you can get
every conceivable article from a pin to an anchor,

from cheese to pork, from a sponge-cake to every
kind of bread in the art of bakery; indeed,
anything from a white mouse to (shall I say?)
a white elephant.

Later on the same evening, December 24, 1881,
I opened at the Corinthian Theatre, on which
occasion I played Narcisse. We had a good
house; the receipts amounted to over two thousand rupees (one thousand dollars). The success
of the play was grand and decisive; the entire Calcutta press was loud in our praise. The next play
taken was Dead or Alive, and the third Hamlet.
This was the largest house ever assembled inside of
a Hindu theatre, and the success was so great that
the Marchioness of Ripon, the wife of the viceroy,
after the third performance, at which she had been
present, sent me the following letter, asking me
to repeat the same play, as she was anxious to see
it again : —

"MILITARY SECRETARY TO THE VICEROY.
"GOVERNMENT HOUSE, CALCUTTA, January 5, 1882.

"Lord William Beresford presents his compliments to Mr. Bandmann, and begs to inform him
that her excellency, the Marchioness of Ripon, has
expressed a wish to see Hamlet repeated by his
company, and the day that her excellency would
like to attend will be Tuesday, January 10.
Please state if this date is convenient, and if so
the entertainment can be advertised as under the
patronage and presence of their excellencies."

I complied with her excellency's request, which was tantamount to a viceregal command, as his excellency, the Marquis of Ripon, has never been seen in a theatre since the time he embraced Catholicism. I repeated Hamlet on the day specified to a house so crowded that days before seats were sold at a premium of ten and twenty rupees.

Lord William Beresford, better known as Lord "Bill" (as he is familiarly called in Calcutta), is private secretary to the viceroy. He has been filling that position ever since Lord Lytton held that office, and it was somewhat unfortunate for me that that noble peer was not still at the helm of Hindu affairs. I should have been socially well treated by his lordship, as I was an intimate friend of his late father, with whom I spent many weeks at Knebworth, and from whom I received upward of a hundred letters, which I still have by me. It was my appearance as Narcisse, in London, that brought Lord Lytton out again, and, after twenty years' silence, induced him to write The Rightful Heir.

Well, Lord Bill is a good fellow, and always willing to do a kindness to a professional man. He is himself a sort of modern Thespis, for whenever the court goes to Simla, which is the residence of the viceroy during the summer months, — a most beautiful spot, at an elevation of ten thousand feet, in the Himalayas, — he arranges all the theatrical amusements and the

entire programme of the summer sports. Lord
Bill has a liking for me on account of my friendship with his brother Charlie, who was a middy
of the Galatea when the Duke of Edinburgh was
in Australia, and who frequently came with the
duke to dine with us. I remember how, on one
occasion, Charlie seemed half to regret that he
was not the eldest son of the Marquis of Water-
ford. "If only I were," said he, "wouldn't I
make the dollars fly ; but, confound it! I'm only
third in *that* race."

One evening the little dinner at my house
included the Duke of Edinburgh, Eliot Yorke,
Captain Haig, Charlie Fergusson (brother to Sir
James Fergusson, now governor of Bombay), and
Charlie Beresford. After dinner was over the
duke whispered to me that he had provided a
little music by way of surprise. Accordingly
Anderson, a fair pianist (who afterward married
Ilma di Murska, and is now dead), in whom the
duke had taken some interest, was introduced for
the purpose of accompanying him on the piano ;
for the duke's little surprise was to be more of
his own fiddling, in respect to which none of those
present were absolute strangers, and certainly,
much as we respected the prince, not very passionate admirers. I shall never forget the long faces
of the boys, especially of Charlie Beresford, when
that announcement was made. He had been the
life and soul of the dinner-party, but now all
changed with him, for he became quite morose.

His royal highness took to the fiddle, but Charlie,
I am sorry to say, was not enchanted by its
strains; indeed, he never seemed fully to appreciate the musical talent of his friend, the duke,
and least of all on this occasion. I could read
in his face the lines of Richard II : —

"How sour sweet music is,
When time is broke, and no proportion kept."

Slyly and noiselessly he got out on the balcony,
and from there he soon disappeared and I saw
him no more that evening.

On the morrow, however, I met him, for I was
invited by the duke to join him in pigeon-shoot-
ing, and Charlie came up and winked at me as
much as to say: "Don't split on me for last
night, old fellow."

Well, if Charlie Beresford did n't like music
at that time, he showed in the late Egyptian War
that he could make his enemies dance to his own
peculiar style of fiddling, and won golden praises
for himself in the din of battle.

During my return visit to Calcutta, who should
come there but Charlie himself, who, since he
was accompanied by his wife, and now had so
many additional responsibilities, obligations, and
dignities resting upon him, from what he had at
the time when he was simply a middy on board
the Galatea, I ought perhaps to call Lord Charles
Beresford. However, the dear fellow was in no
way changed, as the following letter shows: —

"*My dear Bandmann,* — Thank you so much for your kind letter. I shall be delighted to see you again. We are just off on a round of visits; but when I come back I shall come and see you, and we will talk of old times.

"Yours very truly,
"CHARLES BERESFORD."

Calcutta society has only one season in the year, and that is from the middle of December, the time when the court returns from Simla, till about the middle of March in the following year. During that period all India: that is, the white portion of the population, together with all the nobility of Bengal: comes to town.

It is quite a spectacle to see one of these great, high-born rajahs make his *entrée* with his retinue of several hundred courtiers, retainers, servants, and accompanied by bands of music. There are maharajahs who have as great power as the viceroy himself, and who would not budge a jot to do him superior homage. I may take, for instance, the Maharajah of Darbungha, a potentate who has enormous possessions in land, and an income of upward one hundred thousand rupees (fifty thousand dollars) per day, and who is considered one of the most wealthy men in India. He speaks English fluently, and received, as most of the rajahs and maharajahs do, his education under government supervision at the University of Calcutta. He is short, has a full beard, comes seldom to town, always wears his maharajah's uniform, with turban-cap embroidered with pearls of enormous value. He has a beautiful mansion at No. 42, Chowringee, overlooking the Maidan. He took a great liking to me, and frequently asked me to come and see him. His reception of me was always, even from the first, most cordial. I saw on his table a splendid edition of Knight's Shakespeare, and he chatted with me every time I met him upon that topic. What he liked most, of all my impersonations, was Shylock. He invited me to dine with him, and was in every way most courteous and hospitable.

Another of the maharajahs with whom I became acquainted, and from whom I received many indications of friendship, is the Cooch Behar, than whom there is no more intelligent, charming, and enlightened prince in India. He is a man of very different stamp from the Maharajah of Darbungha. No one would take him for a native of India; he dresses and lives like a European, and is married to a daughter of Babu Keshub Chunder Sen, the great theistic reformer, one of the noblest, most impressive, and in many ways most picturesque personalities, not only in the religious history of India, but of the entire world, and of whom I shall have more to say further on.

I had many opportunities afforded me of meeting the Cooch Behar, and hold several interesting letters from him. He lives in a lovely palace called the Woodlands, close to the Zoölogical Gardens, Calcutta, and is deeply read in the poets and dramatists of ancient and modern times, being especially familiar with those of Italy, France, Germany, and England, and is, as might be imagined, a passionate lover of Shakespeare. In fact, the love of Shakespeare is inherent in the Hindu mind, or rather, it is an inevitable blossoming of inherent qualities and dispositions beneath the influence of European education, which all the higher classes in India now enjoy. First comes the Zendavesta and the Vedas; then the Koran, with the Islamic section of the Hindus, and with a very few, who have completely embraced theistic or Christian principles, the Bible; while with others, certainly not a very numerous class, to whom religion is more a philosophy than a creed, all of these — the Zendavesta, the Vedas, the Koran, and the Bible — are equally studied and valued, their reverence being divided among them; then — and it is so with those who belong to all these various schools of religious thought in India, and no matter to which they belong — comes Shakespeare.

The Hindu learns his English through the study of the immortal Bard, and so, from the very earliest years, his devotion is kindled toward this supreme master of the drama, and he becomes to him in after-life "guide, philosopher, and friend." The Hindu is a proud and eloquent creature; he is full of form and dignity; he likes grandeur and magnitude; besides, he loves poetry, and Shakespeare's sublime ideas and magnificent diction touch him to the quick.

But it was my privilege, during my sojourn in Calcutta, to meet with one whose society had attractions for me beyond all others, whether natives or foreigners, and I shall ever regard my intimate, but all too brief, friendship with him as amongst the chief enjoyments of my life and my most sacred memories. I refer to Babu Keshub Chunder Sen, whose name I have already incidentally mentioned, and the news of whose recent death caused a thrill of sorrow that swept over the entire civilized world, and elicited from Eastern and Western peoples alike testimonies to the greatness and beauty and holiness of his character and work, and the general admission of irreparable loss, not only to India and the Hindus, but to the cause of progress everywhere. I am sensible that no words of mine can, even if that were necessary, sketch a complete portrait of this remarkable man, or shape for others a just and accurate estimate of his endeavors; yet, regarding the time passed in his society as amongst the most precious and golden hours of my life, I cannot do other than pay my small tribute to the memory of a friend whose like, in many ways, I cannot hope to see again.

Babu Keshub Chunder Sen was the most learned and enlightened native in India: I may

go further and say, in the entire Orient. He was
the Solon of his country, and took a leading part
in all political, civil, social, and spiritual movements for the progressive enlightenment and
welfare of the Hindus. With a grand, imposing,
athletic figure, a noble bearing, he combined an
expressive dignity which reminded one of the
patrician Roman. He was fully six feet high,
broad shouldered, deep chested, of slightly olive
complexion, mild, eloquent eyes, firm, set lips,
genial chin, black moustache, and long black
hair, which hung carelessly over a well-developed
forehead. The stamp of nobility was upon him,
and he might without vainglory have said : —

> " Mislike me not for my complexion —
> The shadow'd lining of the burning sun,
> To whom I am a neighbor, and near bred.
> Bring me the fairest creature northward born,
> Where Phœbus' fire scarce thaws the icicles,
> And let us make incision for your love,
> To prove whose blood is reddest, his or mine."

He was my *beau ideal* of an " Othello make-up,"
and I told him that I would bring his face on
the stage when I should play that part. He
laughed and came to see it (as he was never
absent from any of my Shakespearean impersonations). After the performance he came into my
dressing-room, and spoke highly of the acting.

" But what did you think of my make-up?"
I asked.

" If it was meant for me," he answered, " I can

only say that I could not see myself in it, for I beheld a handsome man." But the Babu was too modest, for he certainly was the handsomest man I saw in India.

As with most of the educated Hindus, Shakespeare was his favorite topic, and in that subject he was a perfect master. I have greatly benefited in frequent conversations by his transcendental expositions, and looked with pleasure into his inspiring, eloquent eyes, which sparkled with Oriental enthusiasm.

He spoke the English language without the slightest accent, and he possessed that rarest of all gifts, the art of conversation.

In his frequent lectures against Brahmanic fetichism, and in favor of the movement which he called the New Dispensation, he kept his audiences, composed of Europeans and educated natives, spellbound. He was versatile to a high degree, and could discuss any subject, showing a keen and penetrating understanding in all his views.

In religion he was more Christian than Brahman: indeed, it may be said of him that he embraced Christianity, or something so much better than the popular and fashionable Christianity of our Western Christendom, that he attained a beauty in spirit and life that recalled to me, by his presence alone, in a way that no Western type of Christian character has ever done, the image of the sweet and perfect humanity of the

Christ. I read the other day of a man in Broughty Ferry who wrote to his clergyman, the Reverend Murray McCheyne, that he was converted "not by anything you have said, but by your look, sir, as you entered the pulpit." I can easily imagine that hundreds of conversions to the· principles of the New Dispensation must have been brought about in the same way and by that most powerful of all eloquence : the presence and look of a man of singular purity and sublimity of character, such as we know its inaugurator to have been.

Yet, while in his spirit more Christian than anything else, he still adhered to many of the customs of his Hindu fellow-citizens, in dress, mode of life, and domestic matters; and, perhaps, because he could not thereby have done so much good to the cause he had always in view, as he otherwise succeeded in doing, he never fully avowed the opinions of any one of the differing Christian sects, though I am sure he managed to get very near to the heart of Christ himself. The marriage of his daughter, at a very early age, to the Maharajah Cooch Behar, was considered by some of his friends in India, Europe, and America, as a very questionable step; there can, however, be no doubt in the minds of those who knew him intimately, that in this, as in everything else, he was moved by the purest motives, absolutely free of that worldly and selfish policy that some wrongly have attributed to him.

He told me once : " I only desire to live long
enough to be able to destroy the old fetich system,
and lead my people to the enlightened religion
of the New Dispensation," which is, in fact, only
another word for Unitarianism. In this direction
he was to a large extent successful, for Dalhousie's
Institute was crowded to overflowing whenever
he lectured. In the midst of his triumphs he was
called to the great field of rest, where we all one
day have to go. We shall see him no more, and
I presume his mortal body was given over to that
dismal spot on the Ganges, where it was burnt
with sandal-wood, and where his relatives had
to light the pile, and do the last honor to his
remains. How many thousands must have been
within the sombre, lofty walls ! How many
hundreds of thousands must have wept and
sorrowed that day over their loss ! They may
well weep, for with him departed the best and
truest friend of the Hindus in recent times, and
the stanchest adherent of the English crown.
The Queen of England knew this well, and sent
him a volume of the Prince Consort's Life, with
her picture and autograph attached. Peace to
his ashes, for he was a great and good man, and
pushed India a century ahead ; while the Brahmo
Somaj and the New Dispensation still remain to
carry on his work, and to show to coming ages
the immense influence of one man of great, divinely
inspired genius, and, perhaps (who can tell?),
to build a memorial to Babu Keshub Chunder

Sen, in India, no less beautiful and impressive than Christendom is to the influence of Christ.

> "His life was gentle; and the elements
> So mix'd in him, that Nature might stand up
> And say to all the world, This was a man!"

CHAPTER X. — INDIA.

CALCUTTA. — II.

"I pray you let us satisfy our eyes
With the memorials, and the things of fame,
That do renown this city."
— *Twelfth Night, Act iii, sc. 3.*

The exclusively Hindu theatres — Three thousand Hindus witness
Othello and The Merchant of Venice — East Lynne: an incident in
its performance — Leah, the Forsaken — The Marchioness of Ripon
and Romeo and Juliet — What a European can stand in the way
of work — An Eurasian plays Dogberry — A midnight visit to the
Burning Ghaut — The method of cremation as practised by the
Hindus — The miscalled "quarter of pleasure" — The Botanical
and Zoölogical Gardens — "Old Grizzly" — The *cobra de capello*
— The mongoose — No cobras in Calcutta — A bad joke — The
character of the Hindus — New Year's day in Calcutta — Hindu
hospitality — A babu's family bed — Hindu marriages — Hindu
wives — The empalement of widows — The Hindus compared with
the Chinese — Hindu men superior to the women — The ambition
of the men to practise law — The fascination of the law court for
the Hindus — Perjury the commonest crime in the country — Sir
Henry De Witt, the chief justice of Ceylon — How an old judge
of Copenhagen got at the truth — The ways of a Hindu pleader —
Police proceedings with suspects — Hindu servants — A Bengal
judge and his trusted servant — Personal experiences with Hindu
servants — Court-life in Calcutta — The children's garden-party —
The hotels.

IT is a pleasure beyond description to see the
natives of India enjoying a Shakespearean performance; the intelligence and enthusiasm they
evince far exceed that of any European audience with which I am acquainted, and I have
performed in most of the great cities of Germany,
England, and America. After playing all the
rounds of Shakespearean characters, — in some
plays taking, for instance, the part of Othello

on one or several nights, and then that of Iago
at one or more performances of the same play,
at the Corinthian, — I consented, in compliance
with a special request, to play for a few nights
in the exclusively Hindu theatres. I gave them
the choice of my whole répertoire, and they
chose Othello and The Merchant of Venice.
It was a sight of indescribable interest to behold
three thousand black faces turned on the stage,
and there were hundreds of their *zenanas* in the
boxes, who could see us acting, though we could
not see them. They followed the play with rapt
attention, and it was evident from the succession
of pauses, in which one might have heard a pin
drop, and outbursts of applause which would have
drowned a thunder-clap, that they not simply
watched the movement of events and the changed
relations of the personages of the play, but, in a
most philosophical way, entered into the secret,
inner life of each of them, and comprehended
the entire development of the plot; that, in a
word, the subjectivity of the drama was as real
to them, yea, more real, than the mere external
spectacular display. I have never been so well
understood as Shylock as I was that evening
by those three thousand Hindus and Moslems.
They comprehended the most delicate shadings
of character and the finest points in the dialogue.
The success that followed these plays was so
great that I had to consent to repeat them, and
to extend the programme.

Besides Shakespearean plays some of the Hindus exceedingly liked East Lynne. That novel has been translated lately into the Hindustani and Parsee languages, and the success of it has been very great. Miss Beaudet played the principal character a dozen times, and on one occasion a young European gentleman was so overcome by her emotional acting that he fainted in the fourth act, and had to be carried to his home. When he revived he rushed to his mother's room and threw himself into her arms and exclaimed:—

"Oh, mother! what is a home without a mother?"

I know this to have been a fact, for, by a strange coincidence, I was invited to dinner at the very house shortly after, and the mother of the lad told me the story.

The play of Leah, the Forsaken, was next produced, and was wellnigh as popular as East Lynne.

Before leaving for Simla, the Marchioness of Ripon expressed a second wish: this time it was to see Romeo and Juliet: in a letter from Lord William Beresford, dated Monday, Feburary 20:

"Her excellency desires to see Romeo and Juliet; if you will kindly write and let me know what date you would propose, I will submit your letter to her excellency on her return from Darjeeling this week, and will inform you as to the result."

The date I proposed was accepted by her excellency, and she was highly pleased with the performance, and sent Miss Beaudet a beautiful bouquet for her impersonation of Juliet.

My entire season was a marvelous success, my clear profit in Calcutta alone amounting to four thousand pounds (twenty thousand dollars); but it is impossible to tell the amount of labor, worry, and hardship one had to undergo, in teaching the company so as to bring every point connected with each play effectively out, and to give to each of the parts of the respective performances its relative importance, while blending them all into a perfect, symmetrical unity so as to reach a high standard of acting and of art. In thinking even of the golden harvest I reaped, I cannot forget the manifold toils by which it was reached. Although in Calcutta I made further accessions to my company (which at the time I hoped would considerably lighten the work for some members of the group), in a Mr. Dorcy Ogden and a Mr. Denbigh Newton, the first turned out unreliable, and the second was of little use. The company was sometimes in an unwilling and dogged state, perhaps from sheer overwork; but my own indomitable spirit and the constant, joyful co-operation of Miss Beaudet, by sheer contagion, pushed them on, and made it possible for us to perform within three months the following plays: Hamlet, ten times; Othello and The Merchant of Venice,

fourteen times; Romeo and Juliet, Dead or Alive,
six times; Macbeth, As You Like It, Much Ado
About Nothing, Narcisse, East Lynne, eight times;
Leah, the Forsaken, The Duke's Motto, and The
Corsican Brothers, — not to mention others.

After all, it is astonishing what an amount
of work a European constitution can stand, and
my own continued good health, through it all,
has surprised none more than myself. Besides
teaching what were quite new plays to many
of the company, there was constant rehearsing
and aiding all the leading parts, superintending
the outside business management, and looking
after banking account; yet, notwithstanding it
all, I felt quite free of all sense of weariness and
in the best of spirits, on coming out of the theatre
in the evening. On one occasion an Eurasian,
who was as white as a European, and who was
very fond of acting, teased me until I consented
to allow him to play Dogberry, one night, as he
was so very fat and funny. He was delighted
at the concession, but when he. came into the
wardrobe he nearly swooned, and complained of
the heat to such an extent that I had to send
a servant to get him a pankhâ boy. Now, this man
was born in India, and had lived all his life
beneath its skies, and yet he was not able to stand
as much as we were, although he had only to
wear a light domino, while we were dressed in
silks, velvets, and furs.

One night about eleven o'clock I said to Mr. Kellar, the well-known magician: "I am ready to go."

"Well, then, let us be off," said he.

I called to my boy, and in five minutes a two-horse *gharry* (cab) stood in front of my door.

"Jeety!" (quick) I shouted to the driver, and off he drove at a rapid pace over the excellent, well-paved, and, on account of the lateness of the hour, already deserted streets of Calcutta. It took us somewhat forty-five minutes before we reached our destination. When the cab halted, the boy opened the door, and we stood before a high wall at the foot of the river Ganges, whence we could see that smoke was ascending from some place beyond to the sombre skies. We followed the boy through several fields, each surrounded by enormously high walls, till at last we reached a long field walled around on three sides, while on the other we could see the noiseless, dark waters of the Ganges. It was a desolate, most dreary spot, but in the distance we could see some half-dozen shadowy forms moving around what was evidently an object of interest, and watched by them with great care; and here and there, as we drew nearer to the banks of the Ganges, we saw that there were several other similar groups, and could clearly see men heaping up piles of wood and heaps of smoldering ashes: then suddenly quite near to us a pile of wood burst into flame and a dreadful smell filled the night-air, and we knew that we were within the Burning Ghaut of the Hindus.

"But where are the bodies?" I asked, and before the boy could answer, I heard a sound as if a too heavily charged carbolic soda-water bottle had burst.

"Dats de squll, sab, just bu'st, vat you hear making dat noise," and my attention being called to the spot, I saw that the bones of a skull had fallen to the ground and that a body was lying on the top of a pile of wood wellnigh covered by the flames and fast burning to ashes. Soon after we had an opportunity of seeing the entire method of cremation as practised amongst the Hindus.

The simplicity of the proceeding surprised me. A couple of logs of wood are laid on the ground parallel to each other, and then two more are laid across them parallelly, and this process is continued till a pile of a considerable height is built: then the body to be cremated is taken and, so far as can be, doubled up, and placed on the top; more logs are placed two and two, parallel to each other, each successive layer being crossway to the one beneath; then, abundance of brushwood having been placed at the bottom of the pile, the nearest relative of the deceased walks around it two or three times and says a prayer, after which he fires the brushwood with a torch, and almost instantly the entire pile is one volume of flame. It takes usually from three to four

hours to burn a body, and the ashes that remain
of it are gathered and thrown into the sacred
river that flows hard by.   The dreadful silence
of the place, and the mistiness of the night on
which I was at the Burning Ghaut, the towering
walls on three sides of it, and the awful and
mysterious waters of the Ganges on the other,
together with the noisomeness of the dense,
surcharged atmosphere, — all combined to produce a scene most weird and appalling.   I asked
one of the cremators whether the bodies of all
persons, rich and poor, were burnt alike.

" Oh, no, sab," he replied; " rich man burn
himself wid nice sandal-wood — good smell ; poor
man, no *pies* (pennies), sab ; " and at this moment
he made a very energetic forward movement for
backsheesh.

When in Bombay subsequently, I saw a similar
scene on the ground there devoted to these last,
sad offices of the Hindus, but it produced nothing
like the same effect upon me.   I have often
wondered since whether Schiller could have
known anything of cremation, for, if so, how
could he have written in his famous " Lay of
the Bell " —

> " Whate'er the fierce flames may destroy,
>   One consolation sweet is left;
>   His lov'd ones' heads he counts, — and, Joy!
>   He is not e'en of one bereft! "?

After leaving the Burning Ghaut, Mr. Kellar
proposed that we should visit, on our way

home, another night-scene of Calcutta, and drive
through the so-called (but surely miscalled)
"quarter of pleasure." We did so, and to my
disgust I saw streets full of the most horrible
spectacles and orgies of vice I have ever beheld.
We passed houses upon houses crowded with
beautiful, well-shaped Jewish women, all from
the Roumanian districts, principally Banat, Croa-
tian, and Servian, following a trade of infamy and
lust. They are brought over by their masters,
chiefly Jews also, like slaves, for whom they live
a life of degradation, and after they have made
money enough to satisfy their greed are often
married to them. These men are of the lowest
type in the world: innocence and youth and help-
lessness are no deterrents to their villainy: they
have lost all sense of purity, chastity, and honor.
Yet they have their clubhouse, and carry on their
vile trade in the broad daylight; the only restric-
tion being that they are not allowed outside this
quarter of the city, and are under constant police
supervision. I would not have believed it possible, had I not seen it with my own eyes, that
Jewish men and women could so far have fallen.

> " One sin, I know, another doth provoke;
>   Murder's as near to lust, as flame to smoke."

The Jews, as a rule, are very sensitive as to
their chastity, but it is one of the saddest facts
confronted in Eastern travel that the prostitution
that prevails throughout the Orient is principally

carried on by Jews and Jewesses. With disgust
I called to the cabman to turn back and drive
home as quickly as possible, for I felt that here,
even more than at the Burning Ghaut, I had
looked on the horrors and terrors of death.

" But when we in our viciousness grow hard
   (O misery on 't!), the wise gods seal our eyes:
   In our own filth drop our clear judgments; make us
   Adore our errors; laugh at us. while we strut
   To our confusion."

The Botanical and Zoölogical Gardens are very
large and fine, and one of the most lovely drives
of the city lies through them. These gardens
were established as early as 1786, and in the long
succession of years each has added something to
them by way of charm or beauty. There is no
better way of spending a Sunday afternoon in
Calcutta than by paying a visit to them. Everybody drives to the Zoo, to see the animals fed,
at five o'clock in the afternoon. They contain
a magnificent collection of reptiles, tigers, and
monkeys. There is a most venerable bear there,
that has been in the gardens for many years, and
to which special honor is paid; for he is provided
with a cage of great size all to himself. The cage
stands on a mound, and everybody is allowed
to go near him, he is so inoffensive, and there is
not the slightest danger; at least such is the
general supposition both amongst the Europeans
and the natives.

" I would not trust myself *too* near him," I said
to a rather too-confiding gentleman.

" Bless you!" said he. " I have seen the beast
the last twenty years and had lots of fun with
him. I 'll show you;" and he took an empty
paper bag, in which he had carried cakes for the
animals, and shut it up to fool " Old Grizzly,"
who took it and carefully opened it; and while
he was doing so the man played with the woolly
top of his head. " Old Grizzly," perhaps annoyed
over the cheat, or having grown angry at the
succession of indignities to which he had been
subjected by the same visitor, — for I suppose
even a bear loses his patience under such provo-
cations, as the rest of us mortals do, — seized
hold of the man's arm with his two large paws,
through the bars, and was just about setting
his teeth to it, when I gave him a blow with my
walking-stick, which I fortunately had with me,
on his mouth, which somewhat puzzled him,
while I pulled the man simultaneously with all
might out of his clutches; and he escaped the
loss of an arm, leaving only a complete sleeve of
his coat together with that of his shirt and a
part of the skin of his arm in " Old Grizzly's "
possession. The poor man could only say:
" Thank you, sir; if it had n't been for you I
should very likely have been an arm the poorer,
and perhaps a life." He was as pale as a sheet,
and, desirous of avoiding a scene, for I saw
already a lot of persons coming toward the spot,

and not ambitious to be made a hero, I walked toward my carriage with the ladies I had accompanied, and disappeared.

The word "cobra" is a terror to the Hindus. The statistics of India say that upward of ten thousand human beings die yearly from the bite of the cobra. The deaths principally occur in the rural districts, where the Hindus are accustomed to walk barefooted over the fields and roads, and step unknowingly on the reptile; for it is a well-known fact that the cobra does not attack unless he is attacked, or when any one happens to come between him and his hiding-place. It is a dreadful creature, and its bite is incurable. As the full Portuguese name, cobra de capello, signifies, it is the "snake of the hood"; that is, when about to attack it dilates the back and sides of the neck so as to resemble a hood, or, one may say, wings; then it bends itself up, and often jumps several feet forward at its prey. The only animal which will fight this horrible reptile is the small mongoose, about twice the size of a ferret, with a long bushy tail and a sharp nose and mouth. It catches its mighty victim by the back of the neck and literally bites its head off. When bitten itself by the cobra, it is commonly believed that it runs into the jungle and eats of a certain plant which is an antidote, though no one, so far as I could learn, has any definite knowledge of its nature and properties.

The best way of destroying the cobra, up till now discovered by the Hindus, seems to be by means of poisoned milk. The reptile is very fond of milk, and, without for a moment suspecting that his favorite beverage may contain poison, drinks heartily of it, and dies, or becomes so impotent that a man may easily make an end of him.

In the city of Calcutta there are no cobras, although the cellar of the Theatre Royal, where I played part of the season, is said to be infested with them. During the engagement of Mr. Kellar, two of his assistants had to go nightly below to work the automata, and every night when the time approached for them to descend, they grew as pale as ghosts. One of these men assured me that he had seen on one occasion as many as half a dozen cobras jumping about. It is certainly a fact that, when I took over the theatre on my lease, I could not get the coolies to go below to clear the cellar of the old rubbish that had accumulated. I had several batches of coolies, but each ran off every time as soon as they heard what I wanted done, and I was obliged to abandon the job. It was quite amusing: save for the serious thought that would come to one sometimes that possibly a cobra might be hidden in one's own wardrobe: to see my people cautiously handling their dresses and shaking them nightly before putting them on, in the utmost fear that the deadly reptile was lurking in some jacket, cloak, or petticoat. On one occasion, at the morning rehearsal, one of the actors made a bad joke, and frightened the ladies wellnigh to death, by the cry: "A cobra! a cobra!" They never forgave him, and it was a very foolish and a wrong thing on his part. The government pays a premium of eight annas (twenty-five cents) for every dead cobra.

A certain manager of a theatre in Calcutta, who lives half of his life in a state of dazed consciousness, fancied one day there was a cobra in his room, and sent for a snake-charmer, who on coming seemed actually to catch it and demanded payment.

"We will kill it," said the dazed manager, and he was about to knock it on the head, when the charmer screamed, and protecting his "tamed" snake ran out of the room with it as quickly as possible.

The Hindus are, as a rule, kind-hearted, quick in perception, and hospitable. Every New Year's day they send a vast quantity of backsheesh in the shape of cakes and baskets of nuts and fruit to their friends. So that the words seem as true to-day as they were in the time of Aristophanes, who, in "The Acharnians," makes the commissioner just returned from Persia say: —

> " Yes, Orientals estimate their heroes
> By their capacity for food and drink."

I myself, on the New Year's day I passed at

Calcutta, received as many as a dozen large cakes and twenty baskets of nuts and fruits from Hindu friends. The company lived wellnigh exclusively on these for over a month, the supply was so great. The Hindus are especially fond of betel-nut and of lime leaves: one or the other of these they are constantly chewing. They are good for digestion; but they leave a most objectionable, nasty red saliva on their teeth and lips, which makes them look savage. There are other well-flavored and scented nuts which they like, and if you call upon a rich Hindu he offers you a seat on a grand carpet or rug, with a high pillow for you to lean upon, and then you are served with nuts, spices, and delicious sherbets. In the houses of the more modernized Hindus these luxuries will be supplemented by cigarettes, and perhaps some of the party will regale you with a song, which, of course, you are supposed to be pleased with, though too often it is a most unmusical and inartistic performance, being simply a drone and principally coming from the head and throat. At one of the babus at whose mansion I was a frequent visitor, I was surprised, on being shown over the house, to find a bed, in one of his apart-ments, almost eighteen feet wide, and twenty feet long, completely hemmed in with curtains and glass windows, and over which was a large pankhâ.

"That's my family bed, where I sleep with my wives," said mine host.

I was just about to ask him how many, but I stopped, thinking the question might seem offensive, or at least indicate an impolite inquisitiveness on my part; but from general appearances, and the considerable number of pillows, I judged that his wives were, if not as numerous as Solomon's, quite sufficient for the most ambitious man in that direction.

The wives of the Hindus have not the pleasantest lives. Hindu girls are bestowed in marriage very young, sometimes before they are even born, to such and such a son, of such and such a family. They don't see each other till they are fit to live together, which is when the boy is about fifteen or sixteen years of age, and the girl eleven or twelve. From the time they begin to live with their husbands they are locked up, and afterward never allowed to be seen outside their own homesteads. If they are sick, a female physician is sent for; they are not even permitted to eat with their husbands, and dare not sit at the same table with them.

The Hindu conception of woman is that of an unclean thing, and up to a quarter of a century ago the wife was of no account alone whatsoever; and she was taken and burnt alive with the corpse of her husband. It was reported that such a ceremony had taken place somewhere in the interior while I was in Calcutta, and it was openly affirmed that the government has not been able to crush completely and effectively this dreadful, savage custom, but that the priests in the interior have still an occasional wife burning or empaling. This immolation or burning of widows alive at the funeral-pyre of their husbands has never been voluntary, or, if so, in only the merest few instances; and though some fanatics maintain it has been the case, and that the widows follow their deceased lords with meekness and obedience to the burning-stake, they are nearly always intoxicated by powerful drugs and carried away by the fanatical excitement of others, and often actually shoved on to the pyre, while their screams are drowned by the loud and terrible noise of the tom-tom and the shouts and yells of the infuriated crowd.

The Hindus have a great sense of humor and are always ready to enjoy a good joke. In this respect they resemble the Chinese; but in this only. They are not half as clever, but far better-hearted. If the Hindus possessed the brain of the Chinese, and the Chinese the conscience of the Hindus, Europe would have to fear these great nations: but, as it is, the balance of the world's peace is kept steady.

The Hindu women are short, thin, and ugly; but the men are of fine stature and splendid proportions. I have seen many nobly built figures amongst the men, but I have never seen a handsome woman except amongst the Eurasians, who are the offspring of intermarriages; or amongst. the Parsees, who are not natives.

The great ambition of a Hindu is to become a lawyer, or, as he is termed in India, a pleader. There, as in America, the lawyer is allowed to practise both at the bar and as an attorney; but there he is principally occupied in the lower courts, which they call the "small-cause" court, where you can only sue up to a thousand rupees (five hundred dollars). There are four judges in this court, and it is open all the year round; it is on the same basis as the county court in England and the municipal court in America, only that it is always active. The amount of work transacted in this court is tremendous. The Hindu likes to go to law, whether he wins or loses; he seems to derive intense pleasure from merely seeing his name in the law cases as plaintiff or defendant; even from standing up in the court as a witness, and it seems of no consequence to him which side he takes. And since there are so many different castes who hate each other, the quarreling is constant, and the courts are crowded from the beginning to the end of the year.

It is amazing to see the readiness with which they get their witnesses, and the excessive difficulty there is to get at the truth. Perjury is the commonest crime in India, and if the laws relating to this particular offence were to be carried out, at least half the natives would be quartered in the prisons of the country. No caste recognizes the rights of any other caste, and least of all that the *Christian dog* can have any.

Sir Henry De Witt, the chief justice of Ceylon, told me one day he liked the island very well (he had lately been appointed to his present position from the Cape), but that the lying that was carried on in the courts of Ceylon was beyond description. He said that he could not believe one out of every ten witnesses who were summoned before him, and had to rely entirely upon his own judgment. He often thought of following the example of an old judge of the central criminal court in Copenhagen, who, knowing the difficulty of convicting a witness for perjury, placed a constable behind the witnesses with a sharp, thin instrument like a needle, and every time he had reason to think a witness was telling a lie, lifted his hand to his beard, which was a sign for the constable to stick the point of the instrument into the back or leg of the witness; whereupon there was usually a howling on his part, and under a sense of pain, which not infrequently leads to something resembling transient feelings of repentance and pious emotions, even in the worst wretches, the truth was immediately forthcoming.

There is a good story told of one of the clever little Hindu pleaders, who represented the plaintiff in a case in which the pleader for the defendant was not quite ready to proceed, and so desired the consent of the court for the case to stand

over a few days. The judge replied that they
had better arrange that amongst themselves.

"I am ready, your honor," said the plaintiff's
pleader, "and desire to go on."

"I'll beg of you to let the case stand over.
I am really not prepared," said the pleader for
the defendant.

"I cannot, for I have all my witnesses here."

"How many?"

"Twenty-five."

"I'll pay their fees." (The witness fee is eight
annas, that is, twenty-five cents.)

"*Cannot!* I pay double; impossible!"

"Well, we'll put it to his honor again."

His honor decided in favor of the defendant's
pleader that the case was to stand over; and the
pleader for the plaintiff rushed out of the court
wild with rage; but no sooner was he outside
than he met a brother pleader, a great friend
of his, and disburdened his soul thus:—

"Just think, Mullick, had my case ready
against Moocherjee, and his honor ruled it to
stand over; have all my witnesses here, and
everything ready. How damnably provoking, is
n't it?"

"How many witnesses?"

"Twenty-five."

"Well, leave them here for *my* case; it's about
to come on, and I have n't quite enough witnesses
to satisfy me. Of course I'll pay them the
usual fee."

" Accepted."

" There are liars and swearers enough to beat the honest man."

I myself had a case in a certain town in India, where a dishonest babu tried to impose upon me, and dragged me into the small-cause court.

The judge, a most remarkably genial old gentleman, saw through the case at once, and it was decided against the babu. At the close, his honor asked me to step into his private office, and we had a most delightful hour's talk upon art and the drama. This was a most effectual way of settling the other cases that were to come up before him that day, for the various plaintiffs and defendants grew tired of waiting, and settled their difficulties among themselves;

"And *did* as adversaries do in law,
   Strive mightily, but eat and drink as friends."

Shortly before we left Calcutta, Miss Beaudet was robbed of several hundred dollars' worth of jewelry by a servant. The case was immediately given into the hands of the police, who did their utmost to discover the culprit. My suspicion fell upon one of the boys, and I took him aside into a private room, and spoke gently to him. I begged and implored him to give up the stolen property. I even promised to give him twice as much as the smelter or the precious-stone buyer would give him for it. Just then the chief constable, who had seen me take the man into the anteroom, came in, and asked me what I had done. I told him, and he set up a laugh that shook the house, saying, "That's not the way to deal with these fellows; you must give them a good beating;" and turning to the fellow he took him by the beard and jerked his head forward and backward.

"Pig" (the greatest insult to a Moslem), "where is the property? Tell it, or I'll kill you."

The boy never winced, and all he said was: "Nay, sab, nay."

Well, two of the servants were locked up as suspects, and I may say that the way the police try to get at the truth is by a gentle torture. They send a tremendously large-built Hindu policeman to a suspected person at night, who presses his ear, twists his hand or arm, pulls out his thumb, sticks his fist into his sides, sits upon him and squeezes him wellnigh to pulp, till at last he is willing to confess. The law forbids him to use *force*, and, as long as the culprit cannot show serious bruises, the law is quite content.

The Hindu servants are terrible thieves, and have no sense of gratitude.

One of the late chief justices of Bengal, on retiring and going home to England after twenty years of Indian service, provided a rich collection of precious stones, which he intended to distribute among his friends on board the vessel before it left the pier. He put them carefully into a small casket and placed it in a satchel, which he handed to a trusted servant to be carried on board. But when the time to distribute them arrived, and he opened the satchel, they were gone. The chief detective was sent for.

" Who carried the satchel ? " he asked.

" My boy," said the judge.

" Then he 's got them, your honor," the detective responded.

" Nonsense ! man," said the judge : " he 's been in my service for twenty years as faithful as the day. I gave him an annuity and a bungalow for his fidelity. I 'll stake my existence upon his honesty."

" Then your honor must allow me to retire," said the detective, "as I am sure of my suspicions."

" Well, I will not stand in the way of justice being executed," said the surprised judge, "and I will give you permission to do as you like, but you will see how greatly you wrong my poor old Nauth."

The police went at once to the servant's bungalow, quite fresh and new, just given to him by his grateful master, where they found a handsome trunk in the corner of the principal room : also, as it afterward turned out, a present from him : and opened it, and at the top was the little casket containing the judge's jewels, and several

yards of gold trimming of a court suit which the
judge had missed some time back. So much for
a Hindu servant's fidelity.

" When a man's servant shall play the cur with him, look
    you, it goes hard."

The craftiness of these servants in carrying
on their knavish tricks surprises one, even more
than the dishonesty itself.   Their general demeanor reminds one of Iago's words: —

> " You shall mark
> Many a duteous and knee-crooking knave,
> That, doting on his own obsequious bondage,
> Wears out his time, much like his master's ass,
> For naught but provender; and, when he 's old, cashier'd;
> Whip me such honest knaves. Others there are,
> Who, trimm'd in forms and visages of duty,
> Keep yet their hearts attending on themselves.
> And, throwing but shows of service on their lords,
> Do well thrive by them; and when they have lin'd their
>   coats,
> Do themselves homage: these fellows have some soul."

I had one who practised himself so thoroughly
that he could imitate my handwriting most
admirably, and I think there are few persons
who write a hand harder to copy in its various
details than mine, but I must admit that he
succeeded so well that his writing was just like
my own, only somewhat a trifle better, and,
heaven knows! there was need of its being so.
Well, he utilized the art he had attained, in
writing letters of recommendation respecting

himself in my name.   Here is a copy of one of
these : —

" Hassen Al Bey is an excellent servant, honest,
clever, and industrious; and was never known
in any single thing to prove unworthy.   I can
recommend him to everybody."

To this precious document my full name was
subscribed, and never did signature seem so much
like my own.   I found several of such letters on
my writing-table one day, and on searching the
boy a dozen more ' were found, together with
numerous articles that he had stolen from me.
I asked the constable what the boy wanted with
all these letters (they were on my stamped
paper).

"Oh, he sells them to thieves and burglars,
who present themselves to strangers as they come
into the city and are engaged for honest servants,
but afterward rob them."

I half wondered that he did n't borrow the Earl
of Kent's words, from King Lear, to point the
moral of his own great worth: "I can keep honest counsel, ride, run, mar a curious tale in telling
it, and deliver a plain message bluntly; that which
ordinary men are fit for I am qualify'd in: and the
best of me is diligence."

I had to charge the man, and he got three
months' imprisonment.   The disposition to dishonesty is very strong in many of them.   One of

the writers (same position as bookkeeper here), a
babu, who was engaged in a large banking-house
in Calcutta, and who had to give as much as
twenty thousand rupees (ten thousand dollars)
as guaranty for honest behavior, actually ran off
with ten thousand rupees, and this after ten years
of faithful service. But to speak of a happier
subject.

The viceregal court comes to Calcutta, as I
have already said, about the middle of December,
and remains till the middle of March. This is the
gayest, brightest season in the life of that "city
of palaces." Receptions are held twice a week,
and the court gives parties and balls according
to circumstances. One of the greatest festivals
of the season is the children's garden-party, given
annually by their excellencies, and very largely
attended, in the beautiful grounds that surround
the Government House. The Marchioness of
Ripon is the life and soul of all the court festivities, and is highly popular both with the Europeans and the Hindus. The viceroy is not popular.
He is admitted by everybody to be a very religious
man; kind, but overzealous, and too self-centred
and retiring, rarely showing himself amongst the
people, and hardly ever appearing at any of the
rendezvous du monde. He has become very unpopular with the European portion of Calcutta society,
on account of his too strong leaning toward the
natives. The most popular men there, at the time
of my visit, were the lieutenant-governor, Sir
Ashley Eden, and Lord William Beresford.

One thing astonishes me greatly, namely, that in so large and beautiful a city as the metropolis of Bengal, that stands for the whole of India, one cannot get a decent meal, except one dines at a private house. The hotels and so-called boarding-house establishments are beneath contempt — with their tough meats, boiled-out stews, nasty, thick soups, strong curries, flabby bread, starchy puddings, and worse pies. Prepare yourself to starve as soon as you reach India, except in Colombo, where you can get good, wholesome living at the Oriental, or the Mount Lavinia Hotel. Now, farewell, dear, generous Calcutta. In everything, save in thy cuisine, thou hast been so to me, and in that little particular perhaps I ought to forgive thee; at least, I shall suffer no more from it, while memories of a thousand sweet pleasures will remain.

CHAPTER XI. — India.

BOMBAY.

"Hath Britain all the sun that shines? Day, night,
Are they not but in Britain? I' the world's volume
Our Britain seems as of it, but not in it;
In a great pool a swan's nest: pr'ythee, think
There's livers out of Britain."

— Cymbeline, Act iii, sc. 4.

Malibar Hill — Apollo Bunda — The Gaiety, the finest theatre in India — Sir James Fergusson, the governor — The Parsees — The Mazdean religion — The morning offerings at the temples — The Silent Towers — The Parsee conception of nature and life — The Parsees speak English and are great admirers of Shakespeare — Four young Parsee medical students play parts in Hamlet — A Hindu marriage — Hindu theosophy — Juggernaut, the "Lord of the World" — Symbolism in religion.

FROM Calcutta, I conducted my company to Bombay, a journey of about two thousand miles across the continent of India, and now easily made by means of the excellent railroad that connects those far-separated cities.

Of all the large cities in India, Bombay is the most picturesque and in many respects the pleasantest to live in. The city lies close to the sea, and there is always a refreshing breeze for eight hours in the day; then it has a great variety of picturesque houses and antiquities. In the city, or what is called the "Fort," very few people live; most of the better class have their splendid villas on Malibar Hill about four miles from the heart of Bombay, and reached by a steady ascent;

the drive being very delightful, through beautiful, undulating scenery, and commanding fine views of the entire harbor, and if there is a breeze at any season of the year the Malibar Hill is sure to come in for a share of it.

The ladies drive into town in the afternoon to call for their husbands at their banks, offices, or stores, and before they return home all the principal people assemble in their carriages at the Apollo Bunda, a pier close to the harbor, where a band of music plays every evening from five o'clock till half-past six.

There is a fine theatre in Bombay, the finest in all India, called the Gaiety. My reception there was very hearty, especially from the Parsees, who came in great crowds to support me.

I found my old friend, Sir James Fergusson, the governor of Bombay, as cordial as ever; he placed my entire engagement under his special patronage, and came nearly every evening to the theatre. Sir James is a man of true, generous soul and of great simplicity of character, and withal possessing a strong individuality, which remains with him through all the changes of years and circumstances. I met him for the first time on my earlier visit to Adelaide, as I have already mentioned. Lady Edith, eldest daughter of the late Earl of Dalhousie, formerly viceroy of India, was then living, and Sir James and his wife gave me a warm welcome there, both on the stage and in society. Several years afterward a gentleman accosted me one day in the streets of Dundee : —

"How are you, Bandmann? How do you do, sir? Don't you know me?"

"Really, sir, your face is familiar, but I don't know where to place you at this moment," said I.

"Well, I met you in Adelaide : my name is Fergusson."

"Sir James," said I, as he grasped my hand, "how stupid of me not to recognize you."

That was the simple way in which he recalled himself to my memory, and the same fine spirit characterizes him in all the relations of his high office and station.

The Parsees are the cleverest people in India. I may almost say as clever, if not cleverer, than the Europeans. They dress themselves the nearest of all the Orientals after the European fashion, and most of them have discarded even the inartistic helmet which for ages has been worn among them as a distinction.

The Parsee women are very beautiful, and allowed to go at perfect liberty, wherever their own sweet will takes them, without let or hindrance from their noble lords, and to act as they like, just as European ladies. It is a charming sight to see a handsome Parsee lady dressed in her picturesque costume of embroidered silk, and coiled hairdress, walking along the promenades, or driving in her carriage : one is carried away by

her lovely, perfect shape, rounded form, black,
sparkling eyes, and pure, pale skin.

> "Whom everything becomes, to chide, to laugh,
> To weep; whose every passion fully strives
> To make itself, in thee, fair and admired!"

The children of the Parsees are beautiful like
their mothers.

The Parsees are fire-worshipers. Not, as it is
said vulgarly, that their God (Ormuzd, earlier
worshiped as Ahura Mazda) is fire; they rather
worship the divine through the symbol of fire,
or, in other words, they recognize in fire, in all its
forms, a divine energy and fruitful force, and bow
themselves in reverence before this awful mystery
and potency of life. They worship the fire in
the sense of warmth, light, electricity, and life.
They worship the sun as the sovereign power of
nature, that gives fruitfulness to the earth, and
vitality and health to all beings, and pray to it
every morning as the representative to them of
the highest and most potent energy of the
universe. Every true Parsee salams the light
wherever he sees it, — in the rising or setting sun,
or the noon's glory and splendor, —

> "Even from Hyperion's rising in the East,
> Until his very downfall in the sea,"

and brings his offering: if poor, a portion of
cinnamon-wood, which costs a few pies (pence),
or, if rich, sandal-wood, that costs from eight

annas to several rupees: to the sacred fire kept
perpetually burning in the temple,—the symbol
of the divine,—every morning,

> "So soon as the all-cheering sun
> Should in the farthest East begin to draw
> The shady curtains from Aurora's bed,"

as the expression of his devotion. And hundreds,
often thousands, of Parsees are to be seen in the
roads and parks of Bombay, with their faces
toward the sun setting in evening glory, saying
their prayers and salaming this image of the
light and life of God.

There are three closed-in towers, situated .in
the most lovely neighborhood of the city, right
at the top of Malibar Hill, and surrounded by
hundreds of acres of valuable land, all beautifully laid out. These are called the Silent
Towers, because they are the place of the last
offices and funeral rites of the Parsees, who have
their bodies eaten up by vultures, instead of
buried or cremated. I think, in some parts of
Siam, "holy" dogs (not vultures) are kept for
this purpose, but for my part I would prefer the
latter. No visitor is allowed to approach the
Silent Towers within a couple of hundred yards,
but a model is to be seen inside the keeper's
lodge, who, of course, for backsheesh (a magician
everywhere in the East) shows it and explains all.
The priest receives the corpse, which is carried to
the place of the Silent Towers, followed by

hundreds of mourners, ranged two by two, dressed
in pure white robes, and places it on an iron
grating. He then makes an incision on the left
side, where the heart lies, and an old, trained
vulture, which is of huge size and sits on the
highest pinnacle of the towers, swoops down
and has the first pick, while hundreds more,
together with crows and magpies, soon gather
about the body, and in a short time there is
nothing left, save the bones. The blood drops
through the grating into a channel below, whence
it is conveyed to the sea. The bones are taken
away every few weeks or months and burned, and
the ashes of all are preserved together, as those
of one family, which the Parsees are to one
another.

> " Death, having prey'd upon the outward parts,
> Leaves them invisible, and his siege is now
> Against the mind."

The method of thus disposing of the body,
which may strike some as peculiarly repulsive,
is, nevertheless, the expression of a most poetic
idea. In the Mazdean religion, which is in many
respects very philosophical and poetic rather than
a clearly defined set of dogmas, the earth is
conceived as pure and holy and must not be
polluted with foulness. As soon as the light (the
soul) has fled from the body there is nothing but
foul matter left, and this must not be placed in
the bosom of the earth, which is the home of life.

Therefore, in these several ways it is disposed of, and carried, so far as can be, once again into the spheres of life, unpolluted and without taint. Perhaps, however, their great prophet Zoroaster (or Zarathustra), who instituted this method of getting rid of the corpse was, after all, actuated by economic and sanitary reasons, even more than by poetic, and in the far-distant age when he lived anticipated, to some extent, the great lesson of modern times, and surely no small part of religion: that the cleanliness and health of a people are priceless, beautiful things, and that everything ought to be removed as quickly as possible that bears upon it the touch of death, or that by its presence interferes with that best of all sacrifices to the Highest — *the devotion of a sane mind in a sane body.*

> " As this temple waxes,
> The inward service of the mind and soul
> Grows wide withal."

Every Parsee that I met could speak English, and their likeness to the Jews is striking in various respects. They are great lovers of Shakespeare, and were very anxious to show their ardent admiration for whatever talent I may have of impersonating his characters. A number of important persons waited on me, and asked, as a special favor to their youths, if I would allow a few of the students of the Grant Medical College, in connection with the University of

Bombay, to play with me. I promised to do so, and about a dozen young Parsee gentlemen called. I was surprised to find them so familiar with the great poet, and was in a predicament whom to choose, as they appeared all fairly talented. At last I picked out four, to whom I allotted the following parts in Hamlet: *Laertes*, Lalkaka; *Polonius*, Tata; *King*, Setna; *Rosencrantz*, Chackin.

The other characters were, of course, filled by my company. Now, considering that they were alien to the language, and not even Europeans, these young gentlemen did wonders, and I said as much, to the delight of the overflowing audience which came to see them act.

While at Bombay I saw, one night, a wonderful spectacle, namely, a Hindu marriage. The procession lasted nearly an hour, and there were all sorts of devices and odd and curious Eastern fashions. The bride and bridegroom, quite children, about four and six years of age, sat each on a pony, and the presents were carried by coolies on their heads, and to my eyes there seemed at least a thousand laden with nuptial gifts, or discharging some office connected with the elaborate ceremony. There was, of course, abundance of Hindu tom-tom music, in which there was more noise than harmony, and which always reminded me of the fool's lines in Othello: " The general so likes your music, that he desires you, for love's sake, to make no more noise with it"; and the golden temples and images of the gods on large wagons were innumerable. I saw more of the Hindu Pantheon on that occasion than on any other during my visit to India; it seemed that all the gods were taken out, as it were, by their devoted nurses, for an airing. I do not think, however, if we could get at the bottom of Hindu theosophy, we should find that those images are, in any sense, conceived as final, or as in themselves worth anything whatsoever. Whatever glory they have is on account of their typifying some supersensuous idea or attribute of the Unseen; and the reverence and worship seemingly offered to them are in reality intended for the Highest. I half regret that my travels in India did not embrace Juggernaut, the most famous place of pilgrimage in the entire country. What Mecca is to the Moslems, Jerusalem to all Christians, Rome to Catholics, or Canterbury to English Churchmen, that Juggernaut is to the Hindus. The name of the god enshrined in the celebrated temple there, Juggernaut (or, as it is sometimes written, Juggernath), means the "Lord of the World." The image is said to be most gorgeously decorated, and on the occasion of a great festival is carried upon a tremendous car with wheels, which is drawn by the devotees. Formerly it was very generally believed amongst Europeans that, as this car of the god passed through the crowded streets on festal days, a great many enraptured worshipers voluntarily

threw themselves on the ground to be crushed
by the wheels of the god-chariot, as an act of
sacrifice and homage to the Deity ; but all this is
now exploded, for it is known that whatever
deaths attend the festivals of the " Lord of the
World" are due rather to accident than any
intention on the part of those who assemble to
figure in them.

Some years ago the Asiatic Society presented
the French government with a model of the
temple and processional car of Juggernaut. It is
a very precious specimen of Hindu art, its date
being supposed to be 1198 of our era, and is
now amongst the rich treasures of the Louvre.
It is difficult to grasp the exact idea which, to
Hindu thought and piety, is represented by the
God-image, named the " Lord of the World."
But here, perhaps, one theology may assist
another, and we may say that, as Christ and
images of his nativity, passion, and crucifixion
are symbols, " as is the sepulchre in stubborn
Jewry, of the world's ransom, blessed Mary's
Son," for a great number of devout persons, of
God in his relations to humanity, so the image
and the shrine of Juggernaut symbolize to the
Hindus God in his relations to the world.

CHAPTER XII. — China.

SHANGHAI.

"I'll view the manners of the town,
Peruse the traders, gaze upon the buildings."
— *Comedy of Errors, Act i, sc. 2.*
"China dishes."
— *Measure for Measure, Act ii, sc. 1.*
"Well, thereby hangs a tale."
— *Merry Wives of Windsor, Act i, sc. 4.*

An interesting city — The three foreign settlements: English, American, French — Old Shanghai walled around — Population of the entire city not definitely known — The climate — The inhabitants — The influence of the Germans — The clubhouse — The German minister, Herr Von Brand — Shanghai society — A bracelet of brilliants is presented to Miss Beaudet — A peculiarity of the society — The theatre the finest in the East — A little Chinese boy is "made up" and plays the Duke of York — An incident in the performance of East Lynne — The theatre of the natives : its legendary history and its peculiarities — The historical plays — The comedies — A remark of Sir Philip Sidney on the English stage in 1583 will apply to the Chinese stage of the present time — "The Birthday of the Moon" — The "mixed" court — Judge Chên — A smart prisoner.

On the eighth of April, I left Bombay on the Peninsular and Oriental steamer Khedive for Shanghai, by the way of Galle, Singapore, and Hong-Kong — a journey of about twenty-four days. Shanghai is an interesting city, and the sight as you get near to it most pleasing. You cross the bar at Woosung, about ten miles from Shanghai, and soon after steam into the river, an uninteresting sheet of water enough, the scenery flat on both sides, and nothing to please till you catch a view of the charming town, with its beautiful mansions and its extended harbor.

Shanghai is divided into three settlements: English, American, and French. The Chinese city of Shanghai proper is about two miles distant, with a wall around it similar to Canton, where the natives are not allowed to go out or come in without permission. The French settlement is, like all French colonies, the nearest approach to a small provincial town in France. The beauty of the modern portion of the city begins with the English settlement, which runs along the river for miles ; and the street facing it with its long line of grand, palatial buildings on one side, and a thousand masts of fine vessels on the other, is remarkably picturesque.

" With silken streamers the young Phœbus fanning:
 Play with your fancies, and in them behold
 Upon the hempen tackle shipboys climbing;
 Hear the shrill whistle, which doth order give
 To sounds confus'd: behold the threaden sails,
 Blown with th' invisible and creeping winds."

Beyond this lies the American settlement, extending also along the bank of the river a considerable distance; and the street which is thus continued is certainly one of the finest and most beautiful in the world, especially since electric light has been adopted. It is called the Bund, and no one can picture the beauty of it at night, when all the houses are illuminated with seeming myriads of variegated Chinese lanterns, the many-hued rays of which tint and color most fantastically the more powerful electric lights, giving a wonderful picturesqueness to objects which in the daytime seem quite ordinary; add to this a tropical sky, fretted with golden fires; while a fleet of ships lies along the river, some inside and others close to the wharfs, with their different signal-lights full up, from which any one versed in nautical science may detect the merchantmen of every nation of the world.

There are about ten thousand Europeans and one hundred thousand Chinese in these three settlements of the modern city of Shanghai; while in the old walled town (Shanghai proper) there are perhaps hundreds of thousands more Chinese. However, on this point no one can be very correct, for not even the Chinese government itself has arrived at any true estimate or census of the population. The beauty of the European and American settlements arises greatly from their remarkable cleanliness; the only exception being some neighborhoods of the French, which are full of bad odors, and the streets of which are not kept with care.

Shanghai has a long and healthy season, which extends from September to the end of May, during which period, with a few exceptional weeks of pretty cold weather in January and February, the climate. is very refreshing and delightful. The month of June is hot, July hotter, and August " as hot," some European has said, " as hell." Be that as it may, these are the only disagreeable months in the year, otherwise the climate is lovely.

The people of Shanghai, amongst whom the Germans preponderate socially and intellectually, are kind, enthusiastic, and very ready to give support to any effort of culture or art. It is no exaggeration to say that the Germans are the life and soul of this many-sided community, foremost in every public work, and the mainspring of all corporate action.

"Germans are honest men."

They have one of the most comfortable and convenient clubhouses in the world, which comprises, in addition to the club proper, a concert-hall, a ballroom, and a theatre. They are nearly all well-to-do people, many of them rich, and not a few of them persons of high culture.

The time of my visit was most fortunate in having the German minister, His Excellency Herr Von Brand, on a diplomatic mission to Shanghai from Pekin, and whose society I enjoyed very frequently. On two occasions I met him at the house of the German consul, Herr Von Krencki, where I dined with him, together with Admiral Blanc, of the frigate Strosh, and his staff. I also met his excellency at Herr Von Krause's, where I had the pleasure of meeting the Austrian consul, Herr Von Haase (who gave me a letter of introduction to the King of Siam), Herr Guiltzou, Herr Mendel, and Herr Grobien, with other leading citizens of Shanghai.

Herr Von Brandt is one of the most brilliant and best-informed men I ever met in my life, not excepting Lord Lytton, John Forster, Tom Taylor, Lord Southesk, and Charles Reade, who were my intimate friends; these were versed in several branches of literature and art, but Herr Von Brand is familiar with all. I do not stand singular in this assertion, for he is thought of in the East as a second Bismarck in statesmanship, while, as a man, all admit that

" He hath a daily beauty in his life."

It has been his misfortune to be too good a Chinese scholar, and too acute an Eastern diplomatist, to displace him; otherwise he would have made a great mark in Europe before this. But no one knows better than the Berlin government, and those familiar with Chinese affairs, the great good this remarkable man has accomplished in his capacity of minister to Tien-tsin: first of all for the German nation, and indirectly for all Europe and America. Besides securing numerous treaties of vast importance, he has raised his nation to as proud and independent a position as that of England or France in China, and he has shown Li Hung Chang, the cleverest premier (*absoluta*) China has ever had, that he is his equal on his own ground, if, indeed, he has not proved himself his superior in more than one transaction; thus, all things considered, it will be a long time before Germany will have another representative to the Celestial court who will come up to Herr Von Brand in diplomatic skill, knowledge of human nature, and unswerving wisdom.

He has been upward of fifteen years in China, and, as service in the East counts double, has long since been entitled to a pension. But it is to be hoped that he will not retire for years to come; he is too great and too important a man to withdraw from public service so young; for, although perfectly white-haired, he cannot be more than fifty years of age. I hold several charming letters from him, and his brilliant power of conversation and transcendent knowledge I shall never forget.

I grew very fond of Shanghai society, and shall always look back upon the delightful evenings spent there, in which the hours passed as minutes in witty and refined conversation, with pleasure and gratitude. It would defy London, Paris, Berlin, Vienna, or New York, to bring together a more genial coterie than that which gathered on several occasions, after the play was over, at the little *soupés* at Krause's, Von Krencki's, Guiltzou's, Michelson's, or Mendel's. Here were represented diplomacy, the army and navy, commerce, science, and art, and with such perfect geniality and *laisser-aller*, that one was in doubt which was the more to be enjoyed — the champagne so excellent and free or the wit and *esprit* of the society.

Picture a house as large as that of the late A. T. Stewart, in Fifth Avenue, with elegant and spacious reception-rooms, full of precious European, Chinese, Japanese, and Indian art-treasures: these leading into a delightfully cool dining-room, with a long table, capable of seating from fifteen to twenty people, spread with the most delectable delicacies, choice wines, and sweetly decorated with rare flowers, while behind every chair stood a boy in his spotless, white dress, his sole business being to wait upon one particular guest, — and only those who have been in China can appreciate the perfection of these servants, — picture this to yourself, and you will know what Shanghai has to offer in the way of the refinements of society, and get an idea of the beautiful scene in which I met so many distinguished persons. The conversations were of the richest, wittiest, and raciest nature, and the gayety and freedom were of a decorum and dignity which will always characterize the company of gentlemen though men of the world. Never for a moment did conversation flag, nor was a subject allowed to become wearisome, nor a sense of ennui felt.

Miss Beaudet and a few other ladies were usually present at these reunions: indeed, they were quite as much in honor of her as they were of myself; for every one, including Herr Von Brand, had the greatest respect for her as a woman, and admiration for her genius as an artist. On the night of her benefit she received a magnificent bracelet of brilliants from her numerous admirers, and she was universally admitted to be the greatest favorite of all the actresses who have visited China.

Shanghai society is peculiar in this, that the gentlemen have far more importance in it than frequently happens in Europe or America; yet there is no reason why the ladies should not sway the sceptre, save the ladies themselves. The true woman, as in Miss Beaudet's case, is recognized and welcomed at once to the very best circles. But the truth is, and it must be told, that, while the European gentlemen are of a most interesting, refined, and courteous nature, the European ladies, with some honorable exceptions, are the reverse. Perhaps the true cause of this is to be found in the fact that they were spoiled from the outset. Only twenty years ago a European lady was regarded with curiosity and wonder in Shanghai, and consequently whenever a citizen or an official went to Europe to import one of these precious creatures she was immediately lionized by all, fondled and petted to such an extent that in the end she was an utterly spoiled child in society. Now these fair importations have become more frequent, and consequently less thought of and wondered at, and there is little chance at the present time even of becoming, like poor Burns in Edinburgh society, the lion of a season; but the European

ladies settled in Shanghai will not open their
eyes to the fact, and put on all sorts of unlovely airs, and imagine that they are slighted
when they are not, or lionized when no one ever
thought of lionizing; and even continue to daub
in the dark when rapturous regards decline
toward them from their own want of attraction
and loveliness, thinking gentlemen prefer a poor,
painted shrew, to a fair, simple-hearted woman.
In another respect likewise they have to thank
themselves for their present lack of power in
Shanghai society: they should not tolerate ladies
of easy virtue, and easier conscience, who are
able to make a display in dress, fashion, or
carriages, but drive them out of the field by
their own greater charms, fairer attractions, and
sweeter manners; but, alas! they show none of
these advantages, and abandon the ground to the
fast, gay-living women, who are thus left in
possession, virtually without any rivals whatsoever. This is a great pity, as there are many
young men in Shanghai who would like to choose
a wife from amongst the families of the place,
but are now obliged to go to Europe when they
feel inclined to "bear the yoke."

> " I'm ashamed that women are so simple
> To offer war, where they should kneel for peace,
> Or seek for rule, supremacy, and sway,
> When they are bound to serve, love, and obey."

The Shanghai Theatre is the finest in the East.
It was built by amateurs, who occasionally play

in it themselves, and keep it in good order and first-class respectability.

We had no difficulty to manage our plays, but on one occasion an amusing incident occurred. We were rehearsing Richard the Third, and with impatience awaiting the arrival of the boy who was to play the Duke of York. At last a little Chinese lad came with a letter from a friend of mine. It ran thus:—

"*Dear Bandmann,* — At last, after long searching, I have found you a Duke of York, but he has *a tail.* Does it matter?"

I laughed and looked at the bright little fellow in his Chinese clothes, wooden shoes, and long, very long queue hanging to the ground. "Can you speak English, my boy?" "Yes, sir!" was the clear and ringing answer. Here was a youthful Celestial who could pronounce the "R," and who was ready to play an English prince, and well he did it too. He looked capital. His queue, was hidden under a large, blonde, curly wig; his yellow face beautifully pinked; his nose received a white stroke on the top to give it more prominence; his eyes a full underlining to produce greater rotundity; his feet soft leather shoes for greater ease: with these additions to his features, and changes in his dress, the boy was a complete success; and spoke the part as well as I have ever had it done: and for the first time here was Shakespeare uttered in pure English before the public by a Chinese boy. The world moves fast in these days, and perhaps the time may come when the " Land of Flowers " may give a Shylock, a Hamlet, an ` Othello, a Macbeth, a King Lear, to the audiences of London, Paris, and New York, notwithstanding the present wretched condition of the native stage, and that peculiar attribute of the Chinese, held so sacred and inviolable, even to death, the queue; which I didn't find an obstacle to my very successful little Chinese Duke of York.

During our month's stay in Shanghai we played Hamlet, Othello, The Merchant of Venice, Romeo and Juliet, Richard the Third, Narcisse, East Lynne, and Dead or Alive.

On the evening of East Lynne, there was an unusual feature in the performance. The actor who plays Sir .Francis Levison is generally handcuffed on the stage, and on this occasion there was no exception to the rule ; but, unfortunately, the property-man, a native, had forgotten to ask for the key when he borrowed the manacles from the constable, and looked with amazement at the actor when he heard the latter making me a request, after he had finished his part, who was, of course, desirous to be released from his tedious bondage.

" The gee ?   I no got gee."

"How am I to get rid of them, Johnny?" asked the bewildered actor.

"No way me know savie you," was the reply.

"Hang you, fool! I've got to play in the farce; run and get the key!" cried the now enraged actor.

Johnny ran, but did n't come back, and the now much-suffering actor was obliged, after an apology which the audience took good naturedly, to play the lover in the farce handcuffed. But even this was not all, for the constable from whom the Chinaman borrowed them could not be found, and the miserable Sir Francis was obliged either to sleep in them, or to send for a locksmith to file them off, which, when the evening's performance was over, of course he did. Early next morning Johnny sent the key into the actor's room by a comrade, and, as might be supposed, he feared to show his face at the theatre for some days.

The Chinese theatre proper is a peculiar institution in its origin, its nature, its style, and its performances. Certainly, to our Occidental notions, there is nothing charming in it, and all true dramatic art is conspicuously absent. The Celestials do not strive after perfection in acting and the drama, and stand much in need of the advice Hamlet gave the players: —

"Speak the speech, I pray you, . . . trippingly on the tongue: but if you mouth it, as many of our players do, I had as lief the town-crier spoke my lines. Nor do not saw the air too much with your hand, thus: but use all gently: for in the very torrent, tempest, and (as I may say) whirlwind of your passion, you must acquire and beget a temperance that may give it smoothness. O, it offends me to the soul to hear a robustious periwig-pated fellow tear a passion to tatters, to very rags, to split the ears of the groundlings; who, for the most part, are capable of nothing but inexplicable dumb shows and noise. I would have such a fellow whipped for o'erdoing Termagant; it out-herods Herod: pray you, avoid it.

.   .   .   .

"Be not too tame neither, but let your own discretion be your tutor: suit the action to the word, the word to the action; with this special observance, that you o'erstep not the modesty of nature; for anything so overdone is from the purpose of playing, whose end, both at the first, and now, was, and is, to hold, as 'twere, the mirror up to Nature; to show virtue her own feature, scorn her own image, and the very age and body of the time his form and pressure. Now this, overdone, or come tardy off, though it make the unskilful laugh, cannot but make the judicious grieve; the censure of which one must, in your allowance, o'erweigh a whole theatre of others. O, there be players, that I have seen play, — and heard others praise, and that highly, — not to speak it profanely, that, neither having the accent of Christians, nor the gait of Christian, pagan, nor man, have so strutted, and bellowed, that I have thought some of nature's journeymen had made men, and not made them well, they imitated humanity so abominably."

There is a constant strain and stiffness in their speech, movements, and demeanor, which is awkward and ridiculous enough.

However, a very poetic legend lies at the basis of their stage that we can appreciate. In this it is told, and all the Chinese believe it doubtlessly, how, once upon a time, the Emperor Tong-Ming-Wang, of the Tong dynasty, was translated to the moon, together with his wives, concubines,

and all the retinue of his court, and that, while
there, they saw hosts of fair maidens in tableaux;
and it is to this wonderful legend of the voyage
to the moon, with its vision of celestial drama
enacted by Phœbe and her attendant virgins, that
China owes the establishment of its theatre, and
the performance of what are called ancient historical plays.

Every town of the empire has its theatre, and
it is a well-known fact that, wherever the Chinese
congregate in considerable numbers in any foreign
land, they are sure to build a purely national
theatre.　It is so in San Francisco, Singapore,
Rangoon, Honolulu, Portland, and many other
places which have large colonies of Chinese.

In Shanghai, the native theatre is a great
institution, there being no less than four large
ones in the English settlement, and another in
the French, in full swing all the year round.
These places of amusement are open nearly all
day, but from seven o'clock in the evening till
midnight they are crowded.　Many of them employ a large staff of actors, often as many as
one hundred and twenty-five or one hundred and
fifty, all males ; and the stars receive much honor
from the people.　The theatre is usually a large,
square building, and in the private boxes, stalls,
and indeed in every part of the house, the seats
have small tables before them, much after the
London Music Hall fashion, and during the performance you will see the audience regaling

themselves with pears, oranges, mangos, saucers
full of roasted water-melon seeds, small, green
cups of tea, which contrast with the vermilion-
colored sheets of paper on which the programme
is printed, or with large hubble-bubble tobacco-
pipes of brass or silver, while in the intervals of
such festivities they take a cloth soaked in hot
water and steaming, which is handed to them by
a coolie, and wipe the perspiration off their hands
and faces — a custom surely that has much reason
in it, and, in that climate, most refreshing.

The stage is a platform standing about four feet
above the level of the floor of the pit, and illuminated by primitive gas-fixtures in the way of foot-
lights. There is no scenery about the stage, and
the back of it is only a partition of panels of
carved wood. In the centre, however, is the
inevitable large mirror which has such infinite
charms for the Chinese; perhaps every one is
handsome in his own eyes, and the plainest of
the Chinese (though it would surely puzzle even
the gods to decide the point) has untold pleasure
in beholding a reflection of himself. Still, it has
a purpose beyond the gratification of vanity, for
the actors change their robes and head-dresses
in front of it, instead of retiring to the back of
the stage.

The orchestra is composed of seven or eight
old men, who sit around two tables at the back
of the stage, and who, with drums, gongs, cymbals,
flutes, fiddles, and pieces of hard wood, make

as much noise as any band on the face of the earth, and far more unearthly than most of them, and they seem to play the same tune all night. " The trumpets, sackbuts, psalteries and fifes, tabors and cymbals, and the shouting *Celestials*, make the *moon* dance." The plays enacted at the native theatres are chiefly historical, and some of them go on for years before being completed; the whole history of a great dynasty is presented in one play, part of it being given every day. There are, however, lighter pieces, more like our comedy, completed in two or three acts. But even these are presented without scenery, the costumes only being studied, and the characters make up their styles with considerable skill; the dialogue is the main thing, and the imagination of the audience is left to supply all other accessories. The remark made by Sir Philip Sidney, in regard to the English stage in 1583, has been applied by Sir John Davis to the Chinese stage of the present time, and it is most appropriate : —

"Now you shall have three ladies walk to gather flowers, and then we must believe the stage to be a garden. By and by we have news of shipwreck in the same place; then we are to blame if we accept it not for a rock. Upon the back of that comes out a hideous monster with fire and smoke, and then the miserable beholders are bound to take it for a cave; while in the meantime two armies fly in represented with four swords and bucklers, and then what hard heart will not receive it for a pitched field?"

The historical plays are a strange medley, in which acrobatic feats, somersaults, sword exercise, fighting, singing, dancing, very much resembling the Scotch reel, and a thousand and one other things, are mixed up with the slow developments of the romances of history embraced in their plots. It must be admitted that the men are often very clever in imitating the appearance and character of that fair, "tottering lily," — who is never allowed to show herself on the stage, — the Chinese woman.

The fifteenth day of the eighth month of the year, according to Chinese reckoning, is the occasion on which they celebrate the " Birthday of the Moon," which occupies so conspicuous a rank and plays so important a part, in many .of their myths and legends. That night is a great time with the Chinese for worshiping their gods in the temples, and for burning incense in the streets and public places of their cities; and on that night the gates of the cities are open until midnight, whereas on all other days, excepting New Year's eve, they are closed at ten o'clock.

"The Chinese call that particular day the Birthday of the Moon, because, according to their legends, the Emperor Ming-Tai-Tso, the first monarch of the Ming dynasty, — when out with his army and being sore pressed for want

of supplies to sustain his men, — sent out forag-
ing-parties, on the fifteenth day of the eighth
móon; but the darkness was at first so great
that they could not see where to obtain anything
in the fields, until the moon suddenly shone
with great brilliancy, and the soldiers were aided
by her light to go to fields and gather in crops
for food to the army. Why they had not looked
after this in daylight, does not appear from this
legend; that difficulty is ignored for the sake
of the story. The emperor was so much pleased
by the wonderful appearance of the moon at
what the legend makes-believe was an oppor-
tune moment, that he ordered the day to be
ever afterward celebrated as the Birthday of
the Moon. Another peculiar custom still in
vogue has its origin in the story of this emperor's
foraging-party, namely, that it is still the custom
in China that any one can go to the fields or
to the houses of the farmers on this particular
night, and take whatever he pleases, in the
way of grain, vegetables, or food of any kind,
without let or hindrance. The foragers of
Ming-Tai-Tso's army, on that eventful night,
discovered a peculiar root, which on trial, after
cooking, was discovered to be good for food,
and a root to be desired to make one enjoy
mutton-chops; that root was the potato. Old
Ireland cannot claim the potato in the face of
this legend; but whether the Celestial foragers
also found trace of the ancestors of the American

potato-bug, the legend sayeth not. Another interesting legend (already referred to) is that, on the fifteenth day of the eighth moon, the Emperor Tong-Ming-Wang, of the Tong dynasty, visited the moon, in company with his secretary, wives, servants, and retainers, and in that luminary they saw a party of young girls of tender years, who were playing musical instruments and acting tableaux and ancient plays; and to this legend the origin of Chinese theatres is attributed." "Good my lord, . . . see the players well bestowed. . . . Let them be well used; for they are the abstract, and brief chronicles, of the time."

The mixed court at Shanghai is certainly one of the most unique institutions ever devoted to the administration of justice. It was instituted specially on behalf of the foreign settlements, English, French, and American; all civil cases are tried there, in which the plaintiffs are of other nationalities and the defendants Chinese; and the trials of the latter for all criminal offences against the laws of the foreign settlements take place there. The Chinese magistrate, Chên, a mandarin of the seventh order, is the judge of this court; but foreign assessors sit on the bench with him, who have judicial powers, and whose duty it is to look after the strict administration of justice in all that pertains to those of foreign nationalities. I am indebted to my friend, Mr. W. Macfarlane, of the Shanghai *Mercury*, whose "Sketches in Shanghai" contain so much interesting matter, for the following extracts descriptive of this institution : —

"The court is located in the Maloo, the 'hall of justice,' forming part of the mandarin's *yamên*. A terror to evildoers is witnessed at the entrance to the yamên ; close to the street pavement, and flanking the gateway, are two enclosures, or huge cages, formed by strong wooden bars, extending from the ground nearly to the first roof of the porch. They look something like John Bunyan's idea of the cage in which Faithful was imprisoned at Vanity Fair ; they are for the same purpose as the stocks were used in England many years ago ; and here these Celestial cages are filled with prisoners, as part of their punishment, and to make others fear and tremble. The bars are almost wide enough for a lean fellow to wriggle through ; but the awkward thing against such an attempt is that all the prisoners are so well taken care of, lest anybody should steal them, that each fellow is adorned with a huge wooden collar, about two foot square, the framework firmly secured, and an ornamental chain of quarter-inch malleable-iron links attaches the collar to its wearer and joins him to the next prisoner, and so round them all, joining in one inseparable heap half a dozen Celestial vagabonds and all their decorations in woodwork and iron. Their

hands are free so that they can use the chop-
sticks, their supply of rice is plentiful, and they
are happy enough, as they sit there with one
peak of the wooden collar resting on the breast,
the corners covering each shoulder, and the other
peak away up at the back of the head. Their
position is rendered more lively, too, from the
presence of friends moving about on the pavement; cooks and other itinerant street-mer-
chants have their stalls close to the bars, and
the prisoners are evidently comforted at times
with more than prisoner's fare, and most of them
are able to get hold of a pipe and tobacco.

 " We pass through the portals, emblazoned with
demoniacal pictures of mighty Chinamen in red,
blue, green, and all colors in confusion, making
flaming combinations that would be worth money
to a traveling penny-show. We enter a spacious
courtyard, having on the right and left small
houses occupied by retainers of the yamên ; in
front of us is the huge picture of a nonde-
script monster. Is it a dragon ? Well, it looks
wild enough, hideous enough, and, as far as
paint goes, extravagant enough to make half a
dozen good-sized, decent-looking dragons. This
monster is said to be an emblem of 'avarice,'
and it is painted there on a screen, in the open
entrance to the mandarin's official residence,
as a remembrancer that avarice is a sin which
officials are to guard against, and never — hardly
ever — do such a thing as squeeze. . . .

"The first time we went there, many months ago, we instinctively and with due reverence took off our hat; but soon discovered that this was a superfluous bit of etiquette while in a 'mixed' court, and the free and easy manner of the proceedings became more apparent when we observed a friend smoking a cigar. Our notions of the court were upset; we had just thrown away a cigar after a few puffs; we had come into court reverentially with uncovered head; we were out of it in both cases. 'Is smoking allowed?' we asked our friend in a whisper, which the assessor heard, and made reply: 'Oh, yes, smoke away; smoking is the rule here.' At this time, old Chên was taking a cheroot from his cigar-case; he lighted it with a match, and then handed a cheroot to the assessor. Four or five cigars were all going like so many houses on fire in a minute after that; and we never think of dropping a cigar amongst the Celestials at the door, or taking off our hat, when we go to court again. . . .

"Chên sits near the centre of the bench, with the assessor on his right hand. There is room for three or four seats on the bench, and sometimes there are as many occupied, when the foreign consuls may be specially interested in any case. In his winter costume, — with great fur-lined silk coat embroidered in mandarin style, and his upturned cap with peacock feather, — Chên presents a more dignified appearance than in his thin, summer costume. The old man — for he is over sixty, and looks like seventy — seems oppressed with the heat and overcome with fatigue. He often sits bareheaded and is seen to be very bald; there is barely enough natural hair on his scalp to form a queue, the tail which hangs thereby being nearly all of silk. There is nothing very remarkable about his features; his expression is rather pleasant; eyes small, dark, and keen; his nose short but not too broad; his upper lip rather large, only a few gray hairs at each side, and a long distance between these two remnants of a moustache; his cheekbones high, and cheeks fallen in slightly; he is not as sleek as he might have been some years ago; and the wrinkles of age are upon his forehead. To see him sit quietly amid all the squabbling of prisoners and runners before him, one would not think he had so much vigor left in him as he sometimes displays when he scolds a prisoner. On the bench before him he keeps a huge leaden inkstand, with tablets of Chinese ink; and there is a curious-looking article in lead, which is on the table behind this stand. It is in the shape of a human hand, cut at the wrist, and is said to be a representation of Buddha's hand; it stands on the wrist as the base, and the fingers are wide apart; it is much larger than the biggest hand of flesh and blood ever seen; if it were stuck on a broom-handle it would make a good back-scratcher for the

greatest Celestial giant ever heard of. This
peculiar article is the simple device which serves
as a pen or pencil rack, to prevent the bench
being dirtied by the official red ink used in
writing on the documents which come to Chên's
hands. Besides these articles mentioned, there
are of course the small teapot and smaller teacups
always at his left hand; his cigar-case, and a box
of matches that light only on the box, always
directly before him; and there are still two
other things worth mentioning — these are of
simple construction, frequent in use, and yet the
use of them is very hard to see. They are two
pieces of hard wood, about twelve inches long,
and about an inch in thickness and breadth.
When Chên is in a rage, — when he shouts as
loudly as he can, and uses up all the strong
expletives in his vocabulary, hurling his wild
thunders at an unfortunate prisoner, — the grand
climax of his invective is reached when he seizes
one of these pieces of hard wood, and strikes the
other piece, making a tremendous noise that
almost drowns his voice, and which, we suppose,
he considers an effectual means of striking terror
into the heart of the person who is thus so forcibly
and violently admonished. When he is beating
these sticks, he looks as if he were going to shy
one of them at the prisoner's head, and some
of the prisoners look as if they expected it too,
and were preparing to dodge it. . . .

"In this court there is no such thing as perjury,

for the Chinese 'swear not at all.' Lying, therefore, is unrestrained; the biggest liar has most
chance of winning his case against a neighbor,
who is conscientious, or another who tells lies,
but is not 'cute enough in the invention of them.
The criminal who has the best chance of getting
off is the one who tells most lies himself, or who
can hire other liars, better than himself, to speak
in his behalf. And, though the lies are found
out, as they often are, being too glaring, or not
cunningly devised, the prisoner is none the less
thought of, because he did his level best as a liar;
he will only lose his case because he did not do
it well enough. If a Chinaman is in a fix, either
civil or criminal offences bringing trouble on his
head, he can, for a slight consideration in the
shape of a few hundred *cash*, or a few dollars,
if the case is worth it, get any number of his
guileless brethren to declare that black is white,
or white black — either way as the dollars go. . . .

"One of the smartest tricks we have heard
of being done by a prisoner at this court was
when three or four men were convicted of some
paltry offence, and each of them fined twenty
cents, with the alternative of three days' imprisonment. All the prisoners except one made great
lamentation, and tried to excite compassion by
their cries and tears; but he got up from his
knees at once, as soon as he heard the sentence,
boldly stepped forward to the magistrate's bench,
tabled his wealth in payment of the fine, and

hurried out of court. A few minutes afterward, but when it was too late, his twenty-cent
piece was found to be a brass one." "To have
an open ear, a quick eye, and a nimble hand, is
necessary for a cutpurse."

From occurrences of this sort in the mixed
court it would seem that Chên's "pieces of hard
wood," together with all the other symbols of the
authority and the majesty of law, even including
Buddha's "hand," are impotent of effect upon
certain sensitive-souled Celestials, and daringly
set at defiance. Maybe it is there, owing to
Chên's lenient humanity, as Duke Vincentio says
in Measure for Measure : —

" We have strict statutes, and most biting laws
   (The needful bits and curbs for headstrong steeds),
  Which for these fourteen years * we have let sleep ;
  Even like an o'ergrown lion in a cave,
  That goes not out to prey : Now, as fond fathers,
  Having bound up the threat'ning twigs of birch
  Only to stick it in their children's sight,
  For terror, not to use ; in time the rod
  Becomes more mock'd than fear'd : so our decrees,
  Dead to infliction, to themselves are dead ;
  And liberty plucks justice by the nose ;
  The baby beats the nurse, and quite athwart
  Goes all decorum."

  * Chên has been judge in the mixed court perhaps rather more. — [Ed.

CHAPTER XIII. — CHINA.

HONG-KONG.

"The purest treasure mortal times afford
Is spotless reputation; this away,
Men are but gilded loam, or painted clay.
A jewel in a ten times barr'd-up chest
Is a bold spirit in a loyal heart.
Mine honor is my life; both grow in one;
Take honor from me, and my life is done."
— *Richard II, Act i, sc. 1.*

"Defend your reputation, or bid farewell to your good life forever."
— *Merry Wives of Windsor, Act iii, sc. 3.*

"Beware
Of entrance to a quarrel; but, being in,
Bear't, that the opposer may beware of thee."
— *Hamlet, Act i, sc. 3.*

"Love all, trust a few,
Do wrong to none; be able for thine enemy
. . . . be checked for silence,
But never tax'd for speech."
— *All's Well That Ends Well, Act i, sc. 1.*

Hotels in China — An action for libel — The English law — The "Rousby" case — The late lord chief justice of England — The late Sergeant Parry — Mr. Gordon, the scenic-artist — Mr. Willing, the London theatrical advertising-agent — The expensiveness of truth — Sir George Phillippo.

I TOOK my farewell of the Shanghai public in Hamlet, and on the third of June, 1882, left with my company for Hong-Kong. There I made the hotel called after the town, "The Hong-Kong," my headquarters. It is kept by two Parsees named Dorobyee and Hingkee, and considered the best establishment of the kind in China, and it is certainly equal to any of them. They are all bad.

My original intention was, in consequence of the lateness of the season and the approaching hot weather, to limit my stay to a couple of nights; but the pressure was so great, and the success so thorough, that I consented to extend it to six performances. "L'homme propose, et Dieu dispose." I was destined to stay even longer than that, longer than my wildest dreams anticipated, for suddenly I found myself involved in a serious law-suit, and once a man puts an action in the Chinese courts, there's no telling how long it will remain there. However, my own case was settled quicker than many. It was a case of libel, which I felt compelled to bring against a man in Hong-Kong who had, in the most unwarranted manner, attacked my character and abused my good name; and this by a method so pre-eminently un-English that I have only to mention it to show its vileness to all who respect justice after the English fashion, which, perhaps, as I am a German, it may not be unfitting in me to say here that there is no loftier standard in judicial matters to be found anywhere throughout the civilized world. The English law, built on the basis of the ancient Roman "corpus juris civilis," comprised in The Code, The Pandects, The Institutes, and The Novellæ, which the splendid genius of Justinian shaped for the world, and, augmented by the precedents and sanctions of long centuries, is a tribunal by which, if a man is condemned, he is *condemned:* while, if he is acquitted, he is *free* indeed, and may well be regarded as such by all true men.

In 1877 it was my misfortune to appear as the defendant in a case in which the late Mrs. Rousby was the plaintiff, which caused considerable sensation in England at the time, especially in dramatic circles, and certainly much discomfort to myself, for I was the unhappy victim of one of the grossest efforts ever made by one person to injure the character and reputation of another. The action arose in this way: I had translated and adjusted to the English stage the play of Herr Mosenthal, called " Madeleine Morel," from the German, the copyright of which I sold to Mrs. Rousby, subject to certain conditions, among others, these: that no changes were to be made in the play apart from my consent, and that I was to superintend the rehearsals of it. At one of these rehearsals, in a moment of impatience occasioned by wilful and constant violations of the above conditions, I snatched the manuscript out of the prompter's hands and was about to quit the theatre, when I found myself suddenly involved in an imbroglio with him and the stage-manager. The latter laid hold of the book, and remarked that, as the play was now the property of Mrs. Rousby, I had no right to take it away, and the truth of this assertion struck me so forcibly that I immediately relaxed my hold and

left him in undisputed possession of the manuscript. I had acted on impulse, but at the bottom
there was the conviction (which, by the way, the
lord chief justice who tried the case that sprung
from it afterward proved justifiable and correct)
that, although an author or translator sell his
work, he does not sell his brain with it, and no
buyer has a right to trifle with the latter by
making changes in the contents, the form given to
it, or the modes of expression adopted, that the
knowledge and judgment of the author would
not sanction; for if this were permitted the
author's reputation might be injured. Therefore,
though he sell his work and relinquish all claim
to pecuniary advantage from it, he has still the
right to insist that it shall not be caricatured or
marred by the injudiciousness and ignorance of
the buyer or any other persons. Still I felt that
perhaps in my indignation I had gone a little
too far, and left the theatre. But on the next
day something far more serious was made of it,
for Mrs. Rousby was not without imagination,
which all women possess to some extent. In her
case, indeed, it must have attained an enormous
strength and deposed the serene image of truth
and overthrown conscience; for she brought an
action against me in which it was maintained
that I had struck her a cruel, angry blow, and,
to borrow the words of Dicæopolis, from "The
Acharnians," of Aristophanes, which well fit my
own case,

> " forced me into court
> And slander'd, and beslobber'd me with lies,
> And splutter'd like Cycloborus, and slang'd me,
> So that I really felt myself half dead,
> Being dragg'd, all draggled, thro' that case's mire."

The case, however, was tried before the highest court in England, and completely done away with, no stain being left on my name or honor as a gentleman: it was proved that I was a man more sinned against than sinning. It was this old insult that was dished up again by my Hong-Kong libeler, —

> " Men that make
> Envy and crooked malice nourishment,
> Dare bite the best," —

who, not knowing how to sufficiently hurt and sting to satisfy his spite, incautiously and inadvisedly, most surely, for even the devil seems sometimes to be found napping, or, at least outwits himself in ways he deems most sure to bring defeat and wretchedness to others, repeated and circulated the old Rousby accusation.

This I determined to wipe out from the mind of the Hong-Kong public root and branch. Of course it would have been very easy to have moved on, and soon to have shifted one's quarters beyond the libeler's reach. I, however, usually "take the bull by the horns," and I made no exception on this occasion. To me there were only two ways open: either to chastise

the calumniator with a horsewhipping, perhaps
the more effectual ; or to take refuge in the law.
My friends guided me rightly, and, on June 16,
Frazer Smith was committed for trial on two
counts in the police-court in Hong-Kong.

> " Against the undivulg'd pretence I fight
> Of treasonous malice."

It is no desire to play the martyr that has led
me to unearth in these pages a great wrong to
which I was subjected years ago : indeed, I would
gladly have let it rest in the realm of silence
to which I had consigned it ; my sense of
innocence, and the vindication of it in the eyes
of all others by the court of Queen's Bench, being
amply sufficient to render it terrorless ; but since
the story of my tour in China would be incomplete
without reference to the Hong-Kong libel case
that grew out of this infamous action, I feel I
must treat it, once for all, fully here, for, as
Henry Ward Beecher has said himself, "I know
the bitterness of venomous lies." When the
Rousby case (a name I hold in pity and detestation, and which I have here for the first time,
during the years that have intervened, written
down) was settled in my favor, it was my early
intention to place before the public, in printed
form, an account of some circumstances connected
with it which were not explained in court, for
who under such provocation does not contem-
plate turning pamphleteer? In England, in such

cases, the defendant's lips are closed, and he can only speak through his counsel. My counsellors were good and able men, but practised that reservation peculiar to lawyers (and to the clergy perhaps), and many things important to the case were not brought out at all. This to some extent was due, perhaps, to the judge himself; who, vexed that the case was not conducted to his own liking, for he looked upon the matter as a mere theatrical squabble, which ought to have ended by the parties shaking hands and making up in open court, kept intentionally certain particulars relating to the prosecutor in the background, who, as he said, was now standing upon her trial. And I must here say that, had not the decision of the late lord chief justice protected her, I should certainly have subsequently prosecuted her for perjury; for never in the record of the court of Queen's Bench was there a more glaring case of perjury than the one Rousby *vs.* Bandmann.

My counsellors, however, did not sanction the adoption and carrying-out of the pamphlet idea; indeed, the principal of my advisers, the late Sergeant Parry, was strongly opposed to such action on my part. He said: "I implore you, Bandmann, not to do any such thing, at least not at the present time, when your mind is too much excited about the circumstances of the case and indignation so strong in you." Eight years have almost passed, but when I think of the

wrong that was done me in that charge, and
the other wrongs that have followed as a fruit
of it, I feel as deep and strong indignation now
as I did then, at the blackness of the lie that
lay at the heart of it, and to my dying day shall.
maintain my innocence, for no more diabolical
untruth could have fallen from the lips of " the
father of lies " himself. There were upward of
thirty persons present on the occasion the assault
was said to have occurred, but none of them,
save an old man, who lived upon her bounty,
attested to my even taking hold of the woman,
or lifting my hand against her, and the bruises
which she said my hand had inflicted were
known to have been produced in quite other
ways; but there were names and circumstances
in the case which we were obliged to withhold
from fear of incurring great misery to others,
and perhaps destroying the happiness of several
homes. I will name one only of many instances.
A young girl, whose evidence had some value
on my side, was asked by the chief justice: —

" What had you to do so late as twelve
o'clock at night in the streets? Was that a
time for a decent girl to be there? "

The judge then looked at the jury, which, of
course, was synonymous with, " Take heed of her,
she is not to be believed." The young girl
looked at me, but my lips were sealed by the
court ; and she had been warned under no
circumstances to implicate, even by a hint,

other people, therefore she blushed and was silent. Now this girl, smitten as she was by the satirical remark of the judge, might have given him such an easy answer, and such a truthful one withal, for at that time she was on an errand for Mrs. Rousby, who was her mistress, and had two letters, one for ——, and the other for his wife. The one for —— contained the following menace : " Except you send ten pounds by the bearer of this, she has another letter for your wife." She got the ten pounds, which were handed to Mrs. Rousby, and that is what she was doing so late in the street; but she was strictly forbidden to mention the fact, for the name of the person might have ruined an entire family. There were many instances similar to this, which, if they had been allowed to come out, would have given the public a clearer conception of the character of the prosecutor, but which, out of consideration for others, had to be kept in the background. Nevertheless, all this was painfully unjust to me, who was sitting there absolutely innocent of the charge this woman had brought against me. So, too, was the "stand-off" attitude of some persons whose evidence might have given additional confirmation to that which was in my favor. I remember when I met Mr. Gordon, the scenic-artist, in Sydney, on my last visit, he said, in the presence of others : —

" Bandmann, that Rousby case was an infa-

mous concoction of lies. I stood at the back
of the stage and saw the whole row from
beginning to the end. You never struck her
nor pushed her."

" But why did n't you come forward and say·
so as a witness, like the rest ? " said I.

" Well, really, you know, Bandmann, I did n't
want to be drawn into it," was his reply.

And this was unfortunately the way with
several others besides Mr. Gordon; but how a
true man can justify himself in such conduct I
have never been able to understand, for surely
the duty one man owes to another, in such
circumstances, is to come manfully forward and
speak the truth, the whole truth, and nothing
but the truth.

Mr. Willing, the theatrical advertising-agent,
of London, told me that Mrs. Rousby wanted
him to settle the affair with me for two
hundred pounds; but that he knew it was no
good approaching me with such a proposal. In
this he judged rightly, for I was determined
the case should go on, and made no overtures
to settle it outside the court whatsoever. I
wished the world to hear and judge of the
truth or untruth of the charge, and I was too
proud and conscious of my innocence to fear
the result. So for two days the Queen's Bench
was occupied with the grievance of Mrs.
Rousby, whose strong point against me she thus
stated : —

" With one hand he held the manuscript of the five acts, five separate books, with hard, cardboard covers; with the other he took me by the hand, and with the other he clinched his fist and struck me."

The only remark which was made upon this absurd statement was by my counsel, who said: " He must have had three hands, then."

At last, however, the twelve " honest men and true " made an end of it by bringing in a verdict for me, and my character was cleared in the eyes of the world. I discovered afterward, however, that the truth was either not made for the present world, or, at least, can only at times be within the reach of rich men, for that little action cost me for my own expenses fourteen hundred pounds (seven thousand dollars), so that, had I have given my accuser two hundred pounds to have hushed the matter, I should have saved twelve hundred pounds; however, although I was not at that time rich, I had enough to pay those expenses and to spare, and am glad that I allowed the case to go on; for some things are infinitely dearer to me than money, and I regard my good name, honor, character, reputation, as amongst them.* So, though I still remembered what an expensive

---

* Mrs. Rousby, I regret to say, died five months after the above-mentioned trial from the effect of habits which for many years had sullied the splendor of what otherwise would have been a grand career. We would in no case, least of all in present circumstances, " set down aught in malice," but it is necessary for the reader to be informed

thing the truth is, I resolved, notwithstanding, to prosecute my Hong-Kong libeler, and the case was tried before the chief justice, Sir George Phillippo, a wiser, firmer, kinder man than whom was never known. He protected the calumniator till he found it to be his duty to protect me, and then he did me full justice. The jury found Frazer Smith guilty, and the judge sentenced him to two months' imprisonment, and to pay costs (eleven hundred dollars). I am not fond of shining in courts of justice, but, on both these occasions, I could do no other than place myself in their hands, and await the verdict; for I say with my great master, Shakespeare (who, by the way, had his little experience in the court at, I think, Stratford-on-Avon, before Sir Thomas Lucy) : —

"Good name in man and woman, dear my lord,
Is the immediate jewel of their souls :
Who steals my purse, steals trash ; 't is something, nothing,
'T was mine, 't is his, and has been slave to thousands;
But he that filches from me my good name
Robs me of that which not enriches him,
And makes me poor indeed! "

that previous to this trial her *abandonnement* had assumed the symptoms of a chronic disease; and, since
  "Infirmity doth still neglect all office,
    Whereto our health is bound; we are not ourselves,
    When nature, being oppressed, commands the mind
    To suffer with the body,"
her appearance in court as prosecutor in this case must be classed with those many strange doings that preceded the catastrophe — the wellnigh final act in a personal tragedy of unspeakable sadness. — [ED.

CHAPTER XIV. — China.

CANTON.

" What, will you walk with me about the town ? "
— *Comedy of Errors, Act i, sc. 2.*

The *gin-ric-sha* — The German Concordia Club — Herr Streich, the German consul — The European settlements — The old and the modern city — Two circuits of walls — The streets — "The blind leading the blind" — Persons too poor to be beggars — Lepers — Leper villages — Ivory-carving — Embroidery and painting on silk — The prison and its discipline — The mandarins: their exactions and robberies — A typical case — Capital punishment — The prisoners and the wardens — Performance in the hall of the Concordia Club — Edward H. House — Willy Winter — Horace Greeley — The late Charles Reade — A typhoon — The life-saving brigade — Colonel Mosely, the American consul.

My long stay in Hong-Kong, imposed on me by my sense of honor, was, in spite of the great hospitality and friendliness shown to me by the best people of the place, very hard to put up with. Hong-Kong has not many outlets: a walk up the Kennedy Road, a delightful stroll or two to the Peak, or into the country, and you have exhausted the resources of the town and its immediate neighborhood. Besides, one gets tired of being carried about all day in a *gin-ric-sha*, a sort of miniature gig, in which a coolie takes, one may say, the place of a pony in a narrow and light pair of shafts, and which was, a few years ago, introduced into China from Japan, where gin-ric-shas have long been in use as cabs, and where the coolies are said to be of such splendid physique that you can travel by these Japanese man-carriages as many as seventy miles a day.

Under these circumstances I was very glad to accept the invitation of the German Concordia Club, of Canton, to go up there with Miss Beaudet and give a dramatic reading in the hall of their clubhouse. Herr Streich, the German consul, generously invited us to his house, and we went up the river by the Pow Woo, a vessel built on the American river-steamer plan, to Canton, on June 23. The consul received us with the greatest hospitality and made a splendid host.

The European settlement is close to the river and entirely apart from the old city of Canton, which is surrounded by a wall, or perhaps I ought more correctly to say, from the old and modern cities; for here we confront the singular circumstance of a walled city in the centre of another walled city, the fact being that the inner city was the original Canton, but that the suburbs beyond the walls attained to such dimensions that they far surpassed the size of the city itself, and the town was a mere speck at their heart, and another wall was constructed so as to compass them. But if the city continues to grow at the ratio it has during the last five years, they will soon require to build another wall, and Canton will be, in reality, three completely walled-in cities.

The streets of the town are very narrow, from five to eight feet in average, I should say. No wheeled vehicle of any sort can get inside the city proper; much less could it move were it once in, even by the most squeezing process. All travel is done on foot or in chairs, and when a chair is encountered everybody going in the opposite direction is compelled to step into the front of some shop (the fronts are all open, without windows, doors, or any partition), and wait until it has passed. In order to conceive accurately of the multitudinous life that animates these narrow streets, the reader has only to reflect that considerably over one million people are cooped up in an enclosure two miles square. Blockades are not very common in the streets, and yet I do not understand how they are prevented, for the streets always swarm with humanity. A funeral or a wedding procession takes up the entire highway, and a passing fire-department crowds everybody into the store-fronts. People must mind their own business on the streets in order to avoid collisions, and the narrowness of the pathway both tends to enforce the law of self-preservation on the passers-by and to prevent the concourse of mobs.

One of the strangest sights witnessed in the streets is that of the " blind leading the blind." The blind are wont to form coalitions for their mutual benefit. They may be seen moving cautiously along in a procession. I have counted as many as eleven slowly and cautiously advancing in company. Each person takes hold of the

garment of the person in front of him with the
left hand, and with the right keeps a bamboo
pole moving about on the ground so as to
prevent a misstep, which those in front of him
may have avoided simply through good-fortune.
In this way the pitable little band picks its way
along the crowded streets, turning corners and
ascending and descending steps with wonderful
ease. The principal responsibility devolves upon
the leader.

Beggars are not near so common here as
in Shanghai, where they infest the streets as
rats do a wharf. In China, paradoxical as the
statement may sound, a person may be too poor
to be a beggar — that is, too poor to pay the
initiation fee, which admits him to the beggars'
union. In this case he simply lies around anywhere, making himself as offensive as possible,
and even inflicting torture upon himself, in
order to wring pity from the lookers-on. One
afternoon I passed by such a one. He was an
old man, bared to the waist, and as I went by
he knocked his head against the pavement,
thereby producing an audible report which made
me shudder, and surely, though his skull had
been a vacuum before, it must then have gained
at least one idea, that of pain. As he raised
his head from the ground I noticed that long
practice of this sort had produced a large artificial bump on his scalp.

"They are but beggars that can count their worth."

There are lepers here as at Shanghai. Some of them are so horribly revolting to the eye that one feels weak in every joint as one's eye rests on them for an instant in passing by. They sit by the wayside to receive stray coppers of the value of a tenth of a cent, but their home is in a leper settlement three or four miles to the east. Every Chinese city has its leper villages near by, for leprosy is a serious scourge there.

Ivory-carving, and embroidery and painting on silk, are very important occupations in Canton; the workmanship in both departments being exquisite. I have stood for hours and watched the Cantonese carve their wonderful ideas into ivory, or paint and weave into silk the most chaste and artistic designs, and this often in dirty, muddy holes, scarcely fit for human beings to dwell or work in, but without as much as leaving the smallest speck or stain upon their beautiful work. 'T is a marvel of artistic achievement to see the piece of ivory transformed beneath their touch into a complete miniature temple, including even the officiating priests and worshiping congregation, or castle evidently inhabited, or a fortress garrisoned with soldiers.

In relation to the silk industries I must add that the designs are first drawn with white paint upon the material, after which the embroiderer traces them in the loom.

I paid a visit to the celebrated prison of Canton, and was much interested in seeing the prisoners let out of the prison doors to follow their respective trades during certain hours; true, they were heavily chained, but still this custom struck me as a somewhat nearer approach to a conception of the real office of punishment as applied to criminals, than that cooping-up in idleness, or at unproductive labor, simply because they are more painful, which is so common in our Western prison discipline; for these Canton criminals are never for a moment in their prison experience allowed to forget that work is a duty to themselves and to their families — work which ought to be a joy. And work they must, even when in the prisoner's garb and fetters which their own misdoings have brought upon them. The prisoners may be seen about the city in their various shops or stores following their usual occupation during the hours of the day, yet with the convict-brand plainly upon them in those heavy chains, — a warning to all, — being by this means able to support their families and costing the government nothing; very likely, indeed, paying a yearly royalty to the mandarins for being allowed the privilege.

The mandarins, in fact, govern the country, and the empress is ignorant of what goes on in her vast empire. She is only a mere figurehead of the government. The mandarins are the actual administrators. And the exactions and robberies to which they subject the multitudes beneath them are most infamous. Not one of the Chinese dare give out his actual wealth; he is always a " velly poor man," for fear of the mandarin coming to the conclusion, as he inevitably does when a man is found to be in good circumstances, that he has too many riches; in which case the self-called " velly poor man " has to give up a good round sum, and if he does not do it readily and with a certain amount of grace, the mandarin soon finds easy ways of throwing him into prison, perhaps of bringing about his public execution, or of taking his life in some way or other, in short, of laying his bloody hands on the poor Celestial's entire estate.

At the very time of my visit an exciting case of this type was decided in Canton, and cost, as is unfortunately too seldom the case, the mandarin his life no less than his victim, the agent he had employed to execute his diabolical purpose. The mandarin had arrested, tried, and beheaded a man for the murder of another, by whose death he had greatly enriched himself. The man, it turned out, had only been the mandarin's agent in the murder, but hoping to cover up his own crime under a cloak of feigned indignation and justice, he unblushingly threw him into prison, and then consigned him to the block. The case was a most intricate one, but somehow the truth oozed out, and the attention of the supreme government was called to it by

the German consulate, and for once the matter
was thoroughly sifted, the guilt of the mandarin revealed, and the full penalty of the law
enforced. He was beheaded.

" Change places, and handy-dandy, which is the justice?
   Which is the thief?"

Capital punishment in China is very simple.
The culprit kneels with his hands on the
ground, and the executioner, with one stroke of
a two-edged, sharp sword severs the head from
the body. There were forty executions in this
way in the Canton prison on the day before
I visited the city. A life is not worth much
in China, and the punishments for certain crimes
are too horrible to mention.

The Chinese take all this most stoically; they
do not bother their minds over the hereafter.
They believe, if anything, that they go into
complete bliss when they die, and so take death
much easier than life. And well they may, for
the life of the ordinary Chinese is a hard one.

The Canton prison is a dingy, filthy, low-
roofed, stone building of antique structure, with
numerous outhouses; and the prisoners, who were
huddled together, standing and smoking in the
respective yards, evinced the greatest indifference
to everything but the money they asked of the
visitors for having been allowed to look at them.
One fellow told me, with a broad grin on his
face, that he was going to be executed on the next

day for piracy, and begged money for, as I gathered from his words, "a wee little spree." But the ugly crowd of closely confined prisoners (for not all of them are allowed to leave the precincts of the gaol) were not the only ones who besieged us for money; the officials in charge were just as eager as the prisoners themselves. We were glad to get away from the dreadful wretches, and to feel ourselves once more at ease and in safety beneath the hospitable roof of our friend, the German consul.

We gave our dramatic recitations, several scenes from Shakespeare, and performed The Happy Pair, in the handsome hall of the Concordia Club, on the evening of the same day, and left the next morning, with the best wishes of our numerous Canton friends, by the same river steamer, Pow Woo, for Hong-Kong. On arrival there I found the following letter from my friend, Edward H. House:—

"TOKIO, JAPAN, May 29, 1882.

"*My dear Bandmann,*— I am surprised and delighted to find you are so near, and wish I could hope you might come even nearer; but of that I fear there are grave doubts. All I can hear of your intentions indicates that you will go back to Europe by way of India, and not by way of America. If your plans would allow you to visit Japan, I should have a rare pleasure in greeting you again. You are doubtless aware

that no promising pecuniary prospect is ever
open, in this country, to a man of your position.
The English-speaking community is small, very
small, and although you could be sure of one
(possibly two) good audiences, you could not
expect anything like a fair reward for the
trouble and expense of coming here expressly.
That is the reason why I apprehend you will
not come.

"It seems a dreadful pity that you should be so
close, and that I should not be able to shake
hands with you. I do wish that my news of you
were incorrect, and that your route would be via
Japan. You would be here at a fine season of the
year, and you could not fail to enjoy the beauty
of the scenery, and the pleasant ways of the
people. I am rather an invalid myself, but I
would do everything in my power to make your
visit an agreeable one. I was very sorry to miss
you when I was in England last year, and to see
you here would be an excellent compensation.
I do not suppose I ought to expect it, but if you
do come it will be a high gratification to me.

"Yours very sincerely,

"E. H. HOUSE."

Notwithstanding this letter, however, I could
not make Japan fit in with my plans, and I had to
forego the pleasure of meeting my brilliant friend,
whose removal to that country has been so deeply
and widely felt in New York journalism no less

than in the society of that city. Edward House is, without exception, the most thorough and refined critic the American daily press has ever produced; in heavier journalism he, perhaps, has equals, but certainly not many superiors. Willy Winter, who followed him as dramatic critic on the *Tribune*, does things " nicely " enough, but we miss the masterly touches and penetrative insight of Edward House, and certain it is that, had the latter followed the entreaties and advice of the late Horace Greeley, he never would have relinquished his position. A man is known by his friends, and few living journalists have more true and noble spirits among their friends than Edward House ; his intellect is so vigorous and keen, his tastes so refined, and his sympathies so wide for whatever is great or beautiful, that he is sure to win the respect and regard of all with whom he comes in contact. The late Charles Reade was one of his warmest admirers, and though nothing that I might write could equal the beauty of the eulogy I have heard from his lips, I feel a joy in saying that I share the sentiments of esteem and respect no less deeply and affectionately than dear Charles Reade himself did for Edward H. House.

On the seventh of July we were invited out to dinner, but with difficulty reached our destination in consequence of a slight typhoon. It had been expected the whole day, and about half-past seven o'clock it came on, as I thought,

with great violence, but the Hong-Kongese
called it a very slight one. Well, to me it
was terrible enough, and I should not like to
have experienced one similar to that which
occurred a few years ago, in which ten thousand
lives were lost and several three-masted ships
were tossed from the sea-coast half a mile into
the town.

No human mind can conceive the terribleness
of a typhoon that has had no experience of it;
but a very slight one, I assure you, is sufficient.
A picture may be drawn of its awful force when
it is known that five thousand horse-power
steamers may steam with their noses right
against a typhoon and use all their might, and
yet as a rule they are drifted back in a very
few minutes from two to four miles.

When a typhoon comes on, all the sandbank
men, who live on the water by thousands, disappear the moment notice is given of its
approach, which fortunately is generally known
twelve hours ahead from nautical observations;
and warning is given by the loud striking of
a large bell in a lofty tower and the ringing
of many smaller ones through the streets; ere
their sounds have died away the door of every
house is closed and bolted, every loophole is
bunged up, and the greatest precautions are
taken to keep the wind out; and yet the houses
shake as if an earthquake were rattling them.
At such a time the life-saving brigade, one of

the most humane institutions, and principally organized by young Europeans, is on the _qui vive_, with its life-saving apparatus. I asked one of these young gentlemen, after it was all over (a typhoon never lasts more than forty minutes and only about ten terrifically), whether it had been a bad one.

"No, sir," said he; "only about sixteen lives lost."

"Good heaven!" I exclaimed. "Sixteen lives lost?"

"Why, that's nothing," he replied. "In the last, several thousands perished; this was only a little puff."

"Thank you," I thought; "it was enough for me; I don't want to see a worse. If this, indeed, was a puff, what must a full blast be?"

One of my most pleasant acquaintances in Hong-Kong was Colonel Mosely, the American consul, who is much liked for his dry humor and straightforward and _débonnaire_ bearing toward all. I met him in society on several occasions, and had many a good laugh with him. He is still as hearty as ever, and a foreign climate has not aged him in the least.

I was much fêted during my stay, and received the honorary membership of the German Club, which has by far the most elegant of the several clubhouses of that town. Hong-Kong, however, when compared with Shanghai, stands at a great disadvantage on account of its rough element.

It has a vast mixed population, a portion of it very low and ignorant, especially the Portuguese; and the education of even the Chinese of the place is not equal to that of the natives of Shanghai, which as a metropolitan city takes the lead.

About the middle of July, I received a most pressing invitation to visit Manila, in the Philippine Islands, and I was assured that I and my company would meet with most generous support. This, however, I respectfully declined, owing to the sad news that had reached me of the death of an entire opera company from cholera, in that town, and having no wish to place myself and others in risk of that terrible disease. So, on the twentieth of July, I left Hong-Kong, accompanied by Miss Beaudet and other members of my company, by the Peninsular and Oriental steamer Sharon, for Singapore.

CHAPTER XV.— MALAY PENINSULA.

SINGAPORE.

"Why, sir, what 'cerns it you if I wear pearl and gold? I thank
my good father, I am able to maintain it."
— Taming of the Shrew, Act v, sc. 1.

"For the apparel oft proclaims the man."
— Hamlet, Act i, sc. 3.

"Cloth of gold, and cuts, and laced with silver; set with pearls."
— Much Ado About Nothing, Act iii, sc. 4.

"All o'er embellished with rubies, carbuncles, sapphires."
— Comedy of Errors, Act iii, sc. 2.

"Behold! I have a weapon;
A better never did itself maintain
Upon a soldier's thigh."
— Othello, Act v, sc. 2.

"I will wink and hold out mine iron: it is a simple one; but what
though? It will toast cheese, and it will endure cold as another
man's sword will."
— Henry V, Act ii, sc. 1.

"But since all is well, keep it so:
Wake not a sleeping wolf."
— Henry IV (second part), Act i, sc. 2.

"Immortal gods, I crave no pelf;
I pray for no man but myself."
— Timon of Athens, Act i, sc. 2.

The centre of the East — The climate — The great commercial importance of the place — Its magnificent geographical position — Its
produce — The residences and clubhouses of the Europeans — The
Germans in Singapore — The Governor, His Excellency Sir F. A.
Weld, and Lady Weld — The theatre — The Sultan of Sooloo — His
eight wives — His dress and his jewels — A black pearl with the
charm of immortality — His great-grandfather — His sword-bearer
— The ancestral sword — The sultan a cheap guest — A monkey-
hunt — The sultan and his eight wives at the theatre — The German
Teutonia Club — A complimentary ball — A testimonial.

WE arrived at Singapore after a lovely voyage
of five days, and were well received by the

people. The town lies at the extreme south of the Malay Peninsula directly under the equator, and the folk get no particular season there, as the climate, within a degree or so, is always the same, only that, during the months of July, August, and September, the atmosphere is cooler, on account of frequent rains, and consequently the gayeties are then agog and the amusements better attended.

Singapore is the centre of the East. Every ship that goes to China from all quarters of the globe, excepting California, touches at this point, and the entire traffic for Siam, Java, and northern Australia, goes this way, to take in supplies of coal and water, and for purposes of commerce, much freight being shipped there. Ships call for their instructions, and steer afterward for any harbor the advice bids them.

Singapore lies in a magnificent bay, with two grand openings leading into the Malacca Straits, and having landing-piers for miles on miles. It is also the most cosmopolitan town in the entire East, with the exception, perhaps, of Calcutta, by reason of its advantageous position. The produce of the place includes sago, farina, rice, pepper, indigo, and a large variety of spices, and they are now trying tea and coffee, but with little success so far.

The town itself is very large and flat, with lovely outskirts, and beautiful in appearance. The Botanical Gardens and the waterworks,

which are situated several miles from the centre
of the town, are of wondrous beauty, rivaling
scenes of fairyland. The Europeans live out of
the town from three to six miles, and even
their clubhouses are miles away in the suburbs.
The result of this is that most of their houses
are surrounded with delightful grounds, gardens,
and parks, and as there is generally a breeze
in the evening from one quarter or another,
they get more benefit from it than they would
in the closer quarters of the city. Then, too,
they usually select an elevated site for their
residence, and the houses are built in a light
and airy Eastern style, with large verandas and
windows.

Everybody has a home in Singapore, and
lodging and boarding houses are wellnigh
unheard-of institutions, for even the young men
club together in groups of four or six, and hire
a bungalow and set up housekeeping for themselves, and are happier and more comfortable
than they could be in the hotels, which as a rule
in the East are very bad.

The European population in Singapore is one
of the best, if not the best, to be found in
Eastern cities. As in Shanghai, so here, there
are no second and third classes amongst them;
every European one meets has the stamp of a
gentleman upon him. The same superiority
characterizes the ladies, only they are somewhat
too exclusive.

The Germans take a very prominent part in Singapore affairs, and with right; for the nation is represented here by an excellent body of people, generous, intelligent, and genial. We received the greatest encouragement from them and the other Europeans, and I cannot sufficiently express my gratitude to a number of gentlemen amateurs for the generous and ready assistance they gave me in some of my performances. It is needful to say here that I had been obliged to make some changes in my company, and, awaiting a new group my wife had undertaken to organize and send out from London, I spent nearly six weeks in Singapore playing Hamlet, The Merchant of Venice, Macbeth, David Garrick, and other pieces, with capital amateur support which frequently reached a perfection seldom attained by many self-called professionals, and doing an enormous business.

The Governor, His Excellency Sir F. A. Weld, K.C.M.G., and Lady Weld were very kind to us, and frequently visited the theatre, which is combined with the Town Hall, and perhaps the most comfortable for the audience in the East. Pankhâs were pulled the entire evening, and while the actors on the stage have to "sweat," the audience sit under a delightful breeze enjoying the performance.

At Singapore I met the Sultan of Sooloo, who came down from his vast dominion, which comprises the many islands of the Sooloo archipelago, accompanied by his harem, his sword-bearer, and his interpreter, and sojourned some days here on his way to Mecca. The sultan is a little fellow, clean shaven (I suppose he was in the habit of going through that ceremony himself, as I saw no court barber in his retinue: but perhaps one of the imperial mistresses discharged this office, or may be they each took a turn at it), and looked about nineteen, though, in fact, he was already twenty-six: at least, so he told me in conversation later. But in the East, the veracity of the natives is never to be relied on, not even in so personal a matter as their age, which, certainly, they ought to know better than others.

The sultan was tolerably well-off in the matter of wives, for, young as he was, he had already eight, —four of whom he had, with Oriental generousness, taken over from the harem of his predecessor, and each of them old enough to have been his mother; the other four were his own choice, although I could not congratulate him with any degree of candor upon that score, for certainly I never saw four other women so plain and with so few personal attractions as these. Perhaps he has no eye for beauty, or may be his standard in this respect differs from my own, and these women may have seemed perfectly charming in his eyes; or perhaps he went in for plainness from principle as proof against jealousy, which if so terrible to endure, it seems, when roused by one woman, how much more so if roused by eight! Be that, however, as it may, it seemed to me a mystery how this young man, and he a sultan, could have taken all these to himself, when any one of them, I can truly and without hesitation say, would have been deemed too many for almost any other man I have known.

The sultan wore a light coat and a pair of green silk trousers (a great preference, I have observed, with the nobility of the East), a turban, and carried a light Malacca cane. The buttons and decorations of his turban and coat were the most astonishing pearls and huge rubies I have ever seen. Some of the pearls were as large as walnuts, and some of the rubies would have taken a Gould's or a Vanderbilt's breath away. On his forefinger he wore a black pearl, which he told me had the charm of immortality. It had descended to him from his great-grandfather, who lived for over two hundred years. I suppose he attained a great age, and the years in the East, with indolent life, are long, even as counted by one hundred days to a year; but I am a little dubious of the sultan's veracity if we reckon the year in any other way. Well, at last, he told me, this ancestor of his, being utterly sick of earthly life, prayed to Mohammed to intercede for him with Allah — adding, with great reverence that I shall never forget, "There is no God but Allah, and Mohammed is his prophet" — to release him from his bondage, which Allah at

once did, and he ascended to paradise, where he
lives amid palm groves and lovely fountains, and
enrapturing dark-eyed houris. All this he told
me with great seriousness, and then calling to his
sword-bearer he directed the conversation to a
very different subject, producing the "sabre de
son père," a most formidable weapon, which had
descended from the same immortal great-grandfather, and had done duty of execution to thousands of heads. It must certainly have been
a terror in his empire, and I have never seen
a more terrible and cruel weapon. It was of the
shape of a very wide sword-bayonet, not quite so
pointed nor so long, but very wide in the blade,
double-edged at the end, and very thick. The
weight of it was enormous, and must sometimes
have tired the sword-bearer whose duty it was to
carry it wherever his imperial master went; and
I think it was only necessary to drop it gently on
a neck, and it would do the rest of the execution
itself. Besides, its edges were besmeared with
a most deadly poison which would kill a being,
had he the strength of a Hercules:—

> "So mortal, that but dip a knife in it,
> Where it draws blood, no cataplasm so rare,
> Collected from all simples that have virtue
> Under the moon, can save the thing from death
> That is but scratch'd withal."

I took the weapon in my hands (there was no
managing it with one hand), and from that

moment made up my mind that, at all cost, I
would keep good friends with the sultan, and
immediately invited him to dine with me. He
graciously accepted my invitation, and came the
next day; and, O terrors unspeakable! his
sword-bearer, with the immortal great - grand-
father's weapon along with him, who stationed
himself behind the sultan's chair, with one eye
on his master and the other, a most terrible eye,
on me. My situation seemed far from comfortable, but my case was still more disturbed when
I found that, although I had prepared a sumptu-
ous meal for my royal guest, he would n't take
a morsel of anything, save a biscuit and soda-
water. The sultan was the cheapest guest I
ever had. It was a solitary dinner, although two
persons were, in some sort, enjoying it, and a
third party standing with the great ancestral
weapon of the sultan so near! I tried to eat,
but it was wellnigh in vain for terror of thinking
of that awful, poisoned instrument of execution
and of torture, that, at the least wink of the eye
or nod of the head of my imperial guest, might
be drawn from its hiding-place and make an end
of all things "weary and joyful." However,
the affair passed off without blood being shed, and
the sultan even proposed that I should accompany him, on the following day, to a monkey-
hunt. I cheerfully accepted the invitation, and
he called for me the next morning at the
appointed hour in a tremendous, huge carriage

that, I believe, had also belonged to his sainted
great-grandfather. They must have been giants
in those days, for everything was on such an
extensive scale. We took several guns with us,
and drove out into the country about ten miles.
We only shot two miserable little things, not
worth having, but the sport was well worth the
trouble. I saw at least twenty monkeys of various
sizes, but the big fellows were too shrewd for us,
and kept well out of the reach of harm. In the
evening, the sultan, accompanied by his eight
wives, honored the theatre with his presence, and,
although a screen with lace curtains was set aside
for these ladies, they could easily be seen, and the
sultan did n't seem to care a fig whether any one
looked or not; he was evidently more interested
just then in the fate of Romeo and Juliet than in
that of his wives.

Besides the performances at the theatre, we
gave an entertainment at the German Teutonia
Club, where we played one act of Hamlet in
German, and The Happy Pair in English, and
I recited Schiller's " Lay of the Bell." We were
most hospitably treated, and the ball afterward,
given in honor of our presence was a grand affair.
The next day I received from my German friends
the following letter (I give the English transla-
tion): —

"Teutonia Club, Singapore, August 7, 1882.

"*Honored Sir,* — In the name of the members
of the Teutonia Club, we beg to express to you

and to Miss Beaudet our sincerest thanks for the delightful evening you have given us, and request you both to accept the enclosure as a mark of our esteem.

"J. FRIEDRICH, Hon. Sec."

The enclosure was a very liberal testimony in money.

After a number of banquets, fêtes, and other distinctions, we reluctantly left our Singapore friends on the twenty-fourth of August, in order to catch the pleasant weather which the Western monsoon gives to Ceylon.

CHAPTER XVI. — INDIA.

CEYLON.

"Uneasy lies the head that wears a crown."
— *Henry IV (second part), Act iii, sc. 1.*

"Kings are earth's gods; in vice their law's their will;
And if Jove stray, who dare say that Jove doth ill?"
— *Pericles, Prince of Tyre, Act i, sc. 1.*

"Not all the water in the rough, rude sea
Can wash the balm from an anointed king."
— *Richard II, Act iii, sc. 2.*

"The hearts of princes kiss obedience,
So much they love it; but to stubborn spirits,
They swell, and grow as terrible as storms."
— *Henry VIII, Act iii, sc. 1.*

Colombo — The best season of the year — The Western monsoon — The coffee-planters and the coffee-worm — The enterprise of the settlers — The fine roads — Ruin from the coffee-worm — The Singalese — The coolies — A coolie's feat of strength — The best hotels in the East — Mr. Beresford Hope — The Governor, Sir J. R. Longden, and Lady Longden — The commanding-general — Performances in the schoolroom of the barracks — A great success — Gentlemen amateurs — The soldiers of the garrison — The band — Singalese Catholics — Moslem jewelers — Brummagem jewels — Kandy, the capital — The Government House grounds — Lady Horton's promenade — The lake and the walk around it — The legend of the lake — The royal mausoleum — The Great Temple — The fate of a king's wives in olden time — Newara Ellya, the summer resort — A scene of fashion and amusement — English residents — Cinchona — Don Pedro — Elephants — A "rogue" — Mr. Saunders — A Colombo benefit.

I REACHED Colombo, passing by Penang, a dreadful, mean, and dirty place, on the first of September. Any one intending to visit Ceylon and this most charming city, should try to arrange to be there some time between June 1 and October 31, the most delightful season of the year.

During that period the Western monsoon, which eats into steel and iron, and ruins every article of clothing if not hung out in the sun at least an hour every day, is most soothing in its effect upon the lungs, beneficial to all sufferers from heart-disease, and dowered with blessings of health and life for all.

From the opening of June to the end of October Colombo is in its gayest mood, and there is a constant round of amusements and festivities. The governor of Ceylon comes down from Nawara Ellya and Kandy, and the programme of pleasure, during these months, includes numberless races, balls, dinners, concerts, and theatrical performances; and all Ceylon wears robes of gladness and rejoicing. That is, all those who have not been ruined by the coffee-worm, a disease which has made much havoc among the richest and best settlers. Ceylon was, for a long time, the best coffee-producing country in the world; the coffee raised there was of the highest value in the market and most in request. The prosperity of the island was boundless, and the excellent settlers showed their gratitude by a push and an enterprise nowhere surpassed in the British colonies; roads, piers, breakwaters, were constructed with an unrivaled rapidity and grandeur. Any one who travels on the railroad, at an elevation of two thousand feet, from Colombo to Kandy, or the beautiful mountain-road from Kandy to Newara Ellya at a height of three thousand feet, will see what perseverance and enterprise have characterized the settlers in Ceylon. But the prosperity of the best colonists that ever opened a country was not to last long; a terrible disease set in, and out of every one hundred planters sixty were ruined. From year to year it grew worse, till bankruptcy stared in the face those who were, five years previous, living in comfort and luxury, and they found they had n't a rupee to their names. Some, however, were wise in time, and changed their tactics; giving up the culture of coffee, they went in for cinchona (the bark of a tree from which quinine is extracted, said to be so named from the Countess del Cinchon, but more probably derived from *kinakina*, the native word for bark), and came out right. But those who still looked for a release from the disease and continued coffee-planting were only destined to have further disappointment and deeper ruin. Hundreds of miles of coffee-land, which was once worth millions of dollars, had finally to be abandoned.

> " But with fate's almighty powers
> No eternal bond is safe
> And misfortune swiftly rides."

> " This is the state of man: To-day he puts forth
> The tender leaves of hope, to-morrow blossoms,
> And bears his blushing honors thick upon him;
> The third day comes a frost, a killing frost;
> And — when he thinks, good easy man, full surely
> His greatness is a ripening — nips his root,
> And then he falls."

Yet there is plenty of wealth in the island still, arising from the produce of cinchona, rice, and tea. In Colombo, which is the town where the principal commerce of the island is carried on and where the government officials reside, there is but little want to be seen. The Singalese strike one at once as an interesting race, the men with long hair and combs on their heads, while the women wear no adornments of the kind. They are the best-made men of Eastern nations, and the most intelligent, chiefly fitted, however, for indoor work, and certainly not overhonest in their dealings, as our experience at Galle proved to us so convincingly.

The coolies, who emigrate by thousands to all parts of the East, are the workers in the field and at all heavy labors. A coolie will do what no navvy or American negro is able to accomplish; he will take one hundred pounds weight of freight on his head and walk, in one day, from fifty to sixty miles over mountains and dales with it for the moderate sum of four or five rupees. It is true, after he has accomplished such a feat, he generally sleeps a week — his highest enjoyment on earth.

Colombo possesses the best hotels in the East. The Oriental and the Mount Lavinia, a sea-side place about six miles out of town, are equal to any European establishment in beauty of situation, comfort, and elegance. The prices are moderate, from four to six rupees a day, and the cuisine excellent.

The first gentleman I met in Colombo was my old friend, Mr. Beresford Hope (a distant relation of the well-known Conservative member of the House of Commons bearing the same name), who was, at the time, acting as private secretary to the governor, Sir J. R. Longden. He introduced me to both His Excellency and Lady Longden, and made my stay in many other ways very pleasant. But it was not to Mr. Hope alone that we were indebted, for every one we met contributed to our enjoyment. What I have said of Shanghai and Singapore is, in a great measure, true of Colombo. The colonists there are of a higher order, and far superior to those of Calcutta or Bombay.

There is no theatre in Colombo and no large public hall appropriate for theatrical performances, so the commanding-general placed at my disposal the schoolroom of the barracks, which has a good stage and some scenery and is capable of holding six hundred people.

The Governor and Lady Longden were present at every performance. The band was given gratis, sixty performers, if I could have used them, and my first night's play netted over eleven hundred rupees. The second equaled the first, and the other four brought me about three thousand rupees more. I took, in six performances, during two weeks and a half, upward of five thousand rupees (twenty-five hundred dollars), with hardly two hundred and fifty dollars' expenses.

In Colombo, also, I was well supported by gentlemen amateurs, and on one occasion, of which I shall have more to say, a Singalese lady took the part of Emilia in Othello, which she did remarkably well. My supers, carpenters, stage-hands, check-takers, ushers, and the entire orchestra, were all soldiers of the garrison.

Imagine a band of sixty instruments blowing away in a little hall capable of holding about six hundred people. There was a perfect storm of sound, and on the first night it jarred so upon the nerves of Lady Longden and other ladies in the audience, that afterward I reduced it to fifteen; but so zealous were the sixty musicians — and grand military musicians they were, a really splendid body of men — to show their sympathy with me, and each so wishful of doing his part, that no other method could be devised save the casting of lots to see which should constitute the fortunate fifteen. Of course, this was managed by an arrangement agreed upon amongst themselves, so as to avoid the election of too many instrumentalists of one order, and when the result was reached to leave a perfect band of fifteen performers. No incident in my life has ever impressed me more than the glad willingness with which these young military men did everything in their power to help me to make my performances in Colombo a grand success.

The schoolroom stage on which we played had only one set of scenery, and it was so low that when I stood up perfectly straight my head touched the fly-boards. We played three acts of Hamlet all in this one scene, which was rather inconvenient. One of my actors, who played the King, got so "mixed up" that he said:—

"My *thoughts* fly up, my *words* remain below,
Thoughts without *words* never to heaven go."

One thing surprised me greatly at Ceylon, namely, that there are at least a quarter of a million amongst the Singalese who have embraced the Catholic religion, and who have their manuals of devotion and prayer-books, and, I believe, the Bible, or, at least, portions of the Bible, translated into their own language, and who observe all the Catholic rites in a semi-European fashion.

But to turn to another subject: for, as it is hard to forget old grievances, I vow eternal hatred to all swindlers: I cannot refrain from referring again to the Singalese-Moslem jewelers, who are the greatest knaves, in their own particular line, in the entire world. They try to sell you a sapphire, or any other "precious stone," as they call it, "as precious," they will assure you, "as those of the walls of heaven themselves," for the exceeding small sum, for such rare jewels, of five hundred dollars, and, in the end, perhaps come down to twenty-five, which clearly proves them to be about as precious as those of the walls of hell, if, indeed, the world of the lost has any walls, for it were difficult, according to orthodox notions of a "bottomless pit," to understand how any foundations could ever have been laid for their support; yet most assuredly to some such place, with walls or without walls, such rogues ought to go, and a year or two in the Ceylon prisons might not do them any harm. They mean no great wrong, it is said; they only take in the ignorant, who have more money than brain. The calm and close observer who understands stones, or any one who acts as if he does, they treat honestly. I myself have seen the sharpers outwitted by a thoroughly acute dealer in stones, and I have also seen them sell, to a rich Australian squatter for three, six, or eight hundred dollars, a Brummagem jewel, nothing more nor less than a bit of colored glass.

I made a trip to Kandy, the capital of Ceylon, a charming spot, located over three thousand feet above the level of the sea, and yet in a beautiful valley surrounded by still higher mountain scenery. The governor has a fine residence there, where he lives three months in the year. In the Government House grounds there is a most beautiful walk called "Lady Horton's Promenade," because it was laid out by that lady during her husband's term of office as governor of Ceylon. The promenade is three and a half miles long, and winds in the most picturesque and scenic manner around the high mountain which shelters the grounds of the house.

There is another lovely walk or drive around
the lake, which is the principal sight of Kandy.
It has a history: at least a legend of great
beauty has grown around it, and all legends contain something of historic truth. It is said that
one of the old kings of Ceylon, finding that
idleness was the root of all evil, and that his feudal
chiefs were prone, in consequence of that failing,
to give him much trouble, hit upon the novel
plan, for that ancient age, of giving them all some
occupation. They were summoned to his royal
presence in the capital, and came, many of them,
in great state with their retinues and retainers.
The king received them with unusual splendor, and
made known the scheme that had matured itself
in his thought, which was to make a large excava-
tion, for the purpose of a lake, in the royal city
of Kandy. They were delighted with the idea,
and bent their energies to carrying it out. When
the work was completed he ordered them to make
a small island in the centre, on which he purposed
to raise a royal mausoleum for himself and his
descendants, and these schemes were likewise
carried out, and there was the longest term of
peace ever known in the ancient kingdom of
Ceylon. The legend is one of rare beauty, and
contains a suggestive moral for legislatures of
to-day and every age; possibly rightly organized
work for the masses would cure half the disaffec-
tions of modern European society; at least, we
know that in America and Australia, where work

is more abundant, and fair wages and high rewards are held out as inducements to industry, perseverance, and integrity, the spirit of revolt and its attendant evils do not exist to any great extent.

But the king was not buried in the mausoleum on the island of the lake; in spite of his wishes his mortal remains were deposited opposite the Great Temple at Kandy, the largest in all India. During his life, however, he utilized the island for quite other than his original purpose. He was clearly a man of ideas, and, like most such men, sometimes altered his plans, or rather, perhaps, added plan to plan, as in this instance. It is said that the king made the island advantageous to himself as a sort of convict settlement, and not infrequently as a scene of execution for his refractory wives. Whenever one of his beloved better halves (or were they harpies? he had two hundred of them) became rebellious she was rowed over to that insular spot and no more was heard of her. Bones of human beings are constantly being dug up, especially of the feminine class. The king appears to have been altogether a very expert administrator, a veritable Blue-beard in Ceylon history; but, like King Hal of England, in a later age, who resembled him in being, in many ways, a good sovereign to the people and their leaders under him, he manifested a decided disposition to save law and lawyer's fees for divorce on more than one

occasion. I wonder if, like King Hal, he had
any qualms of conscience about his first case, and
got it somehow made easy by the priesthood
and doctors of his religion, and, by-and-by, found
what was so hard to commence very convenient
and agreeable by constant practice of their
doctrine. Man is a strange being, full of con-
tradictions, and when one considers the origin of
the lake at Kandy, so far as legendary history
records it, being in a desire of the king for
peace, and that he might still the warring
passions of his people, and then the brutal use
to which the island in its centre was put,
motives are revealed that seem absolutely incom-
patible in one and the same character, did we
not know that such is the strange composition
of human nature that the most antithetical passions exist side by side.

Quite lately I read of an ancient temple in
Mexico in which were discovered the skulls of
hundreds of thousands of human beings, and it
turns out that the priests were in the habit of
ripping open persons who came to render themselves a living sacrifice to their deity, and of
cutting out the heart, which was offered on the
altar with special devotions, and whole hecatombs
of these victims thus died at the hands of the
priests, who, strange to say, devoted themselves,
in another part of the same temple, to the offices
of mercy, such as tending lovingly the sick, the
afflicted in mind, the homeless, the helpless, and
the needy.

The summer-resort of Ceylon, that is, during the time of the Northern monsoon, from the beginning of November to the end of May, is Newara Ellya, a beautiful valley amid encircling mountains, at an elevation of between four and five thousand feet above the level of the sea. It is reached partly by railroad, which takes the traveler within thirty miles of the place, and partly by coach. The coach-road is through most charming scenery, the whole route being highly picturesque, and the road itself of splendid construction and kept in perfect order. The valley is about four miles long and wellnigh the same in breadth. In the centre of it is a lake seven miles in circumference; the walk around it is most lovely and quite unsurpassed by the lake scenery of any country. All the year round there are European visitors at Newara Ellya, and during the summer season the governor and the *élite* of the people of Ceylon flock to the place and it becomes the scene of every fashion, amusement, and display.

Many English gentlemen, amongst whom a brother of Sir Samuel Baker and a Mr. Saunders, have fine estates at Newara Ellya, and regret to leave the enchanting spot, even in winter-time.

Cinchona flourishes well here because the place is so sheltered by the mountains, amongst which is the Don Pedro, eight thousand feet above the level of the sea, the highest mountain in Ceylon. I made the ascent of it in less than three hours, and beheld many a scene of beauty from its sides and summit.

On my way through the jungle I saw a *chitah* and also a " rogue ; " a " rogue " is an elephant driven out of the herd for bad behavior. Elephants are gregarious, and for one to be driven out by the rest is a very extreme measure of elephantine discipline, and to be thus outlawed once is to be cast off forever, and the life of a "rogue " elephant thereafter has to be passed alone, with no contact whatsoever with the rest of the herd.

Mr. Saunders gave us during our stay a picnic, which we heartily enjoyed, in the Government House grounds, a veritable paradise of sweetness and beauty, seven miles from Newara Ellya.

After a fortnight's stay, I made my way back to Colombo, where I found that my friends, during my absence, had arranged a benefit for me, which turned out a great success. I played Othello ; Miss Beaudet, Desdemona ; a Singalese lady, Emilia ; and the rest of the characters were taken by gentlemen amateurs, who succeeded beyond my expectations. Several days were passed in visits amongst hospitable Colombo folk, — there really seemed no limits to their kindness, — and then we took our departure for Bombay, to meet the new company my wife had organized and sent out from London to support me in a six weeks' engagement there.

CHAPTER XVII. — India.

BOMBAY. — MADRAS. — RANGOON. — MOULMEIN.

> " My ventures are not in one bottom trusted,
> Nor to one place; nor is my whole estate
> Upon the fortune of this present year:
> Therefore, my merchandise makes me not sad."
> — *The Merchant of Venice, Act i, sc. 1.*

Second visit to Bombay — Counter-attractions — An unpopular theatre — Madras — A grand success — Rangoon — A novel theatre — Chinese carpenters — A poor set of Europeans — Eurasians and Albanians — The King of Burmah — Moulmein — Two days in the Gulf of Martaban.

HAVING already described the cities of Bombay and Calcutta, I need only now say that my second season in both of these places, although quite remunerative, was not such a marked success as my first. This was due to outside circumstances, such as an influx of counter-attractions just at the time of our playing in both places. Two other theatrical companies were simultaneously visiting India, having heard of my great success the previous season. One had come from London and the other from Australia. My second engagement in Calcutta was at an unpopular theatre, which also was unfortunate, but, nevertheless, I cleared all expenses, and five thousand dollars besides, out of Bombay and Calcutta in ten weeks.

In February I accepted a capital offer for Madras, the " city of distances," where I met with very generous support at the hands of — as I feel I must ever consider it — a most charming public, and recorded another grand victory.

From Madras we crossed the Bay of Bengal to Rangoon, situated on the opposite coast, a place of no great interest. When I asked where the theatre was, they took me out into the country about four miles from the town, and showed me a large open place without walls, with a stage at the end. I again inquired for the theatre, and I was told that I was in it, but that the wooden framework had been removed by a local society that had given a ball a few days previous, and had had the panels constituting the walls of the hall taken out and had not yet replaced them, but the matter should have immediate attention. I told those in charge of this invisible hall that I should not act without its being walled, and I had to wait for over two days before the Chinese carpenters (they are the joiners all through the East) set the panels back and gave a "local habitation" to the Rangoon Theatre.

I found rather a poor set of Europeans in Rangoon, and even the better class are so completely engaged in rice-shipping, in the spring of the year, that few of them find time, or have the disposition, to go to the theatre. My principal support was from the Eurasians and Albanians. The country around Rangoon did not interest me much. The King of Burmah is a fiend, and lives well back in the interior. He has a peculiar habit of beheading every one who contradicts him, and skulls are consequently very plentiful about his royal palaces.

From Rangoon we went by the British India Line steamer to Moulmein, and here we were obliged to lie two days in front of the mouth of the river, in consequence of the low yearly springtide in the Gulf of Martaban. At last we were rowed up the stream about nine miles, and, to render our position still more comfortable, we were told that it teemed with crocodiles and other "ill-shaped fishes."

We played two nights in Moulmein and were well supported by the people. The club lent us its theatre and made no charge whatever for the use of it.

From Moulmein we went back to Singapore by the way of Penang and Malacca, and there we made another halt and played three times to crowded houses. We could have stayed a month longer, with great monetary recompense, but, unfortunately, the steamer Tanadice, that was to take us to Australia, left on a day which we were compelled to accept; in such cases there is no room for individual choice.

CHAPTER XVIII.— AUSTRALIA.

PORT DARWIN.

"I'll put a girdle round about the earth
In forty minutes."
— *Midsummer-Night's Dream, Act ii, sc. 2.*

Old friends — The governor — The telegraphic importance of the
place — Mineral wealth — Inauguration of the Town Hall — Caste
— The Chinese residents — A cannibal village.

OUR first place of call, after an eight days' voyage, was Port Darwin, and the first object that caught my eye was a white trayman hauling freight from the foot of the bay. It was a pleasant sight, as I had not seen one for over two years. On landing, my hand was instantly grasped by my friend, Joseph Knight, who had become the chief judge of the district of Palmerston, and whom I had not seen since 1869, in Melbourne. Mr. Knight was the architect of the Victoria House of Parliament. He was delighted to see me, and handed me a letter, which read thus: —

"From the Government Resident, Palmerston, to D. E. Bandmann, Esq.

"Come to the Residence and see an old friend, and have lunch. Yours truly,
"G. R. McMINIS,
"Government Resident."

So here, to my surprise and delight, I found another old friend acting as governor of the port. I remembered him from my trip from Victoria to South Australia, in 1870, when we traveled for upward of six hundred miles across country together. I was on my way to Adelaide to fulfil an engagement, and, desirous of seeing the country, I went overland, no easy trip in those days. McMinis was then at the head of the expedition sent out by the government to lay the transpacific cable, which was to unite Australia with the rest of the world. I found him as hearty and kind as ever, and he received Miss Beaudet and myself with the most thoughtful hospitality and made our short stay very pleasant.

Port Darwin lies at the extreme corner of North Australia, and belongs to South Australia, although it is nearer to Queensland than to the former. It is a very convenient point of call for ships on their way to China or to the Malacca Straits, and has attained great importance from the fact that all telegrams from the Australasias have to go from there, as it is the point of connection with the straits, whence messages go by the way of India to Europe. The country round is purely tropical, and it is said to be very rich in minerals, metals, and coal.

The town is fast growing into a place of considerable importance. It has a bi-weekly newspaper, several churches and schools, and about four thousand inhabitants, including the Chinese. On our arrival they had just finished building the Town Hall, a very appropriate structure, and there was a universal desire that we should inaugurate it. The captain was appealed to, and promised to stay over for the occasion, that is, about eighteen hours. My carpenter soon erected a temporary stage, and we played Caste. The hall was crowded, but the fun of the thing was that the Chinese, hearing that the Town Hall was to be inaugurated as a "sing-song house" (their name for a theatre), flocked to the performance to see Caste, a refined comedy in three acts. The bored faces of these usually serene folk were most comical to behold, and no doubt they were happy when the whole thing was over. It could not have been very pleasant to those accustomed to the historical plays and farces of their national stage.

During the day we took a drive to see a cannibal village, situated about three miles from the town, by the sea-shore. We saw some of the cannibals, who, I was told, have had this place assigned to them by the government for residence. The place consists of about thirty miserable huts, and these aborigines, whose appetite for human flesh is a strong passion still prevalent, require great watching and are sharply looked after by the police. It is not seldom that a child, or a stray Chinaman, falls a victim to their ferocity and brutal tastes. They looked upon us with scarcely concealed desires, but the ladies of our party were evidently the special objects of their observation. Perhaps they created a strong craving of their cannibal appetites, and were considered as so many desirable sweet morsels.

Our brief stay at Port Darwin, notwithstanding the fierce eyes of the cannibals, was very enjoyable, and we formed many pleasant acquaintances. Amongst others whom I met was a son of Hingston, the friend of Charles Farrar Browne ("Artemus Ward"), who had formerly been my agent. He was then in government employ as a surveyor and doing very well. We pulled up anchor at one o'clock on the morning of the twenty-eighth of March, and started for Thursday Island, where we arrived on the first of April, a lovely Sunday morning.

CHAPTER XIX. — AUSTRALIA.

THURSDAY ISLAND.

"Here 's nothing to be got nowadays, unless thou can'st fish for 't."
— *Pericles, Prince of Tyre, Act ii, sc. 1.*

"Knew that we ventur'd on such dangerous seas,
That, if we wrought our life, 't was ten to one;
And yet we ventur'd for the gain propos'd."
— *Henry IV (second part), Act i, sc. 1.*

"A very dangerous flat and fatal, where the carcasses of many a tall ship lie buried."
— *The Merchant of Venice, Act iii, sc. 1.*

"I would have men of such constancy put to sea, that their business might be everything, and their intent everywhere; for that 's it that always makes a good voyage."
— *Twelfth Night, Act ii, sc. 4.*

Coral and pearl fisheries — Tricks of the fishermen — New Guinea — Torres Straits — A coral reef — The Tanadice in danger — The coast scenery.

THURSDAY ISLAND is the richest coral-shell fishing-place in the world, and many fortunes have been made there by that occupation. The crews generally go out in small schooners, well-provisioned for a week or a fortnight, and divers go down to get the coral pearl-shells. As soon as they are brought on board, the sorters, most of whom are Malays, open the shell and look for the precious pearl. Of course the search is vain in many cases, but when they do find one their first effort is by every possible means to hide it, and the desire to keep it is so strong that they do not hesitate to swallow it, if they lack other ways of concealment. Indeed, this is a common practice with these knaves. In Ceylon, where the oyster-pearl fishing takes place once a year, the government sells the right of space of fishing by auction. Then the buyer goes out with his crew, and the oysters are raised and opened on the spot, and the pearls sought for; the principal thing for the proprietor to do is to watch the coolies who open the shells. They resort to all sorts of tricks, swallowing them, burying them in their armpits, cutting themselves and concealing a pearl in the wound.

The coral pearl-fishers of Thursday Island are rather a rough lot; they make money easily and freely and like to enjoy themselves, though it is sad to say that the highest felicity of these boisterous fellows is in excessive drinking. One of them, reputed the wealthiest man on the island, came on board, and, as Artemus Ward would say, " he was the drunkenest man I ever seed." It took ten sailors and the captain himself to get him off the ship. They were obliged to tie him in a chair and lower him down to his boat by ropes. I was told that he had made money enough, and that his great ambition was to go to Sydney and stand for parliament. He has a great chance to succeed there !

Thursday Island is the point from which you go to Papua, or New Guinea. We arrived just at the moment to hear the news that the resident authorities had received orders from the prime minister of Queensland, Sir Thomas McIlwraith, to annex New Guinea, on the ground that Germany was going to do it, and Queensland wished to spare the former the trouble by increasing her own possessions.

While on the island we saw some of the most beautiful birds. They had migrated from New Guinea; amongst them there were many birds-of-paradise, whose plumage appeared most gorgeous beneath the rays of the sun.

On the third of April, in the Torres Straits, we were suddenly shaken up in a way that produced very painful sensations, and might have proved, in other circumstances, most disastrous. We struck a coral reef, but it was marvelous how our beautiful and lithe ship Tanadice glided through the danger, when serious consequences seemed most imminent. She actually danced along, and, although she struck the reef three times, she did not receive the slightest damage, as immediate investigation proved. To most of the passengers the matter appeared at first much more serious; for the chief engineer, who stood by me at the time of the first collision with the reef,— pointing out some inhospitable spot on the coast of Queensland, where the natives are all cannibals, and dine off any poor, unfortunate, shipwrecked crews that are cast amongst them, — turned as pale as a sheet, and rushed off like lightning to make his examination of the affair.

The next day we sighted the mail steamer of the British India Line, and our captain sent the third

mate on board with the unpleasant news as a
warning. The point was afterward advertised in
the *Shippers' Gazette.* The fact is, ships are
never safe in the Torres Straits, which are full
of reefs, and, as new ones are perpetually in
formation, there is no more difficult place of
navigation in the world. The scenery all along
the straits is most beautiful, and must be seen
to be truly realized. It is simply incomparable.

CHAPTER XX. — AUSTRALIA.

TOWNSVILLE. — SYDNEY. — MELBOURNE.

"I can easier teach twenty what were good to be done, than be one of twenty to follow mine own teaching."
— *The Merchant of Venice, Act i, sc. 2.*

"Every inordinate cup is unblessed and the ingredient is the devil."
— *Othello, Act ii, sc. 3.*

"Ye have angels' faces, but heaven knows your hearts."
— *Henry VIII, Act iii, sc. 1.*

"Get thee glass eyes;
And, like a scurvy politician, seem
To see the things thou dost not."
— *King Lear, Act iv, sc. 6.*

"O, while you live,
Tell truth, and shame the devil."
— *Henry IV (first part), Act iii, sc. 1.*

Cooktown — Townsville — Cook's River — Crocodiles — A trooper's story — Charter's Towers — Rockhampton — Maryborough — Brisbane — Sydney — A Woman of the People — Temperance reform — The clergy — The Reverend C. F. Garnsey's letter — Lady Loftus — Great enthusiasm — Melbourne — Geelong — Tasmania — Auckland — The Zealandia — Compagnons de voyage — The brothers Redmond — Miss Hampson, the revivalist — "Ever so many sinners" — Captain Weber — Miss Hampson's opinions on Art and the theatre — She tells a story of her early gifts — A poor German pastor — Entertainment on board for the Seamen's Shipwreck and Orphan Society.

ON the fourth of April we arrived at Cooktown, the first point of interest in Queensland. It was once a great mining centre, but has lately declined considerably. We played there one night, while the steamer was waiting for us, and started on the following day for Townsville, a place fast rising into a proud position amongst the towns of Queensland. It has sprung up quite suddenly: an instance of that marvelous genius of life, movement,—one may well say creation,—that characterizes new countries.

Townsville has a stream called Cook's River, crossing which, in a small boat, I felt somewhat nervous, as it is said to be full of crocodiles, and occasionally these unpleasant visitors lift their heads above the surface of the muddy stream and by way of affectionate embrace pull the boatman (he is the handiest because he stands up) down into their watery world, where they sport with him till he is dead, and then lay him out in some nice sunny spot on the bank of the river to decay: for the crocodile is an epicure in appetite and must have his meat just so, never eating his prey fresh: and when decomposition has set in, he makes a holiday feast of the body and lies down to sleep contentedly in the sun. They have pretty much disappeared as civilization has moved on, but up in the interior of the country they are still numerous in this river.

A trooper gave me a stirring account of his incidental encounter with one of these terrible creatures. He was in pursuit of a criminal, and had good cause to suspect that he was concealed on the opposite side of Cook's River. The government had set a heavy price on the man's head, and the trooper was determined by every means in his power to trace and capture him. He was on horseback, and the banks of the stream were bare for miles, but at a distance of about a hundred yards he saw, as he thought, a long log near the water's edge, and made his way to it that he might tie his horse to it, and then swim across the river in search of the offender. Just as he was close to what he had taken for a log, to his horror it rose to a great height and he saw himself confronted by a crocodile of enormous size, which had raised itself to its full length in the air; his horse reared frantically, and he was nearly off his saddle when the monster glided noiselessly into the stream. Now, his own life was safe enough if he had hastily beaten a retreat, but in that case he would have been obliged to give up the hope of finding the outlaw and to forego the reward. With the courage and nerve of a true soldier who must do his duty although sure death look him in the face, he rode along the bank some little distance and then plunged his horse into the river, which at that place was only about twelve yards wide, and made for the farther side. Just, however, as his horse swam near the opposite bank the crocodile, which must have been a close observer of his movements, peeped out of the water, but the trooper, with the adroitness of a man in imminent peril, seized his carbine and hit the monster a severe blow on the proper point, and to his unspeakable relief it immediately disappeared, mortally wounded, in the bed of the stream. The trooper and his horse reached the bank in safety, and his courage and resolution were rewarded in his finding and, after a tussle in which he proved that disciplined strength is able to cope with confirmed brutality and recklessness, capturing the ruffian, who for years had been a terror amongst the people of that neighborhood; and he received the considerable monetary reward that had been set on his captive's head by the authorities.

We played Shakespearean pieces at Townsville for six nights, and then passed on to Charter's Towers, a capital mining-place; then to Mackay; then to Rockhampton, a most important, perhaps the most important, northern town; then to Maryborough, a wretched, mean spot; then to Gympie, a dead mining-place; and so reached Brisbane for a second time, and I was surprised at the marvelous growth of the town in the interim. We played a splendid engagement at the new theatre. From Brisbane we passed on to Sydney, where I purposed at the time to stay but three weeks, but remained over four months. We played one piece, A Woman of the People, for upward of two months to crowded houses, and it is said that the play had an unusual moral significance, its influence on the crowds who flocked to witness it being in kind and degree quite unexampled in the history of the Australian stage. I cannot give too much praise to Miss Beaudet in connection with this performance; she was at her best, and elicited universal eulogium, and it is owing to her powerful and splendid acting that much was done toward lessening the cursed hold of drink on the men and women of Sydney, and for the sweetening and sanctity of a thousand homes. The leading clergy were much affected by these results, and the Reverend .C. F. Garnsey, rector of Christ Church, addressed the following letter to the Sydney *Herald :* —

"CHRIST CHURCH, SYDNEY, July 31, 1883.

" *To the Editor :   Sir*, — For many years past I have abstained from the theatre, from the feeling that the ordinary plays presented to the public missed their object as expressed by our great dramatist, the immortal Shakespeare, whose end, both at the first and now, was, and is, to hold, as it were, the mirror up to nature, to show virtue her own feature, scorn her own image, and the very age and body of the time its form and pressure. Rather it seemed to me that the aim and intention of too many of the writers for the stage was to pander to unwholesome tastes and feelings, and to present scenes at once gross, sensational, and corrupt.   Having had the opportunity of witnessing the performance of A Woman of the People, I have no hesitation whatever in expressing my conviction that it achieved, in a very marked manner, the desired object I have indicated, and must influence many who are able to see it for good.   It is a true picture of life, powerfully exciting the good impulses which the Creator has

implanted in our breasts, and holding up to scorn
and detestation that well-known character in the
world, 'the jolly good fellow,' who, in his own
absence of self-restraint, becomes the ruin of
others and the blight of many homes. It is free
from coarseness and vulgarity, while it points
most strongly to the one moral, the evil of over-
indulgence in drink.

" C. F. GARNSEY."

The excitement in the city was intense; everybody went to see the play: the pulpit and the
pew, the church, the wineshop, and the alehouse,
saints and sinners, — all were represented, and
crowded pit, galleries, and boxes, night after
night and week after week. It was a sight that
did one's heart good: to see so many white
cravats and unmistakable high-cut vests scattered
amongst the " gods " above and the mortals
below, and one could but hope it might do them
good, and tend greatly — at least so far as Sydney
was concerned — to break down that partition of
bigotry and uncharity that has so long existed
between two, when rightly considered, kindred
institutions — the Pulpit and the Stage. The
spectacle, recurring as it did every evening
throughout the long run of the play, brought
to mind with new force the words of Wagner
to Faust in Goethe's immortal masterpiece: —

> " An actor, oft I 've heard it said, at least
> May give instruction even to a priest."

Lady Loftus, the wife of the governor, was present, and was charmed with Miss Beaudet's acting. The play was placed under the united patronage of all the temperance societies in Sydney, and for five weeks the house was regularly sold out within a quarter of an hour after the doors were opened, and the enthusiasm was unparalleled by anything I have witnessed in connection with the stage. I cleared upward of fifteen thousand dollars by this piece alone.

We paid another visit to Melbourne for two weeks, and by special request we performed four nights at Geelong. I did not, however, know, when I complied with it, the real character of the place, or I might not have gone at all. It is one of those pseudo-religious towns in which opera bouffe and variety-shows are the only proper thing.

On the second of November we went once more to Tasmania, by the way of Launceston, and here I may say that I finished my tour, save for my stay at Honolulu on my way back to America, of which the remaining chapter of this book is the record. I had important business to attend to in New York; and there was an additional reason for bringing my tour to an end, in the domestic affliction that had visited the home of Miss Beaudet. Her mother's life was despaired of, and, with the devotion of a true daughter, — art, fame, and money were all of secondary consideration in such a crisis, —

she wished to return. The heart of the thorough woman asserted itself beyond the art of the actress; and on this sad news reaching us, we at once prepared for our return voyage.

We traveled by the way of New Zealand to catch the Pacific Mail steamer in Auckland; and found on board the Zealandia quite a pleasant company of travelers, amongst whom I may mention the brothers Redmond, the well-known Irish members of Parliament, whom I found very charming and highly intellectual gentlemen, and greatly enjoyed their society. The Australian revivalist, Miss Hampson, a lady who by nature seemed to have been intended to be very graceful and pleasing, but whose peculiar religion seemed to have rendered graceless and unattractive, was also one of the passengers. Her audiences in Australia, she informed me, had been large, and she had "converted ever so many sinners." She was evidently worn out by her miraculous doings, and was traveling for rest. By accident, or the cunning intention of Captain Weber, one of the most genial men I have ever met, who perhaps thought I needed the revivalist's wonder-working power to be exerted on me, my seat was placed opposite to Miss Hampson's at table. I was thus naturally thrown into somewhat closer society with this lady than others; for one must be courteous, and Miss Hampson traveled alone. I had several conversations with her,

and purposely avoided every subject that might
jar on her feelings, seem wicked in her judgment,
or worldly to her sentiments; even the word
theatre was banished, because "the theatre is
such a wicked place, you know." But the fatal
moment came; for, on one occasion, Miss Hampson spoke with great enthusiasm of nature, art,
and things that are beautiful, and quite un-
consciously we drifted into a tabooed subject;
and, as the devil would have it, gentle reader,
that subject was the stage! Alas! I had been
misled by the lady's conversation in thinking she
was capable of a wide and general view; but as
soon as I mentioned the word theatre it was all
over, and the revivalist stood before me, to use
certain famous words more appropriately than
than they were originally by Lord Beaconsfield,
"inebriated with the exuberance of her own
verbosity," in all the superstition, conceit, and
cant, the current coin of the class to which she
belongs, who speak of what they know nothing
on the hearsay of those who know no more
than themselves. I was not at all annoyed by
what the lady said about Shakespeare and the
stage: the first she considered "obscene;" the
latter a place of "diabolical wickedness." I
listened with the patience of a Job to her
ignorant calumnies, bigotry, and intolerance,
and then said:—

"Have you ever been to a theatre?"

"No! me go to a theatre? Who do you think
me, to go to such a place?"

" How do you know anything about it then? "
I asked.

" I can imagine it."

" Have you ever been in a picture-gallery? "

" They are not needed by those who have ·
visions of heaven."

" Have you ever heard an opera? "

" No."

"Why do you think, then, that you would not
feel edified by hearing a Patti or a Nilsson? "

" Because no voice can come up to mine."

At this point she regaled me with a story,
which reveals so well the immeasurable conceit
that so often characterizes such very humble,
saintly souls as her own, — to whom all the world
and every interest of life is wicked, save the
prayer-meeting or the rude, vulgar, revival
service, — that I cannot withhold it from the
reader.

"When I was a child," she said, "of about six
years of age" (I doubt if she ever was a sweet,
simple-hearted, six-year-old child), " Jenny Lind
was just making the round of her charitable
concerts. She came to our town, and, as she
generally required a foil, a lady who had to sing
before her, that she might triumph all the more
afterward, we were, of course, expected to put in
our programme such a singer. Our pastor said:
' We will give her a foil this time which she shall
never forget!' and when the evening arrived, and
the hall was so full that not a pin could drop to

the ground, our dear pastor — now, alas, a sainted
memory — lifted me on a chair and said: 'Sing
to me, darling.' I would have gone through fire
and water for him, I loved him so. Well, I sang.
I don't know what it was: it came like inspira-
tion: but when I had finished there was such
applause and enthusiasm that Jenny Lind was
thoroughly forgotten. The excitement was past
description, and Jenny Lind came and flung
her arms around my neck, and, sobbing as
though her heart would break, she said: 'My
child, I cannot sing after such an ovation; my
talent would fall flat after your heavenly gift.'"

I need scarcely say that, as Miss Hampson
related this triumph of her early years, the tears
of self-satisfaction glistened in her spiritual eyes;
those eyes which had looked on the thousands
she had saved from everlasting damnation, and
which had so eagerly, many a time no doubt,
looked to the amount of the collection that is
usually a conspicuous part of the programme at
meetings in which such spiritual work is done.

After this conversation I heard, every morning,
opposite to my cabin, where Miss Hampson had
her quarters, a sort of guttural chant, which
perhaps Miss Hampson considered divine, and
devised for my special benefit, but which generally drove me early into my chair on the
hurricane-deck; for I preferred' the cackling of
the geese to that heavenly melody. I am afraid
all this seemed very wicked to Miss Hampson,

but I really could n't help it, and this much is
clear to me: that her voice, if it had ever
rivaled, which I doubt, the matchless melody
and richness of Jenny Lind's, had sadly deterio-
rated; and that, if it were ever inspired from .
above, it was certainly on later occasions now
inspired from below — from a lost world.

There was a poor German pastor, with his
wife and six children, on board, who had steerage
tickets, and, therefore, rather a rough time of
it. The girls, some of them grown-up, had to
mingle with the general steerage company, and
had no place of privacy or comfort. I spoke with
Miss Hampson about these poor young gentle-
women, but she no doubt thought it was outside
of her lofty sphere to administer to worldly comfort. Her calling was beyond such trifles, though
it is well to remember that He, whose disciples
true Christians are, cared with great tenderness
and compassion for the poor, the suffering, and
the innocent lambs of the flock.

I afterward spoke with Captain Weber, who is
well known to be a kind, noble-hearted man, and
he immediately moved the whole family into the
second cabin, where they had separate rooms and
all the comfort they could wish. The parson was
very grateful, and we became great friends. He
did not preach against the theatre, but held, with
other noble-minded priests and men, that whatever is good and beautiful is a gift of God, to
be respected, admired, loved. He was a man of

fine insights, — of that poetic thoughtfulness and
sweet temper that

"Finds tongues in trees, books in the running brooks,
  Sermons in stones, and good in everything."

During the voyage we gave an entertainment
for the Seamen's Shipwreck and Orphan Society,
of Sydney, and realized a nice sum. Miss Hampson, of course, was not present; she was either
praying for the conversion of souls, or enamored just then more likely by her own melodious
and heavenly voice.

I can strongly recommend the Pacific Mail
steamers for comfort, speed, and safety, for I
always feel sorry to leave them. One is at
home the moment one enters one's cabin.

CHAPTER XXI. — HAWAIIAN ISLANDS.

HONOLULU.

" Give them friendly welcome every one:
Let them want nothing that my house affords."
— *Taming of the Shrew (introduction), sc. 1.*

"Give me the cups,
And let the kettle to the trumpet speak,
The trumpet to the cannoneer without,
The cannons to the heavens, the heavens to earth,
Now the king drinks to Hamlet!"
— *Hamlet, Act v, sc. 2.*

Old friends — His majesty, King Kalakaua — *Aloha!* — King Kamehameha V — Lunalila, his successor — His admiration for his ancestor, Kamehameha I — Lunalilä's character and habits — A visit to his suburban cottage — Stories of him — "Firewater" — The old Hawaiian laws against spirituous liquors — The repeal of those laws a great misfortune — A land of " brotherly love " — The Hawaiians — The probable total extinction of the Hawaiian race — The causes — The Hawaiian nobility — The prosperity of the islands — The white man's blessings — The Hawaiian kings have an open eye for business — King Kamehameha's *poi* factory — King Kalakaua's service of city cabs — Residences of the upper class — The new royal palace — The throne-room — Produce, manufactures, and shipping — The reciprocity treaty with the United States — International communication — The position of the Chinese — The scales turned toward America — The government seemingly monarchical, in reality a republic — The king's power — The privy council and legislature — Electoral representation — Government expenses — King Kalakaua's the most prosperous of all reigns — The king's appearance, character, and habits — John Cummins, the king's friend — His influence over the natives — A *hula* — Waimanalo — The Pali — Good Mexican mustangs — "The world moves" — A Hawaiian reception — Sugar-mills — The king's arrival — A great banquet — The *hulakui* — Hawaiian music — The public taste of Honolulu — The theatre — The public library — Celebration of the prime minister's birthday — Colonel Spreckels — The king's political views — Christian Chinese — San Francisco again, after traveling seventy thousand miles by land and sea.

WE arrived at Honolulu on the twenty-third of December, and were besieged by old friends,

Dr. and Mrs. Magrew, Paul Newman, the attorney-general, and his majesty, King Kalakaua, who urged us to stay at least for one week and give a few entertainments, and, although we were anxious to get to New York, we could not withstand the pressure; besides, Miss Beaudet had more reassuring news of her mother — the worst was past; and so with relieved minds we consented to remain a week or two.

Aloha! (the native expression for welcome, good-day, God bless you, etc.) is not merely the audible greeting of the stranger as he places his foot upon Hawaiian soil; but, in a way that he is not able fully to explain, an impression that means this and a great deal more spreads itself over his inner consciousness and brings with it a sense of happiness and a feeling of almost absolute contentment with his environment. There grows up within him a feeling that here he would like to remain at least for some time, and that feeling is strengthened and deepened by what he sees around him during his journeyings about the islands, and by his contact with the people. This feeling came over me on the occasion of my first visit, and on every successive one which I have made the feeling has become stronger, and my mind has become more and more sensitive to the attractions of the island.

During my visit in 1871 I had opportunities of becoming intimate with the then reigning

king, Kamehameha V; and also with Lunalila,
who succeeded him on the Hawaiian throne, but
who was not permitted to enjoy his sovereignty
very long. He died after a very short reign.
Of all the princes he was the most beloved and .
mourned. He had a geniality of nature which
was to a high degree charming, and could win
the hearts of his subjects quicker than most
sovereigns win a kindly thought. Hardly a
day passed during my stay that Lunalila did
not spend a few hours with me in my cottage,
and play and chat with my little girl, of whom
he was very fond, and took a great delight in
telling her marvelous stories of the heroism
and achievements of his great ancestor, Kamehameha I. He understood the child-mind as
very few other men I have met have done,
and my little one loved him to come; under
the spell of his voice her imagination became
all aglow, and no doubt she often felt herself surrounded by fairies, or maybe one of
the little princesses in the court of the great
Kamehameha I. Lunalila lived at that time
in one of the beautiful suburbs of Honolulu, a
few miles from the town, where he enjoyed the
sea air and the life of a free and independent
citizen. It is sad to say that he was very
much given to that worst of all evils, " firewater,"
and that this habit shortened his otherwise good
and noble life. He was of a most lively disposition, a man of excessive fun and merriment

of soul, and hated intensely conventionality in manners and in dress. On one occasion he urgently asked me to pay him a visit at his little suburban cottage. I promised to do so, and my friend Dr. Magrew made up a party consisting of Mrs. Magrew, my wife, the doctor, and myself, and drove up to the Diamond Head summit, the loftiest rock in Hawaii, close to the seashore, near to which his cottage was situated. I recollect that when we had almost reached our destination the doctor and I noticed the future king on the top of a cocoa-palm, busy decapitating some of its heads, in the garb of Adam before he met Eve. We, of course, with our wives by our sides, could not place him in the predicament of calling upon him in this costume *au naturel* (alas! the world has lost its innocence), so we drove right on, as we perceived that he had noticed us, and gave him time to come down and to get into clothes, if not more innocent, at least more conventional. This he understood very well, for when we returned to the cottage, about half an hour later, we were received by him attired in a most tasteful white dress, and were conducted with great courtesy into his scrupulously clean and comfortable parlor, where we found the New York *Herald*, the London *Times*, and the latest fashionable society papers of England and America lying on the table.

On a certain occasion Lunalila presided at a

public banquet, at which King Kamehameha V
was expected. The king was late, and the guests
were tired of waiting, and it is reported that
Lunalila rose and said: "Gentlemen, we will
wait no longer for the king; we will let the
band play, 'God Save the King'; and, if his
majesty does not appear during that time, we
will let the band play, 'God d—— the king.'"
His majesty, it seems, did appear, and the second
part of the musical programme suggested was,
happily, not gone through.

When a prince, Lunalila had generally an escort
of native boys with him, who carried a parcel
under each arm, which had the suspicious appearance of a neck of a bottle peeping out of some
corner or other; for in those days the natives
were prohibited alcoholic drinks, and could only
get them clandestinely. The law at that time
was very strict relating to alcohol, absolutely
prohibiting its manufacture, the act of selling
or providing it for others, and rendering punish-
able its use. That law, subsequent facts have
proved, was not a bit too stringent; for since
its repeal the population of the Hawaiian Islands
has decreased seventy-five per cent. Here is
an item for every temperance lecturer; but
none save those who have traveled in that
beautiful country and partaken of the hospitality of the natives and come to feel a great
respect for the many noble qualities of the men
and women they have met there, will realize all
the pain and sadness of this deplorable fact.

I may well call the Hawaiian Islands the
land of "brotherly love." The Hawaiian is, by
nature, of a happy and generous disposition. He
looks on life as a thing of joy. He moves in a
sphere of laughter and love. I have never seen
an angry Hawaiian. You may abuse him and
ill-treat him, but he laughs and takes it quietly.
Civilization has no power upon him. He is a
child of nature, who sings and laughs and loves,
the whole day long, and only under compulsion
or necessity will do anything else. He hates
work, especially manual labor. He has all the
instincts of a gentleman and is happy in his idleness. He will spend twenty-four hours in a round
of amusements, and, when through, commence the
same over again, and so on, week by week, and
month by month. Such a being is especially
susceptible to the influence of "firewater," and
its havoc has been tremendous; for, in less than
ten years, the population has fallen from one
hundred thousand to forty-seven thousand on
these islands. Small-pox and leprosy, introduced
by the Chinese, may, no doubt, have had something to do with this; but, to a great extent, it is
due to the effect of excessive drinking amongst
the natives; and, if things continue as they are
in this respect, there seems nothing to be looked
for, save the total extinction of the Hawaiian
race. When I say "total extinction," I mean, of
course, of the pure, native stock from a true
kupuna (source). During the last twenty-five

years there has been considerable deterioration in racial purity, owing to frequent intermarriages, and to the still more frequent promiscuous intercourse, against which there is no restraint, or little, at best, in the habits and customs of the people; so that a pure *kuaukau* (genealogy) is, even now, somewhat difficult to find.

The principal nobility of the Hawaiian race are nearly all married to Europeans or Americans. Her Royal Highness the Princess Liliuokalani, the heiress-apparent, is married to His Excellency John Owen Dominis, an American. Her Royal Highness the Princess Likelike to Mr. Archibald Scott Cleghorn, an Englishman; another princess to Mr. C. R. Bishop, an English banker, and a large number of native and half-caste ladies to Europeans; so that there seems every reason for thinking that within a few decades, at most five or ten, the pure-blooded Hawaiian will have disappeared. All who love poesy and natural sentiment will deeply regret this, for there is no other race on the globe so generous, hospitable, and kind. They have opened their country to the white man, and have told him to come in and take what he likes. The white man has done so, and carried with him his blessings: new industries, cant, and brandy. The first have done wonders, and will make these islands a source of jealousy, perhaps an object of strife, to the various nations of the civilized world. The second, up till now, has left the people

untarnished from the sheer force of their native
nobleness, and the third has reduced the race
to its present deplorable numerical condition.
In their primitive state, they lived in their
scrupulously clean grass-houses, with a few goats,
and a patch of *taro* (a native vegetable similar
to the potato) land before them, spending their
lives in fishing, hunting, singing, and *hula kin*
(dancing), and were, in many respects, a strong,
noble people. But since civilization has come
amongst them, with its accompanying tempta-
tions and coils, they are rapidly dying out.

Confronted by this and similar facts in other
countries — New Zealand, for instance — makes
it a thing devoutly to be wished that the pro-
found knowledge of natural laws and moral
sequences, the exquisite wisdom, and — may I
not say? — divine philosophy, that lie in Friar
Lawrence's soliloquy should be uttered elsewhere,
and in other ways, than by the Franciscan in his
cell. It would be well if it could be dropped
from off his lips into the heart of human society,
or carried on some mighty voice " as the sound
of many waters" far and wide throughout the
world; and nowhere, for friendship's sake, could
I desire it spoken in stronger, but at the same
time sweeter, accents, — with the rousing power
of the thunder, yet with the "persuasive tongue"
of pure eloquence, — than to the people of that
fair, sea-girt isle, Hawaii, for

" I have loved her ever since I saw her: and
Still I see her beautiful;"

whose happiness I wish, with all my soul, to last
forever : —

"The gray-ey'd moon smiles on the frowning night,
Checkering the Eastern clouds with streaks of light;
And flecked darkness like a drunkard reels
From forth day's pathway and Titan's fiery wheels:
Now, ere the sun advance his burning eye
The day to cheer, and night's dank dew to dry,
I must upfill this osier cage of ours
With baleful weeds and precious-juiced flowers.
The earth, that's nature's mother, is her tomb;
What is her burying-grave, that is her womb;
And from her womb children of divers kind
We sucking on her natural bosom find:
Many for many virtues excellent,
None but for some, and yet all different.
O, mickle is the powerful grace that lies
In herbs, plants, stones, and their true qualities:
For naught so vile that on the earth doth live
But to the earth some special good doth give;
Nor aught so good, but, strain'd from that fair use,
Revolts from true birth, stumbling on abuse:
Virtue itself turns vice, being misapplied,
And vice sometime's by action dignified.
Within the infant rind of this small flower
Poison hath residence, and medicine power:
For this, being smelt, with that act cheers each part;
Being tasted, slays all senses with the heart.
Two such opposed kings encamp them still
In man, as well as herbs, grace and rude will;
And, where the worser is predominant,
Full soon the canker death eats up that plant."

It is not my purpose to give a description of the marvelous commercial progress these islands have made during the past fifteen years, but I cannot pass silently over the gigantic strides Honolulu has made from the time of my first visit, in 1871, to that of my second (1882–83). A few remarks on the subject, though by no means exhaustive, may be of value or interest to many who may read these pages.*

When I was in that Garden of Eden in 1871, the native beauty of the place was in its fullest splendor, but commerce was still in its infancy. King Kamehameha, however, even then had an open eye to business, which seems to have been a characteristic of many of the Hawaiian monarchs. He had, amongst other enterprises, started a *poi* (a native food made of taro) factory on his own account; just as the present king, Kalakaua, is the proprietor of the greater number of the city cabs. But still the city was in a primitive state of growth, and trade was only beginning to gather about it. Since then large warehouses, wharves, and factories have been built, and private dwellings risen, which will compare favorably with the most palatial mansions of the great cities of Europe and America. The residences of Colonel Spreckels, Justice Judd, Mr. Cleghorn, Mr. Bishop, Dr.

*The reader who is desirous of fuller information is referred to the capital work, entitled "The Hawaiian Handbook," published annually by Thomas G. Thrum, Honolulu. — [ED.

Magrew, and those of numbers of others, are
specimens of exceptional elegance, grace, and
beauty. The new Royal Palace, too, is a structure which would do honor to any city in the
world. The throne-room is of remarkable beauty, .
and has few equals in Europe itself.

But these are social matters: the wealth and
prosperity of a country is founded on its produce,
manufactures, and shipping interests; and it is
in these respects that Honolulu has made
such marvelous advancement. Since the United
States has extended the reciprocity treaty to the
Hawaiian Islands, the coasting-trade alone has
increased from one steamer, twenty-six schooners,
and eight sloops, of a tonnage of sixteen hundred
and twenty-five, in 1875, to ten steamers, thirty-
eight schooners, and three sloops, of a tonnage
of fifty-four hundred and thirty-five in 1882;
and the sugar-planting interest has assumed such
enormous proportions that the estimated value of
it is calculated to be upward of sixteen million
dollars. The exports of domestic produce, too,
such as sugar, rice, oil, bone, hides, wool, syrups,
and fruits, reached the value of eight million one
hundred and sixty-five thousand nine hundred
and thirty-one dollars; while the import trade was
four million nine hundred and seventy-four thousand five hundred and ten dollars. International
communication has greatly been facilitated; and
where there only used to be a monthly postal
service, there is now a weekly one both to and

from America, and a monthly one to and from Australia.

The Chinese threatened at first to take the leading position in Hawaiian affairs; but the prompt action of the last government, headed by an influential American cabinet, put a check to the ambition of the Celestials and a limit to their power, and turned the scales toward America.

The government of the Hawaiian Islands, although seemingly managed on monarchical principles, is in reality much more like a republic. The king, in idea, is the supreme power, but in fact he has very little to say, and still less to do, in active work of government. This is carried on by the privy council and the legislature. The privy council consists of the four ministers, who form the cabinet for the time being. Those at present being the premier and minister of foreign affairs, His Excellency W. M. Gibson; the minister of home affairs, His Excellency C. J. Gerlick; the minister of finance, His Excellency I. M. Kapena, and the attorney-general, His Excellency P. Newman.

These ministers are responsible for all their actions and advisory influence over the king to the legislature, which meets every year, and is the actual ruling-power of the country. The members of the legislature are elected by the people. Some idea of the growing importance of the country can be formed from the fact that the

outlay for government purposes, including the
civil service, amounted, in 1882, to two million
one hundred and ninety-six thousand and six
dollars; and in 1883 to three million five hundred
and sixty-three thousand one hundred and sixteen dollars; the expenses of his majesty's household alone during the latter year being one
hundred and forty-eight thousand five hundred
dollars; out of which his majesty received fifty
thousand dollars; the queen, sixteen thousand
dollars; the heiress-presumptive, sixteen thousand
dollars; while twenty-two thousand five hundred dollars were appropriated to defray the
expenses of his majesty's tour around the world;
the remainder being allotted to the household and
other expenses of his majesty. But even these
large demands on the pockets of the people were
not seriously felt, owing to the great prosperity
of the country. From its present splendid
position and its revenue, there can be no doubt
that, whether in consequence of the fortunate
spirit of the time or to exceptional circumstances,
King Kalakaua's reign has been the most
prosperous in the history of the monarchy of
the Hawaiian Islands; though it is generally
admitted that Kamehameha's was the most
beneficial to the people in general.

Kamehameha V was a very simple gentleman,
who was fond of driving about in an American
buggy to look after his poi factory and extensive business, of presiding over lotteries estab-

lished throughout the land, and of saving money for the people; and, be it said, of being *wulie wulied* (gently soothed on the forehead) by the hand of a *wahine* (sorceress). Lunalila cared only for his personal enjoyment; but the present king, Kalakaua, is made of "sterner stuff."

In appearance Kalakaua is somewhat portly, but of a most dignified bearing, refined nature, and gentle manners. When he receives his visitors he generally wears a suit of white flannel and a large, black necktie; and his deportment is easy and graceful. I knew him before he was king, when he was still in the post-office as a clerk. Lunalila, of whom he was somewhat jealous, introduced me to him. His reception of me was most courteous and hearty, and he arranged a *hula* (festival) with his old friend, John Cummins, in honor of myself and several other guests from San Francisco. The hula was to take place at the summer-resort and sugar-plantation of his friend at Waimanalo, about fifteen miles from Honolulu; where Kalakaua has a pretty little cottage allotted to him for his exclusive use.

Of John Cummins it is difficult to give a pen-and-ink portrait, but those who have visited these lovely islands and met the king's friend will acknowledge the truth when I say that he is one of "nature's gentlemen."

> "There's in him stuff that puts him to these ends:
> For, being not propp'd by ancestry (whose grace
> Chalks successors their way), nor call'd upon

For high feats done to the crown; neither allied
To eminent assistants, but, spider-like,
Out of his self-drawing web, he gives us note,
The force of his own merit makes his way;
A gift that heaven gives for him, which buys
A place next to the king."

Born of an English father, from whom he received the name of Cummins, and a native mother, he looks more like a Mexican nobleman, or an Arab sheik, than a Hawaiian. A large-featured man, with a fine forehead and slightly bronzed skin, he bears the stamp of generosity, goodness, and nobility on his massive countenance. His greatest joy is to confer happiness on others, and he uses his fortune to assist the poor and to give pleasure to his friends. It was greatly owing to his influence with the natives, who are deeply attached to him, that Kalakaua ascended the throne. I may style him the Hawaiian Warwick; for in appearance and dignity he recalls the celebrated "king-maker."

On the day of the hula we started for his plantation, at nine o'clock in the morning. There was quite a cavalcade of ladies and gentlemen on horseback, decorated with *lais* (wreaths of flowers presented by the native ladies to the gentlemen, and worn around the neck as the sign of friendship), left the Hawaiian Hotel for Waimanalo. It was a fantastic sight to see this motley company of horsemen and horsewomen, the ladies riding cross-legged, in all sorts of fancy-dresses, through the town.

About eight miles from Honolulu we arrived at the dreaded Pali ; a pass in the range of mountains behind the town over which our route lay, which only fifteen or twenty years back was considered an impossibility for an European lady, and an extraordinary feat of skill for a man, to descend. The descent is so steep, abrupt, and sudden, that even those who have made the journey several times feel somewhat uneasy on each successive occasion. On this journey, however, our horses, good Mexican mustangs, were wonderfully sure-footed. They picked their way with the greatest caution, and never made a mistake, whether they had to jump over a ditch or balance themselves upon a precipitous rock ; so we were borne safely over the entire pass, which in some places well-nigh takes one's breath away and makes one's hair stand on end. It takes a good rider (or rather a good horse, for the rider has little to do with it save manage to keep his brain cool and himself in the saddle) about twenty minutes to descend the Pali, and the sense of relief that ensues is unspeakable. Those few minutes seem an eternity, and every inch of the way a jeopardy of life or limb. Beyond the pass the country opens in a glorious panorama of beauty to the eye, and Waimanalo is reached after a journey of some seven miles through the most lovely undulating scenery imaginable. We made a halt for refreshment within two miles of our destination, at the summer residence of Colonel I. H. Boyd, a fine young native gentleman, and one of his majesty's staff. His residence is on the top of a huge mountain, and I was somewhat surprised to find iced champagne, delicious sweetmeats, and cake, awaiting us ; the Australian bush damper and tea would not have aroused my curiosity, but that iced champagne and cakes of Huntley and Palmer should be served on the top of a mountain thirteen miles away from Honolulu, and in a country that only a hundred and six years ago was still undiscovered, is certainly enough to justify wonder, or at least an astonishing proof of the quick pace at which " the world moves " — in quite another sense than Galileo's — in these days. After these refreshments and a redecoration of the gentlemen with lais, and a thousand expressions of alohas, we took our departure, and soon reached the highest peak in the neighborhood, where a scene opened to view of surpassing beauty, leaving on the mind impressions never to be effaced. Beneath us, in the valley of Waimanalo, we could now see the rich sugar-plantation, sugar-mills, *keaniani polisates* (village houses), and charming meadowlands that constitute the estate of John Cummins ; while beyond these, spreading far and wide, the ocean, serenely quiet: the blue above, the blue below, smiling at each other.

Having at last reached the village, a couple

of dozen of servants came forward and took charge of our horses; while the king's musicians and dancers (who had gone on before) struck up their instruments and received us in true Hawaiian fashion. Our noble host conducted us to our quarters, and all the ladies were provided with *kalakoas* (beautiful native robes). My own quarters were with the king's chamberlain, Colonel Judd, Captain Morse, and two other gentlemen. We only had one bed between us, but there was ample room for us all, the bed being seventeen feet long by nine feet wide. In all my travels I have only seen one bed larger, and that was the "family bed" of the babu, in Calcutta, which I have already described.

As soon as the ladies had changed their dresses, tiffin was served in European fashion, after which the guests were left at liberty to roam about. Some of us went with our host to inspect the sugar-mills, and I was very much impressed with what I saw; the machinery was of the most perfect kind: every modern method had been introduced, with the result of minimizing toil and securing satisfactory results.

At three o'clock his majesty arrived, attired in a dark-blue suit with a crimson sash, and covered with lais, accompanied by Colonel Boyd and a trooper. He looked like a true knight of the mediæval times. He was received with great ceremony, and the band struck up the national anthem, "*Hawaii Ponoi.*" I, taken somewhat by surprise, was standing in my shirt-sleeves, but the king, holding out his hand to me, said: " That's the very way I like to see you, Bandmann; this is liberty hall here! " His majesty had a few pleasant words for every one, especially for the ladies; and after playing several games of billiards with some of us, and partaking of refreshment, he retired to his cottage for rest and to prepare for dinner. This was the sign for all of us to do the same, and while the band played one piece of music after another, the order of the day — a couple of hours' rest — was generally obeyed by the guests, during which a banquet was prepared in a large hall.

At six o'clock we reassembled to partake of this great native dinner, and I may say that no expense or trouble had been spared to make it a splendid success. The table was raised about one foot and a half from the floor; there was no tablecloth, but it was covered with beautiful mountain-evergreens, and decorated with flowers — lilies and roses of all kinds. The guests sat on mats and carpets, spread on the floor; each was provided with a soft pillow to lean against, in Eastern fashion. The king sat at the centre of the table, and the ladies were appropriately placed amongst the gentlemen, who somewhat predominated in number. The table was literally covered with all kinds of strange dishes, prepared in all manner of novel ways. There were meats, poultry and game, vegetables

and fruits, served in every conceivable mode;
boiled, stewed, roasted, fried, and raw. For the
first time I tasted *luan* (native) dog, which to
my palate had the flavor of tender English suck-
ling-pig. There were dishes of luan pork, mutton,
and beef; fish, chicken, and duck; sweet potatoes,
prepared in all styles; three different sorts of
poi — owena, shua, and *apuwai; eike barnarnarno,*
in all shapes; ham and eggs, sea-eggs; *opih,*
wana, kukui nuts; and at least forty or fifty
other dishes, served with beer, lemonade, milk,
and iced champagne of the best quality; while,
during the whole repast, the king's singers regaled the guests with melodious native songs,
and kept us in pleasant wonder and cheerful
astonishment.

After dinner, his majesty's dancers performed
the *hulakui*; this is a native dance, which it is
hard appropriately to describe. It was formerly
danced by men and women in their natural
state; but now they cover their bodies, from
the loins to their ankles, with a sort of petticoat
made of long weeds. The dancers go through
a most varied programme, in which there are
very wonderful contortions of the body and
gymnastic feats; while the singers describing
the performance act somewhat after the manner
of a Greek chorus. There is certainly a great
amount of agility necessary to its execution,
and the wild humor of the dance is fully understood and appreciated by those who are familiar

with the native language and history; but to
those unacquainted with these and not initiated
into their secrets, it will seem coarse and devoid
of interest.

The king asked me, later, whether I could not
oblige him with a recitation, and when I wished
him to name the one he desired, he replied:
" Something earnest; it will do my people good."
So I recited Hood's Dream of Eugene Aram,
which was received with prolonged applause.
Miss Beaudet and a Mrs. Brown, a lady from
San Francisco, gave some songs, and afterward
the company took to dancing, but not the
hulakui; we had had enough of that.

At eleven o'clock supper was announced, and
once more the company sat down to a splendid
repast. There was little sleep that night, for
a hula means a continuation of festivities. Still,
I managed to get a few hours' rest in my huge
bed; I may here say *my*, for that night I was the
sole occupant of it, and had infinite space — a
world — to roll about in. But I did n't want
to roll: I wanted rest.

On the next day, after breakfast, his majesty,
attended by his singers, musicians, and dancers,
was escorted to the steamer Waimanalo by the
whole company. We journeyed by our host's
railway, which leads from his establishment to
the wharf, where, as the vessel left the little
harbor, re-echoing cheers were given for the

genial and perfect gentleman who reigns over
the fair Hawaiian Islands. The remainder of
the party then started homeward by road, and
the king, having arrived at Honolulu some
hours beforehand, drove⁻ out to meet us, and
soon we were all assembled once more at the
Hawaiian Hotel, where our festivities were
prolonged till the next day, when the guests
gave three cheers for John Cummins, and one
and all declared that no nation on earth, for
real, sincere, and liberal hospitality, equals the
Hawaiians.

The Hawaiians have lovely voices, and remind
one in many ways of those mysterious wanderers
over Europe—the Gypsies. Their music is weird
and sentimental. There is a romance in their
melodies which sets one thinking. In this they
more closely resemble the European than Eastern
peoples; for while the Hindus and the Chinese
sing a sort of high drone through the head, a
weary, melancholy chant at best, the Hawaiians
sing from the full chest and exercise the whole
gamut of the voice. During our stay we had
many opportunities of observing this. There
were serenades nearly every night, given to high-
class people, such as the prime minister, the
attorney-general, Dr. Magrew, and others, with
whom we dined or spent the evening.

I was very delighted to meet, during this
visit to Honolulu, my old friend, the English

commissioner and consul-general, James Hay
Wodehouse, whom I had not seen for thirteen
years, and to whom I was, in the first place,
introduced by the Duke of Edinburgh. He was
as kind as ever to me, and his charming wife,
a thorough English gentlewoman, contributed
a great deal toward our success. So did my
dear friend, Dr. Magrew, and his gifted and
beautiful spouse.

In regard to the public taste of Honolulu, I
may say that the *bon ton* of the best society is
of no inferior order, and that it improves considerably with every year; that the spirit of the
higher social classes is pervading, to a wonderful
extent, the whole life of the city. The plays,
Narcisse, The Merchant of Venice, and Hamlet,
were the most appreciated, and my houses were
crowded every night I played. We were only
three: Miss Beaudet, a Mr. Charles Lobbett, one
of the actors sent to me by my wife from London,
and myself. I had disbanded the rest of the
company. It would have been impossible for
us to get on without an additional staff, and, to
my great surprise, I found a couple of ladies
and several gentlemen in Honolulu desirous of
assisting us.

Among the amateur gentlemen who were most
anxious to give a helping hand was an old
Australian, a Mr. C——, who is in business, but
a man of true poetic soul. He loves Shakespeare

as he loves the fresh air, sunlight, sea, and skies, and has the great bard's works in his heart but, unfortunately, not in his memory. He was willing to play any part, or, for the matter of it, half a dozen, if required, in any play. He knew them all by heart, and moved familiarly in the whole Shakespearean world; but when he came to speak them he got so mixed that the inevitable result was a complete breakdown. But I shall ever be grateful to him for his good intentions and disinterestedness in trying to assist me.

The theatre in Honolulu is far beyond the requirements of the city, and worthy of any first-class provincial town in the world, and it is to be deplored that good theatrical companies do not frequent these islands oftener. On one occasion I gave a benefit for the public library, when I played Narcisse to an enormous house. The trustees of the institution gave me a testimonial in the shape of an illuminated address in acknowledgment. The following is a copy: —

" *Daniel E. Bandmann, Esq.: Dear Sir,* — The generous and material assistance given by your company to the funds of the Honolulu Library and Reading-room Association, through the rendering of the play of Narcisse, at the Music Hall, last Tuesday, as a benefit to the association, calls for our hearty thanks, which please accept; and we request that you will also convey to Miss

Beaudet, and others who assisted on that occasion, our obligations and sincere appreciation of their kindly help.

"Sincerely wishing you a prosperous future,

"We remain, very truly yours,

"BEAUFORD B. DALE, *President.*
M. M. SCOTT, *Vice-President.*
H. A. PARMELEE, *Secretary.*
A. L. SMITH, *Treasurer.*

ALEX. J. CARTWRIGHT,	ALFRED S. HUTWELL,
C. M. HYDE,	WILLIAM JOHNSON,
WALTER HILL,	CHARLES T. ROGERS,
HENRY WATERHOUSE,	A. MARQUIS,
H. R. HOLLISTER,	*Directors.*"

"HONOLULU, January, 1884."

Before leaving, we received an invitation to the celebration held in honor of the birthday of Mr. Gibson, the prime minister, which was a grand affair, the king, the nobility, and all the gentry being present. The king's own band, numbering seventy performers, played, and the royal dancers sang melodious native glees under the veranda; while all Honolulu society, in silks and laces, crowded to congratulate the worthy old premier, who has been for upward of twenty years in Hawaiian service. It was a very impressive occasion, and affected me more than any other reception I had ever attended. There was a cold spread good enough for Paris, London, Berlin, Washington, or New York, and champagne was liberally and freely served to all comers.

Mr. Gibson is a man of great culture and sagacity, with an experience in Hawaiian affairs unequaled. There is a common impression that Colonel Spreckels manages the islands by reason of his great wealth and vast enterprises, but that is an erroneous view. He has done a great deal toward the development of the country and has great influence; but the government is in the hands of the people, while the controlling influence and tendency of Hawaiian institutions are decidedly American. The king's political views are American, and, though he is not very popular with the people just now, he is a shrewd, thinking man, who is capable of accepting good advice, and will, no doubt, some day become universally beloved. The masses wanted the dowager Queen Emma for their sovereign, and felt their disappointment keenly; but they are now gradually finding out that Kalakaua gives them prosperity and fame, and will soon see that he is the right man in the right place.

> " May he live
> Longer than I have time to tell his years!
> Ever belov'd and loving may his rule be."

The Chinese still have very considerable influence in Honolulu, and a great many óf them make profession of Christianity. I visited their church. There were about a hundred assembled listening to the Chinese clergyman, who was reading the gospel to them in their native tongue. I watched him closely, and for forty minutes he never evinced the slightest interest in the sacred narrative he was reading, by variation of countenance, look, or gesture. He read right on in the same monotonous singsong several chapters from the New Testament. It was a purely mechanical performance, very badly done, and evidently gave him much pain, and still more to his listeners: especially to those who could not understand him.

On the twenty-first of January, we left Honolulu, and after a rough journey of seven days arrived at San Francisco; having been absent about three years and a half, and having traveled during that period upward of seventy thousand miles by land and sea, and having played nearly seven hundred nights. Out of the seven hundred nights, we gave fully two thirds to Shakespearean performances — principally Hamlet, The Merchant of Venice, Macbeth, Othello, Richard III, Romeo and Juliet; the rest we occupied chiefly with Narcisse, A Woman of the People, East Lynne, Dead or Alive, and The Corsican Brothers.

> " The end crowns all;
> And that old common arbitrator, Time,
> Will one day end it."

NOTE TO CHAPTER IV.

THE MAORIS.—Any who may wish to know more of the lights and shadows of the history, character, and life of the Maoris, than has been told in this chapter, should turn to "Old New Zealand, etc. By a Pakeha Maori. With an Introduction by the Earl of Pembroke." To this singularly interesting book we desire to acknowledge our indebtedness for valuable facts.— [EDITOR.